Contents

BOBBY - THE SCALPER

Vijay Kumar Pagadala

1. Bobby's Intro

The year 2023, the month of December.

The Indian stock markets and the global indexes were heading toward new heights; besides; a fear was brooding about the recession and the geopolitical issues. The Nifty gained 17 percent, and the index was at 21650 while Sensex was about 1.9 percent, and its index rolled up to 780 points. The GDP was at 6.5 and the annual inflation was at 5.69. The Nifty Bank index, which has mostly large caps, has good liquidity with the bank stocks. The PSUs and other corporations played well, but the retailers were re-adjusting their active positions. The US markets reacted with the falling inflation data, slowing the growth.

Twenty-seven years old Bobby Shacal copied the prices and charts of selected shares on his pen drive. He has been doing the record-keeping for the past few months and could not find the exact reason for the uptrend of the capital markets. He studies the charts, analysis, and data of the stock markets. The movement of stock prices, indexes, and trades proved no relevance to anticipate a complete range picture of the present financial markets.

He did not understand who was gaining from the markets and decided to analyze the hourly and four-hour timeframes. After a short while, he opened other charts, which gave no reason to support the market's trend; he shut the system and went to his favorite Nikitha coffee shop. The reality was the huge transaction tax paid by anxious investors and greedy traders. Though it's charged at a nominal rate, it's an unseen expenditure in day-to-day participation in the market. A few trading platforms initially levied the least brokerage; the registered user trusted and ignored the taxes of their daily transactions. Subsequently, the Zero brokerage service providers were busy with the new account openings. Bobby ordered a cupcake and coffee and read the financial reports of the selected companies. Four companies reported fair figures and the other two had heavy expenditures and posted huge losses. He ignored the PL statements and the unusual annual projections of the company after comparing them with other similar, peer groups.

Later, he saw the flashing prices in red he included in his portfolio on his mobile. The charts indicated a buy signal, and the shares were in an overbought range. Some advised the same share to sell while others suggested buying; it's meaningless and hard to get the right price. He realized the tips and recommendations were business by the experts. The charts and the analysis were job opportunities for the professionals, while the real operators were the *genuine market movers*. A few sectors and indices are below average, and the charts displayed higher-ups in the present situation. Similarly, the US markets were trading with the recession fears, and the FOMC was yet to announce the rate cut.

There was no point in searching for the real value of the share prices. In the volatile markets, there are certain well-known companies that benefit from bullish sentiment. It was time for the European markets to open he searched the other world markets. He observed the shares of a few companies listed in the European stock markets. At present, the automotive sector is on the rise. He took a tissue, wrote a few notes, and ordered another coffee. Later, he returns home and searches for the job opportunities'. Bobby's father, Ram Shacal, returned from the office, placed two orders, and had lunch and asks,

"Where's your son? Still roaming on the streets?"

"He went to the market to get vegetables."

"For how long will you lie? Make him understand the responsibility and ask him to take up a job."

Bobby heard his mother and left the house from the kitchen door. He returns after ten minutes; his father stares at him and leaves for his office. Mother and son were relaxed; they knew if they had lunch with his father there would be verbatim and remarks, and no one would enjoy their food.

Ram Shacal works for a small private local transport company. He struggled hard to attain the present position as a manager and educated his son in a good college, though with an insufficient salary. He has a strange habit of speaking about his son while having the food. Often, his wife gets annoyed at his rude behavior toward his son and warns him not to scold while having food. At least for once, he comments on his son and says he's wasting the precious time of his life. Bobby's unsuccessful attempts to get a job become an issue, and everyone loses their peace of mind.

Bobby spends most of his time at a coffee shop and researches the factors affecting the index to lose its steam or fire up the spirits of enthusiast investors and traders. There was the news of the inflation numbers expected in the afternoon; it shouldn't pull the market down, as it's only 0.3 percent down from the past announcement. The index was declining, which made the market reverse. He checked the other political news, and only the ruling government's proposal of new taxation on imports was in discussion. Still, it was a debate for approval and implementation in the parliament.

He checked the international news, the usual election shouts, the GDPs of a few countries, earthquakes, and the terror attacks. All these recurring issues shouldn't push markets down, was his opinion. Should all this useless news be necessary for the upcoming countries and their economies? He didn't find any link or a reason to relate the aspects to the emerging healthy markets. A frustration builds inside him when he witnesses such irrelevant issues spoiling a good trading day. He wants to stop such useless factors from pressurizing the index to go down and wishes the markets to run independently and unaffected by the media hype. He could not pacify himself that the trading now is a profit-yielding business. Bobby thought of the world's stock exchanges and their management and realized that none was safeguarding a common person's hard-earned money. Of course, trading is not for small or seasonal investors if they are not properly educated about the market risk and reward. Who cares; governing bodies only need the taxes to fulfil their promises? He thinks about the earnings of the retailers and small traders. Are they receiving the profits or paying in additional funds, to sum up, to average the loss? To his knowledge, only a fraction of smart investors profited, and the rest were hoping for another good opening tomorrow to test their trading challenge. Moreover, this goes on and on as his father does, daily.

The common investors or traders assume and try to dictate the market as per their ideology and knowledge. Eventually, none of the market participants can forecast a correct, right move in the fast-moving markets and in the present circumstances.

Bobby returned at eight pm, heard his father grumbling, and went to his room. He knew his father's intraday trade were squared off in loss. He saw his portfolio; it has good shares of six sectors worth three lakhs and eighty-six thousand. He viewed the trade settlement and checked the brokerage and the taxes. Checks the book value, EPS, and 20, 50, and 100 EMA of the shares of his father's portfolio. He pitied his father; it wasn't his fault, and many times warned his father not to go for an intraday trade. Unexpectedly, Ram returned from the office, saw his son before the computer, and was furious.

"What are you doing with my portfolio?"

He admonished his son and called his wife. She comes running from the kitchen.

"Look at him, is this what he does in my absence? And you never tell me and support him always. Does he know about the stock market and trading?"

"Dad, I am aware of your trades and the stock market. I was just checking the losses in your portfolio. You can sell these shares, they are at all-time high."

"Now, you teach me the rules of the market. You take up some job, earn, and then talk to me. I have to learn from a jobless and lazy attitude person?"

He stares at him and his wife in anger and sits before the computer. His wife holds her head and returns to the kitchen. His father warned him not to get involved in his money matters. Bobby took it easy, and from then on, he never discussed the stock markets with him. His love for him didn't allow him to get annoyed; he knew his frustration for loss and happiness after the trade's profit.

In the intraday charts, the shares should move to a positive breakout, to new highs, but a few reversed and settled at the lower levels. After observing such negative breakouts, his father often frustrates and abuses the stock market and says the market is a gambler's den. He knew his frustration wasn't on him or for losing money but for the wrong guess in intraday trade in the stock market. It hurts Bobby if his father loses money in his trade, not only for his father's money but also for all innocent people losing their money in the intraday trade.

Bobby's subjects were finance and business administration. Once, he was selected as a junior-level manager, but the job assigned to him was at the front office of an online trading firm. His salary hardly earned him cupcakes, coffee, and beers. Later, he resigned and is now idle at home. Sometimes, his mother gives her saved money for his expenses. Even that was an issue to his father, and he yelled at her. After his drink, he was a lovely father, and his son knew, but his mother was worried about his health.

Bobby saw his father receive a call and leave for his office. She served him breakfast and asked him to take a job and assist his father. He smiled, and asked her not to worry. Later, he helped his mother in the kitchen. She loves him for his help and kisses her son on the forehead. Her motherly acts make him happy.

At a quarter past two pm, after his father left for the office after his lunch. Bobby switched on the computer, signed in, and saw sell orders of the intraday trade. The index dropped sharply; he modified and short-sold triple the number of shares his father bought in the morning. After fifteen minutes, he squared off the trade and made a good profit. Before his mother entered the bedroom, he logged out and returned to his room. After two months, Bobby's mother suffered a heart stroke and passed away. The father and son were having a tough time spending at home. Bobby cooked and served as his mother did and was taking care of his father. Shortly after a few days, his father retired and was spending most of his time with alcohol and passed the days in grief. Now, his intraday trading was a full-time job, and regularly he lost the money, either by placing the wrong orders after the drink or trading on worthless share tips below their face value.

A false **belief** often convinces him to believe that the share prices would rise, but gradually, a few shares dropped below the face value, and he lost thousands of rupees from his savings. Later, in frustration, he started revenge trading with his retirement benefits. When he loses his money, he drinks and weeps with the memories of his wife. Bobby spoke and convinced his father to trade as per his view and on selected shares. Surprisingly, Ram agreed and bought the shares his son recommended, and in the afternoon, he gained ₹2200. In the evening, he went out, bought his drink, and packed food for them. After the dinner, his son explained how to maintain patience and mental balance and go steady with the market trend. His father tried for the next three days and started believing and trusting his son's recommendations. One day he lost on the recommended shares, and his son again selected other shares and averaged the loss. By the closing time of the stock market, his father had fetched ₹2000. He thought his father was angry and tried to explain, but his father was happy, smiled, and coolly said it does not bother him.

Daily, Bobby screens for active shares, selects, and gives three to five shares with entry and the targets to exit the trade with mere profits. Now, Ram started trusting his son's ability despite a few hundred losses, and Bobby was happy for his father's trust in him. Ram Shacal earned at least ₹1500 to 3500 in intraday trade. In the evening, both started going out for a walk. One day, while returning, Bobby asked his father to draw a part of the profit earned from yesterday's intraday trade. His father was surprised; his son explained to him to spend some of his profit for a purpose and gave him a reason to celebrate. He said one must not save the whole profit for *unpredictable next day's market.*

Bobby knew his father could not give up alcohol, a diehard habit, and didn't want to get deprived of his choice of drink after his retirement. Therefore, it was a better idea to reduce the quantity than ask him to stop at once. Traders should also spend their profits for their daily needs; it gives them joy and self-confidence of their hard work.

Bobby said if one tries to save all profits for tomorrow, greediness will overtake, and one might lose not only yesterday's profits but also the deployed capital. His father was impressed, and surprisingly, nowadays, he is more addicted to the day trading and stock market than his night liquor parties. They reached a bank and asked his father to draw some money from the ATM; he happily went and returned with ₹2000. Bobby was glad, took a few notes from him, bought a fine malt whiskey from the liquor store, and gave it to his father. After nine pm, Ram settled with his bottle in the living room and enjoyed his drink alone. After a few minutes, he called his son and gave the leftover money to him. He said it's a long time since he gave something to his son and said it was a small tip for helping him to win the market. Bobby refuses, and his father remembered his wife and spoke of her. He saw the tears in his father's eyes were ready to drop and knew he would start weeping, so he took the money and went to his room. He took a small plastic box and placed the notes; it was his mother's moneybox. Now, his father gained confidence and regularly traded from nine thirty to mid-afternoon.

Later, his son takes charge of the trades of his father. After lunch, Ram takes a nap, and they go for a walk in the evening. It has become a routine for the father, and his father's health slightly improved after a lung infection.

2. Bobby & Sidhu

Bobby and Sidhu are childhood friends and studied at the same college. They developed a hobby of tracking shares, prices, and company profiles from their college days. They bet on the closing prices of the shares and the next day's opening. The bet was just a few beers; either win or lose, they would have their share of pocket money spent at the favorite pub once a week. Sidhu was more interested in the analysis and major breakout of the indices, while Bobby was confident and precise with a few selected shares and indexes substantially; his predictions proved correct. They meet once, or twice a week, to discuss the markets and share research to study for next week.

Sidhu works as a software programmer and works for an international organization. He's perfect with his codes, strategies, Algo, and Auto Trading Software—ATS. His company is well-established with the HFT with Algo and ATS applications widely used by traders for all segments. The company is ready to launch the latest version of the software at a reasonable price for retailers and day traders.

They ordered their regular beer and snacks. Bobby opened his laptop and showed the charts and price movements to Sidhu. Both exchanged their strategic views and are building self-confidence to establish their office. They want to start an online trading platform, an Asset Management Company, and wealthy investors to finance their dream project. Their predictions proved sixty percent correct. Overall, a six percent profit over the loss-making companies and in the bearish market was quite a surprise. Bobby opened a chart and asked,

"You see this chart and tell me the price it should open and close tomorrow."

His friend frowned at the chart and replied,

"If you go by the price action and volumes, then don't see the charts."

"Of course, but as a lame investor or aggressive trader, what do you suggest?"

"Well, if the trade volumes and stock options are taken into consideration, it should fall and go for a correction by three to six rupees. If the price action's applied, it should go up further next week."

"Exactly, even I guessed the same, and so, let me try my presumption next week."

Sidhu took a sip of his drink and asked,

"Bobby, why don't you try the options, man?"

"Ah! Until someone asks me to take care of his portfolio, I don't want to try with my father's money."

"You want to gain experience and profits with other's money and portfolio, right?"

"Yes."

"You want to play with other's money for your gains; it's not a good idea. And if you lose, how do you repay?"

"Hey! I am not, and in fact, always work cautiously with the mutual consent of my partner. Let me explain, I'll use the money, hedge it, give them the profit, and take a small fee for my hard work."

"You surprise me; even you planned a fee for a dormant idea. Count the stars, big bull."

Sidhu laughs; Bobby's silent, and watches him for a short while. He thought he could be wrong with his idea and decided to rework his plan again. To his knowledge, five shares are underperforming; they discussed it last week. Meanwhile, Sidhu scribbled the shares on a piece of paper, their prices, entry, target, and exit, and showed. Three shares are under Bobby's observation; he smiled, took the paper, wrote his new mobile number, and returned it to his friend.

"Sidhu, what's the speed of an order execution?"

Sidhu stares at him and replies,

"Well, the Stock Exchange is timed at 1 to 2 nanoseconds. It's the fastest in the country with a low latency and response time. NSE is trying to reduce it to 1 and further to 0.5 in the future."

Bobby nods and speaks.

"You mean, there's no chance of tampering; let me say, there's no way one could stop or control an order once submitted and before hitting the trade execution."

Sidhu gives an affirmative reply,

"No way! The latest software is built to reduce uptime delay and maintain the low latency."

Bobby thinks for a while and questions him,

"Does speed vary from one server to the other, or the data transfer from retailer to broker, or stock exchange's system? Sometimes, I find the orders get executed immediately after I submit them. And other orders, I observed, they don't reach the exchange on time, and later it acknowledges with a few seconds delay."

Sidhu stares at him and explains the procedure.

"Usually, broking houses use HFT—High-Frequency Trading, with ASP coordinating with the latest and fastest processor to place their orders. Brokers slice and route small lots through their terminals in order to receive the HFT rebate offered by the exchanges. However, some brokers negotiate terms before placing bulk orders. Just buy, sell, and earn; why do you need this information?"

"Because I found differences in brokerage from one broker to another and is there any checkpoint to find the flaw? If so, I'll blow the whistle."

"Leave it buddy, it's just a fraction. So, now what's your plan?"

"I have to open a trading account, take you four fools in, invest, and win the market."

"Why do you need partners? Can't you do it yourself?"

"No Sid... I can raise money, but it won't be enough for my project. I need at least forty to fifty Lakhs to implement my start-up project."

"I'd better explain to you later, I have to call Naveen and Vinay to discuss this project."

"Bob, I don't understand your plan; now explain to me in detail of your plan."

"Sidhu, if I want to trade, I can open my account and play, but I want three or four to follow up on my strategy. We should bet a share, a company, beat the market right from the opening till closing, and earn enough for four of us?"

Sidhu frowns, folds his hands and suggests,

"Then, you should register as a broker with SEBI, get the clients, and provide tips to your customers and traders."

"Do you know how much one has to pay to register as a stockbroker?"

"I think, it is rupees ten Lakhs."

"No. It's fifty lakhs now."

"No, Bobby, it's just ten I believe."

"It's ten only if registered for a proprietor's trader and without Algorithm trade and twenty-five Lakhs with Algo and client based. To get all services and nationwide trading terminals, it's fifty."

After a while, Bobby continues in a cool voice,

"I don't want to earn for my tips or suggestions and squeeze innocent investors' money. I'd love to give *free trading tips* to my followers, and I have other plans for paid services. I have to dissuade desperate investors from using their hard-earned money for their anxiety to become overnight millionaires. Many had lost thousands and lakhs of rupees with such dreams; I have a deep sympathy for them and one of them, is my father; even he decided to pump in his pension benefits to beat the market, just to win."

"Yes, I agree there are many people, but we can't convince or stop them from playing in the tough market. It's an addiction."

"That's the reason, Sid... I don't want to become a stockbroker but want to help innocent people to play safe with their savings."

Sidhu's confused. Thinks for a while and questions Bobby.

"Well, then what are you up to?"

"I don't know."

Later, they leave the pub and, on the way, Bobby meets a neighbor and asks him to invest in his researched company's shares. He mentioned the prices and targets and asked him to stay invested for a week, as they are to report good third-quarter results. He spends a few minutes with him and reaches his home. The hot sun was raising the temperatures of the active traders with the sliding index with no known reason to them. A few closed their positions, and others still clinging to the falling points. Clever cats short-sold the shares without stop loss and closed with small profits, and Bobby was one of them.

He squared off all except one and calculated the earnings; it showed the utilized funds as two lakhs plus brokerage and transaction taxes. The profit margin was around just four percent it's not bad based on the present market situation. The NSE and BSE indexes were diving; the players panicked, still holding their positions indecisively, and were even afraid to square off the shares bought, hoping for a turnaround to scale at least a few points up. The index stabilized for five minutes and descended another twenty points, and Bobby covered his short position and closed all trades in his father's account.

₹ $ £ €

Bobby remembered his father; Ram Shacal was hospitalized with chest pain. He had a strange obsession even while in the hospital. Doctors declared only a few days for him to live, analyzing his health condition. Ram's last wish was to win the market before his death, and one day Bobby took his laptop and was with his father, waiting for the markets to open. His father had his medicines, saw his son, and smiled. The pale face and weak body of his father brought tears to Bobby's eyes. He walked out of the ward to control himself. The next moment, there was a scream from inside. He ran into the room and saw his father smiling, and raising his hands in the air with excitement. Bobby saw he placed four buy orders of thousand shares each on his recommendation for intraday: maybe it's his last day—*the last intraday*. The buy orders were executed in a matter of minutes, and they were promptly increased by two, three, and nine rupees. Bobby bent over from beside his father and saw the shares; the volumes and prices were increasing for the other three shares.

The average traded price was constantly changing and above three times the price his father bought. Ram Shacal was smiling like an innocent child. He asked his father to place the sell orders after the shares reached the anticipated target price and left the room. Tuesday was his father's lucky day. He wished and prayed for a satisfactory and profitable trade. He went to a tea stall, had a cup of tea, and called his friends; they told him that his suggestions were earning two to three percent on their investment just in twenty minutes. He was glad and returned to his father's ward. His father leaned back on the pillows, and head facing up, both hands dropped to his sides. The laptop slid and tilted from his lap and rested half on his left leg and on the bed. He stopped, and his heart squeezed, noticing his father. Bobby slowly approaches him; Ram's eyes are half closed, and his mouth dropped, exposing his cavity. At once, he leaves and returns with a doctor; he checks Ram and declares he's dead.

One day, Sidhu called Bobby and spoke of one of their college friends. At first, Bobby didn't agree but after hearing, about the miserable state of life, he was convinced. It was a dreadful promise he made, and he was busy for three months and accomplished his mission and hobby with good returns. That gave self-confidence and willpower to play with the money and the markets.

3. Nikitha meets Bobby

Ms. Nikitha's beautiful face with sharp whispering eyes attracts everyone. She takes pride in showing off her twenty-nine-year-old sexy figure with her brisk walks and bouncing breasts. A flat stomach, round buttocks, and attractive T-shirts and jeans draw in men of all ages, and every customer notices them frequently. Nevertheless, her customers are making her wildest dreams come true by paying her bills, and she expresses her gratitude by dressing sexy and attractive every day. Her talkativeness, facial expressions, and pretense were purely for business and money; a false makeup for social interaction was a tactful act of attraction. However, a few customers were anxious to get her in their lives and invited her to join them for parties, and she politely ignored them.

Her dream of owning a coffee shop was fulfilled by the bequeath she received. She sold the old house in Jafferkhanpet, Koyambedu, and fetched huge money from the deal. She left Chennai and settled in Hyderabad. Invested in the coffee shop in the prime locality at SR Nagar and established as a young businessperson within a short while. After the renovation, she's left with a few Lakhs in her account that she kept safe for her expenditure to buy gold ornaments.

The renovation wasn't necessary as the business was doing well. Out of the three bakeries in the locality, one was gutted in a fire accident recently and her idea of modification and redesigning yielded better profits by the increased footfalls of customers to her shop. For the past two years, fifteen and thirty-two percent profits were registered. Her target and breakeven seemed achievable in another year with another twenty-five percent of profit. She was satisfied and was looking for a ready-built house in the prime localities of

Hyderabad. One day, a young man briskly walked in at eleven in the night, after the coffee shop closed. He was searching in the dustbin at the corner of the table. A waiter enquired, and he said he was searching for the notes he had written on the tissue. After a few minutes, he collected his coffee-stained and crushed tissue and left. Nikitha watched him and from then on, she has been keeping an eye on him for the past few weeks, the tissues thrown in the trash and along with the bill. He's one of the regular customers in the mornings and evenings; he orders a Samosa or club sandwich and coffee, and later, he updates the figures on his laptop.

He spends an hour at the corner single table. After updating, he throws away the tissues in the dustbin before he leaves. He was tracking the stocks, futures, and indices of the stock market. Before closing, Nikitha picked up the trash and checked the torn and crumbled tissue papers. She regularly took note of the shares mentioned on the tissues, and their prices and entered them into her laptop. Later, checked the latest price and compared the price she entered a few weeks ago.

She was surprised at the price of three shares and was excited to see her share price double. Closed her eyes and thanked him. Nikitha had dinner and was watching the American markets. A sudden fall and rise of the Dow Jones and S&P 500 after thirty minutes of the opening surprised her. She checked her portfolio and marked two stocks from the nifty watch list that her customer scribbled on the tissue paper a few days ago. She viewed the closing prices, placed the offline orders, and set the morning alarm. She's decided to meet him, was aware of his knowledge to spin the money for her quick returns, and believes he's her *Quick Money Machine*. She has a dream of a big house in the Jubilee Hills locality and loves the gold ornaments that are going to be fulfilled. Due to the lack of funds, she was using cheap imitation jewelry. Her routine begins with half an hour of yoga practice and later, checks her shares worth four lakhs. Her ambition is to earn through the share market, and faster than her coffee shop's sales.

Dreaming about a possibility is good, but ignoring the present opportunity and chasing an evaporating cloud is a dangerous aspiration. Matters can turn to disaster if an idea is fueled by greed for big money.'

At thirty minutes past nine am, she checked the market and left her flat. On the way, she called two suppliers and ordered the day's requirements. The online sales for the delicacies are increasing, and she has made the arrangements and tied up with the local door delivery and party service providers. She reached her shop, seven tables were occupied, and the students were the coffee and books preparing for exams.

At eleven am, she saw him entering the shop; he was of five-six height, has a fair, beautiful face, was clean-shaved, and slim, and appeared as a female model dressed up in male attire. He opened his laptop and was scribbling something on a tissue. Later, he ordered coffee and biscuits. After a few minutes, Nikitha walks to him.

"Sir, may I interrupt you, for a while?"

He smiled at her and offered her a seat. She thanks him and takes the chair. He closed his laptop and stared at her. Meanwhile, the coffee and biscuits arrived. She asked the waiter to get her a coffee too.

"I am Nikitha."

She introduced herself and extended her hand.

"I am Bobby."

He replies, and they shake their hands and exchange glances.

"Sir, regularly I see you watching the stock market and updating the prices of the shares."

He interrupts her, smiles, and speaks.

"Call me, Bobby. Bobby Shacal."

"Ok, Bobby, are you a stock broker, a trader, or an investor? I didn't understand you and your business."

"I track the share prices, and their movements and search small profit-earning stocks."

She raised her eyebrow, smiled, and asked,

"Do you invest? I mean trade regularly, please suggest good shares, and I am interested in investing in the stock market."

He watched her right index finger tapping on the rim of the coffee cup. He knew she was intruding and, besides, interfering with his private and personal preferences. None should ever peek into someone's interests unless known better, but now he's aware and she already did. Was she a genuine investor or a seasonal trader? He took a bite of the biscuit, took a large sip, and said,

"Nikitha tell me how much you know about investing and trading in the stock market."

"Well, to be frank, none... I copied your shares for a long time and invested. Today, they earned me a good profit, three times the return on my investment. I am glad and sorry for stealing your information."

"That's good news, wonderful, and I am surprised, Nikitha."

"Please, don't take it the other way, and I am more interested in shares than the coffee shop now. My aim and targets are to get good and quick returns in a short time... I could be wrong, but I can't resist my appetency to earn."

He stared at her for a short while and asked,

"If my shares didn't fetch you a profit, were you to blame me for the information?"

She smiles, bends over the table, closer to him, and speaks in a low and sweet voice.

"No. I know you are doing a perfect analysis on the shares, and that inspired me."

He did not expect such a frank and fair statement from a smart businesswoman. She leaned back and stared at him. He assumes she's now relieved of her guilt of stealing his information and was feeling sorry. Realized, she's more eager for the money and wealth than a devoted businesswoman who stays focused on regular profits, and in the long run. Her desire waved him a wrong sign; her eagerness for a money multiplier idea scared him. However, her bold and blind decision to invest in a vague tip encouraged him.

Nevertheless, she earned good profit and that satisfied him. But if she lost? He imagined her anger and frustration and realized that he would be disdained on his next visit. However, it's not his fault, yet, he felt that his casual behavior had sparked a dormant wealth volcano from a well-established businesswoman. Besides, she has no right to blame him; still, he's afraid of such blind belief and inspiration while dealing with the money matters.

He felt guilty for his carelessness and for his unmindful exposure. He has the potential to convince and expect people to believe in his stock advice on logical approaches but, he never encouraged others. Now, he's determined and can suggest his tips to investors. His idea of winning the market encouraged and was confident with her investment. Her interest and his untried, unoffered investment advice yielded good returns.

"Bobby, let me again apologize."

"Nikitha. It's ok, but I suggest you be careful while investing in the stock market. Do not put your money on such tips, ok?"

"From now onwards, I won't; I'd seek your advice before investment. Will you be my stock advisor?"

He nods and she excuses herself as a waiter beckons her to the cash counter. He saw her stylish walk escaping the elbow of the customers on her way. Her perfect body was doing a ramp walk. For a few minutes, he observed her smile, conversation with the customers, and sexy gestures and liked her. Later, he checked eight shares and took a tissue, saw her and she was watching him. She waved her hand and smiled. He knew his every moment was watched; wrote three shares on a tissue, buy price, stop-loss, and target price, placed it on the table, and waved for the check. Nikitha took a print and presented it personally. He saw the bill, placed the money in the tray, and said,

"These three shares may fetch two times your investment if you hold for a few days, but please don't invest all your money... Be patient and wait for the right price and the target price."

"Thank you, Bobby."

She said and took the tissue. He saw the bill; it was fifty percent discounted. He shut his laptop and took the bill to the counter. She saw him and raised her left eyebrow.

"It's a small discount for my investment guru, Bobby."

"No, I don't; Do I deserve it?"

"Yes! You fetched me a total profit of eleven thousand and six hundred."

"Oh! Well done, what was your investment?"

"It's one lakh and fifty-two thousand."

"How long did you hold the shares?"

"Just twelve days."

4. The Scalper

Bobby checked his email; there were job offers, and one email caught his attention. The subject was written as A Millionaire's Trade–Scalper, he saw the date and time; it arrived just half an hour ago. Clicked open and read the mail; it mentioned three shares and a question mark and asked him to predict today's closing price of the shares listed on Indian stock markets. He observed the signature stamp; it is a symbol of a head with snakes, no initials or sender's name, and the sender's mail id's 'Mudusaa.' He remembered the Greek guardian 'Medusa', a female with snakes as her hair and was deliberately misspelled. It appeared as a prank and spam, but it was not; it challenged his research.

There were twenty minutes for the markets to close; two shares were the same, his father regularly traded, and one was out of his watch, a mining sector's share. At once, he searched the mining sector's average and industrial potential earnings ratio. He read the company profile and observed the past six months' charts, volumes, and the prevailing price. He calculated the figures, noted the approximate closing price based on the volume, and trend, and sent the reply. Selected a few shares due to declare a bonus in the next month and sent the mail to his friends. The next day, as usual, the markets were trying new crests on the NSE and the BSE stock exchanges.

The big screen on the Phiroze Jeejeebhoy towers was glowing with sixty percent in green figures. The market closed and his guess proved correct. Later, he received a call from an unknown number and asked for his address. He did not understand why the caller wanted his address and unwillingly gave his location. After a while, a car arrived, and a stranger enquired about him. He approached Bobby and introduced himself as a Personal Assistant working for an organization called Mudusaa Associates Limited. He's in his mid-fifties, and by his attire and the luxury car, none would think him to be a PA. Remembered the email asking for the closing prices of the shares. He asked Bobby to accompany him if he needed a job and pointed at the car he arrived. Bobby was surprised, and without a word took his laptop, locked his house, and sat in the car. The car was moving towards the airport, and Bobby asked where they were heading, and PA replied coolly.

"Mumbai."

None spoke throughout the journey and they reached RGI airport, Shamshabad, Telangana. PA gave the boarding pass and asked him to wait at the lounge. Meanwhile, Bobby called Sidhu and said he was going to Mumbai to attend an interview, and Sidhu wished him good luck. After the announcement, PA arrived, and they boarded the flight. They occupied the executive class; it was the first experience for Bobby, and he could not distinguish the difference between the classes of the flight. After the takeoff, PA started a conversation and detailed about the company, its operations, and its financial status in India. Bobby was surprised after hearing it was more than a few thousand Crores in turnover. After a while, he asked,

"Why does your company need a non-professional?"

"Well, a need never tells you when it's needed; a requirement is an option, a choice, and necessity's a must and for everyone. Either for a maximum or least in our daily life."

Bobby smiles, nods, and agrees to his strange metaphor and is silent. Later, PA explained why they were hiring him and his job. He Spoke of the stocks, futures, options, mutual funds, AMCs, and the shares he traded in the stock exchanges of the world. Bobby understood the requirement and knew it was a company's requirement; besides, it's also a necessity for him. He agreed it was a need, requirement, and necessity, and all were *scholarly arguments and debatable*. But he did not understand why he chose him and forced; for a job, everything baffled him. A strange job offer; no one would believe him if told to his friends. He was answering a hundred questions inside his head, closed his eyes for a while, and relaxed. An air hostess wakes him, smiles, serves soft drinks and refreshments, and walks away. PA was busy on his laptop; one after another, three mobiles started ringing, and he answered one.

"Don't stop jogger and keep jogging and watch the target volume."

He disconnected the call, took his second mobile, and answered the second call.

"Put a strict stop loss; do not forget the trigger. and follow the jogger."

He took the third call and asked the caller to hold. He checked his laptop, frowned, and said,

"You can follow the jogger and walker but call me before you reach volume. And remember to leave a good up and down movement for the runner, wait for my call."

He turns his head, looks at Bobby, and smiles. His smile expressed authority and confidence in whatever he was doing. Meanwhile, the flight landed, and a chauffeur received them, and the BMW was moving towards central Mumbai. He dropped Bobby at an apartment, gave the agreement documents and the key, and asked him to report to the office after two days. Bobby took the key, and it was tagged with a visiting card and after two days, he was to resume his office.

₹ $ £ €

It's a two-bedroom flat converted into an office on the tenth floor in the new trade center in Chembur, Mumbai. Bobby was given three terminals in one of the master bedrooms; Sunil Gaikwad, the manager, uses the other one. There's no office assistant; a part-time maid comes in the morning and evening and cleans the office. Three individual trading accounts were registered in Bobby's name with different stock broking houses, but the trades were done with the company's money. Gaikwad took the signed agreement document, smiled sarcastically, and told him that the PA was the owner of Medussa Associates Limited. Bobby was asked to manage three accounts one after the other with the different trades. At first, it was very confusing, but later, with his quick and alert decisions, he mastered the trades in a short time. Daily, after the market's pre-opening, Bobby studies the index, EMA, and moving trends and screens a few shares. Later, he prepares the list and sends the file named 'Trademel,' a PDF, to his boss and his manager Gaikwad for their records.

Sometimes, Sointhara, his MD, gives his choice of stocks, and they usually are swing and positional trades. Days rolled away without notice, and Bobby had become a *scalping machine*. Bobby swiftly places the basket orders with a strict stop loss. His predictions, accuracy, and swiftness while executing the orders were often discussed in the closed meetings of the company. The agreement documents mentioned that he should not use the Algo or the readymade trading strategies. The clause emphasized that he must build self-made trading strategies. If ignored, a penalty was mentioned as per the trade value, and legal action would be taken against him. At first, it scared Bobby, but his confidence overruled the strange clause of the agreement.

Gaikwad gives the list of shares to Bobby to trade for the day. He stays in his office until the closure of markets and observes Bobby's scalping activities. Later, he takes a print of all positions—buy, sell, intraday, positional, options, and futures of Nifty and Nifty Bank transactions.

He uses simple price action on the charts with RSI and MACD, which surprised a few experienced traders in his office. The shares of Nifty 50, Sensex and a few reputed companies are regularly traded, and the profits were never below three to six percent of the day's investment for the past three months. Sometimes, he uses the EMA with small timeframes for large scalping. Usually, he's busy at the closing hours of markets, and his hectic job never allowed him to see the day's profit.

However, he has an idea as to how much he has earned for his company. After the coffee break in the evening, he takes prints of all trades and presents them to his boss before leaving the office. He also maintained an official as well as a personal trade journal on his laptop. After Bobby leaves, Gaikwad scrutinizes the trades and places payout orders of the day's earnings, leaving sufficient cash for the next day's trade. After a while, he mails the total business transactions and figures to his MD at the Mumbai corporate office.

₹ $ £ €

Nowadays, Bobby started preparing a list of the next day's selection of the shares to trade; Gaikwad disliked him for his independent decisions regarding the trades in the markets. The manager's job was to be present, idle in the office until the markets were closed. Surprisingly, one day he was impatient and asked Bobby thrice about the positions held in the afternoon. Then, he received a call and left the office in a hurry without a word. Later, he called Bobby and asked him to lock the office before leaving.

Bobby was ready to leave and received a call from the corporate office in Mumbai. The accountant asked him to wait; it was half past five pm, so he went to the coffee shop on the ground floor. After waiting for ten minutes, the accountant arrived; they had coffee and went to the office. The accountant asked Bobby to find the two cheques that were dispatched to his manager in the morning. He called his manager twice but did not answer. Bobby went into Gaikwad's room and searched on the table. Under the pile of letters, he saw the blue-bordered corporate envelopes. Three envelopes were opened; two had two cheques, one was in the manager's name with the rupees eighty-two thousand dated last week, and the other two cheques were in his name for rupees fifty-six thousand and sixty-five thousand with today's date. He took the cheques and observed, took a snapshot with his mobile, came out of the manager's room, and asked for the figures written on the cheques. The accountant took a printout from his diary and tapped with his index finger at the figures. He took the cheques and said he would prepare new cheques.

Meanwhile, Bobby saw his name twice; two payments were made in his name, and the figures entered on both cheques were marked as paid. There was a whirlpool chasing Bobby; he felt like a three-minute single red candle eroding the earned profits within seconds. He presumed it was the pay for the present month, but instead of a single cheque payment, why was his name written twice and for different figures? Was it a bonus or a special perquisite? He could not guess the reason behind the double entry of his name in the register. Later, Bobby locked his office, gave the keys to security, and left. He relaxed on the sofa for a while, closed his eyes, and within minutes he dosed off. A wrong call disturbed him at eight pm; he refreshed and changed into a white shirt and blue jeans and went to his usual bar. He ordered his drink and remembered the payments and the salaries of his company. He was informed about Sointhara's profitable management of national, international, and other business entities' construction businesses.

Six months passed away unnoticed; other than the trades, he and Gaikwad hardly spoke of any general topic. His manager, Gaikwad's job, was to supervise, scrutinize, and deal with the money matters of the day trades. Bobby did not bother to find out the salary of his manager earlier, and now he's eager to find out the real facts after the cheque discrepancy.

5. Hameed's Business Proposal

Karan Reddy's ancillary in Bollaram IDA was running three shifts a day. The production of small and medium-sized automotive molded rubber products is more in demand with the introduction of the latest high-end vehicles. His unit supplies to major vehicle manufacturers, but the payments were received too late. Even the other similar units were running three shifts but not as prompt in deliveries as Karan's unit. He planned for the expansion of his business with the new die and mold-based products and wished to be incorporated as the best SME status for his business. The equipped capacity was not fully utilized, and sometimes he takes up local orders to run the regular shifts. After three years in production, hardly there were any new business prospects other than the regular orders.

Karan left for Mumbai, to negotiate with a private travel company. The company has thirty-four vehicles and they need regular service and replacements of spares at their garage. One of his clients referred the company; he spoke and wanted to meet the company's Managing Director. The next day, he arrived at the Chhatrapati Shivaji Maharaj Terminus and took a cab to the hotel in west Andheri. Had breakfast and reached the garage on the Gujarat highway. He met with Mr. Omkar, MD of the Travel Company, middle-aged, with bulging eyes, half bald, and with a round beer belly. They discussed the products and the garage's monthly requirements. Later, after an oral confirmation, Omkar asked for a regular supply of spares on a credit basis for three months. Karan assured him but agreed to two months credit as he was quoting one percent lower than the present market price, and a final agreement was signed. Although it was a financial deficit for his company, he was obliged to supply spares to Omkar's garage so as not to leave an opportunity to his competitors. Before leaving, he was introduced to one of Omkar's friends, Mr. Hameed, a scrap dealer who deals with steel strips, die mold waste, and silver foils. He was a broad-shouldered, average-height, fat man in his sixties. His baldhead, sharp eyes, and small, tight-lipped smile gave the impression that he was not an easily convincing type. Surprisingly, he was more interested in Karan's business and invited him and Omkar to his house.

Karan and Omkar went to Hameed's house. They traveled for half an hour and arrived at an old, big bungalow beside the Powai Lake, Andheri East. The house was known as Hameed's Mansion. It was four floors with various creepers and plants hanging from each floor. The colorful spotlights created a wonderful view from the street. Hameed was known for his kindness and generous donations for all festivals and occasions. He was often referred to as a decent businessman who easily mingled with the people on the street.

They are received by Hameed's assistant, who took them to the penthouse on the fourth floor. The living room is designed with transparent, thick glass on three sides, and it gives a clear view of the Powai Lake and the street around. There are three heavy foamed couches and a low table in the middle of the room. The minibar is at the corner beside the door, and next to it is a beautifully carved Malaysian dining table. They were served with soft drinks, and after ten minutes, Hameed arrived in a white T-shirt and grey shorts. He shook hands and sat on the couch before Omkar and Karan; meanwhile, a waiter arrived who was waiting at the corner of the room.

"I thank you, friends. It's a long time since I had a cool party. Omkar and Karan, what would you like?"

The waiter took a step forward and was waiting for their choice.

"I'd prefer scotch,"

Omkar said.

"I'll go for a beer."

Karan answered nervously. Hameed asked the waiter to prepare a Godfather for him and asked his guests,

"For snacks, what do you like?"

"I'd go with kebab."

Omkar said and smiled.

"Tandoori chicken, please."

Karan said, and the waiter bowed and left.

"So, how's business?"

Hameed asked Omkar.

"As usual, unpredictable weather, TRA checkups, and foreign tourists decrease due to social security reasons."

"Hameed, I heard your brother-in-law's looking after a part of your business?"

"Of course, he does; he's a Chartered Accountant."

"Well, then income tax people could hardly find any..."

"Omkar, I never did anything against the law, and if did and they couldn't find it... then, it's their fault."

Hameed chuckles. That was an arguable debate Karan thought and smiled, but it did not continue. The waiter served drinks and snacks. Hameed lit his cigarette and asked,

"How many years have you been in the manufacturing, Karan?"

"Ah, just three years."

"Now, what makes you come to Mumbai?"

Karan told them about his expanding capacity and production targets. Spoke of the competitors of the local market and their deals of the business. He explained of the quality and said that other manufacturers compromise over the low-quality spares for frequent and regular requirements of business from their dealers. He expressed his dislike for such practices and said his intention for a regular supply of genuine and long-term commitment of business from the other states. He explained to them about the setting up of a large steel die-cast and mold plant with a large capacity for his expansion project.

"We should appreciate your devotion and sincerity towards the business; what do you say, Omkar?"

"Yes, we must, and I like his business strategy, Hameed; he charges one percent less compared to the present market price."

"Oh! That's praiseworthy; I see people with an idea of quick and huge money in a short time. But his view of business convinces me to take a part in his business if, he agrees?"

Hameed said and stared at Karan, and they were watching him. Karan finished his beer and said,

"Well, if you can get into a partnership, you are welcome, but I run a small business, sir, so... I can take only one as a partner; please don't take me the wrong way."

"I am not interested, Hameed may..." Omkar said.

"It's a long time, Omkar, running, filing quotations, and lifting the scrap, and it takes away all my energy and happiness. Now, I think... I should take some rest and learn the business of manufacturing, designing, or any stationary business that should leave me with some time for myself."

After a few days, Hameed expressed his view. Later, they spoke of the rising prices, government policies, politics, and the other related issues that affected their business in the past year. And at last, before saying goodbye, Hameed asked Karan a final word. Karan invited him to Hyderabad for a better understanding of his business. The automobile industry was extensively turning to the latest technologies and new designs. A steady growth of 26 percent for the year 2013-14 and around 36 percent in 2014-15 for two, three, and quadricycles. In 2023, the automobile industry is aiding the Indian economy with a growth of approximately 4.8 percent and with a CAGR of 36 percent with EVs introduction by 2026, making it the fourth largest in the world. After a few days, Hameed sent his brother-in-law, Anwar, to visit Karan's factory in Hyderabad. Anwar arrived in Hyderabad, and drafted an agreement and prepared financial terms and conditions. He rechecked his figures and investment, and an estimated breakeven was posted for the fifth year. Later, he compared his data for installed capacity utilization and actual production. He prepared a separate sheet for commercial vehicles and industrial heavy-duty machines. He drafted a factsheet, and the results after his approximate value gave a satisfactory appreciation over the investment.

The total cost of the steel die and mold industry was more than a few crores in addition, as estimated, and the major contributors are yet to be finalized. He compared the infrastructure and facilities provided by the newly formed Telangana state's SEZs—Special Economic Zone benefits much better than those in Maharashtra state. In Mumbai, they could easily arrange loans from local and international banks, but Anwar is particularly focused on the Telangana region and mostly in Karan's business.

The industrial area at Bollaram IDA was an ideal and potential landmark for his business. Now, the raw material can be easily re-routed to various smelting factories in a few states. As the state of Telangana being a new developing state and with its geographical position, it was close to the other three states to which the collected scrap can be transported easily. Now, the transport expenditure would be minimized if they supplied the scrap directly to the smelters.

6. Sointhara, Fulkeery & Gaikwad

Mr. Fulkeery's new business, Astrapee Industries, is in Navi Mumbai. He invested in his new steel and aluminum companies and also traded in the stock markets daily and was satisfied as a better market player. Sometimes, he lost a few blue-chip shares with over trading; it was negligible if compared to his fifty percent earnings in the past four months. The ability to guess the right price earned him twice or thrice his day's total money traded. Only a few acquired a trade secret in the present market scenario. Even the regular market players did not dare to invest as he did with the logical technique. His aggressive trades are often highlighted in his friend's circle and even a few challenged and lost their bets.

The annual report of the steel and aluminum industries posted good results. Fulkeery's wife and two children are in the USA, and he stays with his new girlfriend in Vashi, Thane District. At six am, he goes for a walk, sweats for an hour, returns and checks the opening of the markets and share prices, selects a few shares, and places the orders. The betting on the horses was not attractive nowadays, and he was losing money with his unruly wrong bets. Earlier, he was regular to the race clubs in the country. Moreover, all his business partners and friends were acquainted at the racecourse only. Now, the most profitable win was in the stock market rather than the horse race.

He sent a message to his friend and planned to meet in the evening at the club. Fulkeery met his friend Sointhara in the regular room, 'Mist,' where the confidential meeting takes place. Usually, they meet once a month or fortnight. Earlier, they managed many businesses as partners in the past years, but due to some financial constraints, they had to break up their partnership. Yet they still maintain a good friendship and have a common goal; to win in the stock market. Sointhara is well known for his liberal donations and the social events in the city. His business flourished after taking up international construction contracts. His company won awards and accolades, and there is a chance to receive another award as a successful entrepreneur of the year. Both friends spent some time discussing their businesses over drinks. Fulkeery gave a cheque for sixty-six lakhs to Sointhara. It was an interest-free loan taken a long time ago. Sointhara frowned and said the money should not be a *cause or a reason* for their friendship. Later they hugged, shook hands, and walked out of the lounge.

Gaikwad waits until Sointhara leaves, and he meets Fulkeery. They occupied the table beside the bamboo grove. Gaikwad gives a print of the transactions of the trades. Fulkeery studied the paper for a while and said,

"I am not satisfied with the earnings, Gaik."

"Sir, I followed the portfolio of Bobby, but the entry and exit differed, but it didn't affect the overall trades."

"You take a look at the past ten days' trade; my earnings are ten percent less than Sointhara. You played the same shares as your assistant did. But see the profit margin of your boss and mine."

He scoffed at his words and lit his cigarette. Daily, Gaikwad copies the list of shares Bobby trades in the market. Later, he executes the trades for the same shares, but the timing was not going well with his entry and exit of the intraday trade. Every month Fulkeery gives a cheque to Gaikwad for an amount to invest in the stock market and, with a note, what he wants in return. Usually, it would be a twenty percent profit on his investment. Gaikwad deposits the money in his trading account and trades as Bobby does, and for the past two months, the returns were hardly ten percent on the investments. Now, Fulkeery explained his new idea and wants Gaikwad to include his stock investment in Bobby's trading accounts. He asked Gaikwad to double the share quantity of his investment than Sointhara for day trade. Gaikwad understood his plan and said that he would double the share quantities in Bobby's trades and deposit Fulkeery's money along with the Sointhara funds. Gaikwad collected his commission cheque and assured Fulkeery that he would go as per his idea.

₹ $ £ €

Gaikwad reached his house at eleven pm. His wife was waiting for him in the portico. He asks her to have her dinner and goes into the bedroom. She took his bag and removed his lunch box. Two cheques fell on the floor; she picked them up and saw the figures. Both cheques were in his name; she was surprised and did not understand why and who paid such big money. It was not the time for a bonus, or the annual appraisal, and a doubt sparked inside her mind. She places them back in his bag and walks into the kitchen. Mrs. Saritha Gaikwad is an English lecturer at a private college and takes tuition classes in the evenings. It has been ten years of their married life, and she did not conceive. She enjoys spending time with the children. Despite the medical checkups and expensive treatments, she couldn't become a mother yet. Many times, she thought of adopting a child, but her husband did not agree and said he could not take in an orphan child. They fought over the issue for a few months, and to fulfill her wish of spending time with the children. She started giving free tuition to primary-class children. Even he did not tolerate her getting the children into the house and helping them with their studies.

Nowadays, she often gets disturbed, panicked, and depressed. She's always with negative thoughts and feels guilty for not bearing a child. Her loneliness and hopelessness made her feel ashamed and intolerable of the discussions at parties, weddings, and social gatherings. The involuntary childlessness and depression symptoms were more inclined toward suicidal tendencies. Whenever there's a talk or a discussion of children or motherhood arises, she weeps and shuts herself in her bedroom for hours. If she's at the college, she hides in the washroom and weeps for a while, and it lightens her heart. A gynecologist suggested she should undergo counseling and short-term therapy CBT—Cognitive Behavioral Therapy. She didn't like going to another doctor and did not agree to attend the classes by other medical professionals. Finally, she decided to live her childless life and endure the pain in silence.

Saritha wanted to go on vacation to Ooty and booked three tickets. Her husband was surprised and questioned about the third ticket. She said that a cute girl was going with them. He didn't like going with an unknown girl. Finally, he was convinced and prepared to take the girl along. Meanwhile, Gaikwad deposited the cheques at the bank and returned to the office. It was the closing bell for the stock market, and he checked the squared-off trades. Gaikwad's personal investment was yielding eight percent profit for the day. He calculated the past fifteen days' investment and profit and was satisfied. At four pm, he received Trademel from Bobby, and the figures reflected a good profit for the day's investment. He compiled a breakdown of the day's market activities and emailed it to his MD and later to his second boss, Fulkeery.

₹ $ £ €

Within a few months, the NSE and BSE reduced the lot sizes of Nifty, Nifty Bank, and the other indices; it was good for the single trade per day type of traders and if the trade went in their favor. For the multi-lot traders, it proved profitable only when the market maintained a steady move either up or down. Besides, the low margins of the options were attracting inexperienced participants with no prior knowledge of the trading. Moreover, the work-from-home culture encouraged most of the employees after the pandemic. The liquidity was expanding in all indices, and finally, most of them lost their money without a strict stop loss, entry, or exit. Thus, the probability of the profit was low with market volatility. Some experts believed that the impact of the low margins resulted in good revenue for the *stockbrokers* and the *exchanges* as well. Bobby was still at the office, and he was observing the charts. It's Thursday; the expiry of options, and unexpectedly, the market declined more than the anticipated downtrend. The Nifty Bank was the worst hit, and Bobby searched for the shares, which hit new lows and highs. He spotted twelve such shares, and charts predicted a gradual rise based on 50 and 100 EMA crossing over the charts.

However, the charts indicated a positive move; he wasn't confident with the price, volumes, and ROI of the shares and called his friend, Sidhu. They spoke for a few minutes, and meanwhile, he received three calls from Mrs. Saritha Gaikwad on the office phone. She was enquiring about her husband, and he told her that he left the office. She asked him to call or leave a message stating that she was unable to reach his mobile and mentioned her health condition. Bobby called Gaikwad, but he did not answer, so he left a message to call home. He picked some shares for the next day and checked the balance in the trading account. It showed double the amount than today's morning balance. He checked the pay-in and saw the new fund transfer into the trading accounts.

Usually, after the day's trade, first there would be a payout from the trading accounts; instead, now there's a new pay-in. It appeared suspicious—a malicious activity—and Bobby was hesitant to trade in the next trading session. He was suspicious, as Gaikwad maintains the trading account's user IDs and passwords.

Anyway, he decided to go with the few blue-chip shares that were beaten down recently in the market. He made a list of shares and marked them for the pre-opening of the market. The clock displayed nine pm; he shut his system and took Gaikwad's address from one of the security staff. After a search of ten minutes, he reached the house. Saritha Gaikwad was pale and lying on a sofa in a semi-conscious state, with a medical prescription in her hand.

7. Business Entities

Nikitha was on her way back from a Twin Cities Hoteliers Association meeting. At the parking lot, Karan was introduced to her by the association's recently elected president. She already knew him; he was a regular customer of her coffee shop. Karan was with Anwar, and he introduced Nikitha to Anwar. Later, when she was searching for an auto, Karan said he would drop her off at her coffee shop, and she smiled. After getting out of the car, displaying her courtesy, she invited them to her coffee shop in the evening.

At seven pm, they arrived, and she ushered them to the table and ordered coffee and special delicacies. Again, they introduced themselves to her jokingly and started discussing the prime businesses of the twin cities. Later, she told them about her coffee shop and business turnover. Karan and Anwar spoke of the die and mold industry, and Nikitha was interested in the business. Anwar presented the agreements and other financial papers to Karan. After seeing the figures, Nikitha was bewildered, excused, and went and was attending to the customers. After half an hour, Karan asked for the bill, Nikitha smiled, walked them out of her coffee shop, and said goodbye. She returned to the cash counter and was busy until the closing hours. After closing her shop, she collected the food from a takeaway and reached her rented flat in Banjara Hills.

In the morning, Karan took his business partner Anwar to his factory. Karan explained the manufacturing process; later, they discussed the unit's expansion and the land acquisition to set up the unit. Anwar called his brother-in-law, Hameed, and informed him about the unit, land, and other infrastructural assessments. They had Hyderabad's special Biryani and returned to the hotel where Anwar stayed. Karan arranged a meeting with the bank manager at three pm. Anwar was handling the other arrangements, and following the meeting, a loan was to be processed. Karan returned to his flat, and his wife and two children were ready and waiting for him. They went to a movie, had dinner at a restaurant, and returned late at night. His thoughts woke him at four am and he was thinking about the deal and, unreasonably, did not like the business deal with Anwar. Something was strange with him, his casual talk, and he thought of speaking to Hameed before proceeding to the final agreement.

Karan went to the bank and met with the bank manager for the loan. He needs someone to ensure his loan, repayments, and surety. He remembered Nikitha and called her. She was excited to speak to him; he asked her to meet him at the hotel in Begumpet. Karan was in a white pinstriped suite; he picked her up from her coffee shop and went to the hotel. Nikitha wore a light blue Tussar silk sari with a yellow border and a matching blouse with long sleeves and looked gorgeous. He couldn't stay calm and appreciated her beautiful attire.

"Nikitha, you are beautiful today."

"Thank you."

"You're looking elegant too."

"No? Not before a gorgeous businesswoman like you."

He ordered and took out the papers and gave them to her. She took them, read the first page, and saw him. He told her about the expansion of his unit with a new die and mold project, of PVC parts manufacturing, and rubber products used in various commercial and industrial automobiles. Briefed her on the project and his estimation and explained to her about his financial position and the bank loan. He requested her to visit his unit once, and she was glad and agreed. They were discussing their businesses and before leaving, he asked if she could be one of his sureties. She hesitated and asked him to take her as a business partner after a while. He enquired about her investment in the coffee shop, assets, and liabilities. She told him the present net worth of her business and said she could finance his new project. They planned to visit his unit next Saturday.

₹ $ £ €

There was a rally of a political party and a meeting in the evening at SR Nagar on Saturday. The police issued a public notice to the establishments to close early, sensing anti-social elements trying to disrupt the meeting. Nikitha closed her coffee shop at five pm and was waiting for Karan. He arrived and took her to his ancillary unit. He showed her his plant and they spent some time roaming in the industrial area. After loading the consignment for delivery, they started from Bollaram. The roads towards Secunderabad are blocked so she invited him to her flat in Banjara Hill for dinner to avoid traffic constraints. He asked what she takes with dinner, and he said he prefers whisky with food. She said she would prefer beer; he asked her address and ordered food. They reached the flat and were busy discussing the process of acquiring the loan and finance.

Meanwhile, the food was delivered, and they tossed their drinks for the beginning of their new business. After a few minutes, they were speaking in singular and joking with one another. She excused herself saying she wasn't comfortable in a sari, but he insisted, asked her not to change and praised her body. Winked at him, went into her bedroom, and returned in a transparent nightdress; a lovely atmosphere surrounded them and they were attracted to each other.

'The alcohol was tempting their desires to ignite, but time was reminding them of tomorrow's responsibilities.'

It was midnight, and Karan was ready to leave. Nikitha hugged him, promised, and said that she would cook at home next week and invite him for dinner. He smiled and said goodnight. Nikitha received a message from Bobby, instructing her to purchase only two shares that were expected to gain momentum in the future. She promptly added the shares to her buy list. While contemplating Karan, she admired his diligent efforts to expand his business and was drawn to his polite and appealing behavior. Lately, he had been visiting her coffee shop every two or three days, spending time there before going to or returning from his factory. She envisioned him as her ideal partner and resolved to meet him in private.

However, thoughts of Bobby, who was similar to Karan but younger, lingered in her mind. With her thirtieth birthday approaching, she hesitated about being with someone younger. Faced with a dilemma, she deliberated between choosing a younger man or someone her age with wealth. Despite her high aspirations, she ultimately convinced herself to choose Karan. Her decision was like a flickering candle, bizarre and casting moving shadows.

Bobby arrived in Hyderabad for official work and invited his friends to his house in Madhura Nagar. The party was filled with jokes, laughter, and songs. He mentioned that he wanted to rent or sell his house and move to Chembur, Mumbai. His friends did not like the idea and promised to find a good tenant and secure a higher rent. However, Bobby was determined to live in Chembur and had already checked out a new two-bedroom flat near his office, although he hadn't negotiated with the builder yet. After the party, the friends went for a bike ride on the necklace road and had dinner before Bobby returned home at midnight.

The next morning, he went to one of the banks, changed the address, and transferred his account from the home branch in Hyderabad to the Chembur branch. Later, he went to his favorite coffee shop. Nikitha was surprised and excited to see Bobby entering her coffee shop after a long time. She went forward and offered him his usual table. She ordered coffee, cupcakes, and samosas and sat with him.

"A few days ago, I was just remembering you, Bobby."

"Wow, thanks, and someone cares for me."

"How's your job in Mumbai? How much do you earn at your office and with trading?"

"Just enough, for my coffee and cupcakes... I am living in an expensive city."

"How did you like the city? Any girlfriends?"

He smiled and moved his head, saying no. He finished his coffee and observed her. She appeared different; he saw a change in her and remembered his last visit. A few months ago, she was active, attractive, and expressive. Now she appeared different, with a grown-up look and mature behavior. She saw him watching her, adjusted her T-shirt, and said,

"Hey, what are you watching?"

She gives a seductive look, moving her shoulders. He stared at her and said,

"Nikitha, I don't know... Can't say, but you look very different now."

She smiled and excused herself for a while. He saw her briskly walking towards the cash counter. and a little fat on her body enhanced her physical beauty. He remembered his old days in the coffee shop, scribbling on the tissue papers and meeting her one evening. She returned after five minutes and joined him. He ordered another coffee, placed his mobile aside, and asked,

"How's your business, Nikitha?"

"Ah! Fine, just doing well, but not as good as before."

"You should have opened another branch in Secunderabad."

"I thought of it, but now I am into other business."

"A new business?"

"Yeah, and how long are you staying in Hyderabad?"

"I'll be leaving a day after tomorrow."

"I owe you for your trade tips, Bobby."

"Oh! Forget it, it's nothing."

"Are you free tomorrow?"

"Don't bother, I'll accept your treat on my next visit."

She leans forward on the table, looks into his eyes, and speaks.

"Bobby, I have to discuss a few important matters with you. I believe you to be a true friend rather than a customer."

Bobby mocks at her and says,

"Let's discuss and I'll argue first."

"I am serious Bobby; I have no other friends."

"Ok, where do you stay?"

"I'll message you my address and we'll meet after eight pm."

"Ok, do I have to pay the coffee bill now?"

"Of course, you have to..."

She says, extends her hand, and confirms again.

"Eight pm, tomorrow, I'll be waiting."

₹ $ £ €

It was half past eleven in the morning, and Bobby was busy analyzing the total investments and profit earned from the past year's transactions. He realized that Sointhara was involved in market trading through four traders. Player one buys shares for intraday trade, and if the market advances, the second player buys the same shares for five or six rupees higher than Player One. The third player then buys the shares for three or four rupees more than the second player. Meanwhile, the fourth player shorts the total volume of shares of the other three players and waits for the market to respond to the index fluctuations.

If the index advances, then the first, second, and third players sell their shares at the targeted price and close their accounts. The fourth player squares off his position for the day or takes the delivery. Similarly, if the index declines, the first, second, and third players short the shares twice or thrice the quantities bought and wait. The fourth player completes his deal by purchasing the entire volume that other players have shorted, reselling it after the delivery. Bobby did not understand why he appointed him when the other scalpers were doing a good job. Surprisingly, he finds that the two trade accounts are in the company's name and the other two are registered in individual names. Later, Bobby assumed that his MD did not want this information to be in public and to be known to his friends.

He remembered his first day with his MD on the flight from Hyderabad to Mumbai. It was a weird experience, when he introduced himself as PA to MD. He smiled to himself and left his office in Banjara Hills for lunch and went to the Nagarjuna Circle in Panjagutta. Had Pav Bhaji and Pani Puri, spent some time and returned to the office. Now, he understood, what were the nick names meant? The first player was called 'Jogger,' the second 'Walker,' the third was 'Stroller,' and the fourth was 'Runner.' He took the sheets and checked each trading session of four players.

The first player—Jogger, bought the shares at the opening of the market and in huge volumes for intraday trade.
The second player—Walker, bought double the volume of the Jogger with one or two rupees higher than the Jogger.
Later, the third player—Stroller, purchased three times the volume of Walker and two to three rupees more than Walker.
Finally, the fourth player—Runner shorts the total volume of the other three players.

The act of price rigging is against the rules of trading. The speculations might go unnoticed for a while, but eventually, the authorities would undoubtedly track them down.

One day, the index gained more than eight hundred points in Nifty Bank and three hundred points in Nifty, and the three players fetched a profit of rupees one crore, five lakhs, and sixty-two thousand rupees. The loss of the fourth player was forty-three Lakhs and fifty-nine thousand. The total profit at the end of the day with the swing and positional trades was rupees one crore, two lakhs three thousand, including the stamp duty and security tax. The figures on other days showed even more than three crores. The turnover for a month was around fifty to eighty crores, and the average profit per day was eight to twelve percent. Bobby was amazed at checking the figures and appreciated the strategy deployed with such a huge amount in the present unpredictable market situation.

He wondered why his boss did not go with the options and futures. Realized that he had no time or a reliable person to deal with on his behalf. One question bothered him: why were the trading accounts registered on individuals rather than on the corporate account when it's financed from the company's account? Later, he was studying the offshore trades of the US, UK, and Germany. Forty sheets displayed the trades of Dow Jones and SP500, FTSE, and DAX and the investment, transactions, and profit. The total turnover was more than six to eight crores per month. He searched for the scalper's names and addresses, but to his surprise, they were marked as J1, W2, S3, and R4. He guessed that the first two accounts were in the company's name, and the other individual accounts were on S3 and R4.

Bobby couldn't understand why his MD, Sointhara registered the scalpers trading as AOP—Association of Persons. Later, he realized that the trading activity must reflect as AOP, which generates a regular income and entitles the legal entities. Subsequently, he runs the big show, being the sole financier for the activity of scalping by the professional traders.

Later, he was checking the local civil contracts of Metro Rail, FOB—Foot over Bridge, and the new expansion project of the two railway stations in the twin cities. Until now, the projects were done as per the tender's value and the time, but one was lagging and had huge escalating costs than the original project cost in the old city. An unanswered question was still pricking him; as this breakup of the reports can be done in Mumbai itself, then why he's sent to Hyderabad and gets the financial report posted from here? Now, he is one of the scalpers; he didn't understand the exact business and the strange deals of the organization. He sent the reports to his Mumbai office and saved this information, thinking it could be a worthwhile opportunity in the future if something goes wrong against him.

Surprisingly, that was a boon for his survival.

8. Nikitha's Wedding Plan

Nikitha prepared her choice of food and was waiting for her young friend. Bobby arrived at half past eight pm in a white T-shirt and jeans, and she was excited to receive him. She offered him a soft drink, placed a plate with Samosas before him, and said,

"Bobby, I am happy to see you. After opening the coffee shop, I have no friends, I mean true friends, except, you."

"True friends! You have many business friends, why true friends?"

"Yes, true friend, with whom I can speak open-heartedly. I have many issues to get clarified."

"Yellow low-neck T-shirt, casual trousers, a little makeup, and you can talk for hours in your dressing mirror or with any businessman."

He said and laughed. She stared at him for a while, observed herself in the mirror of the sitting room, and spoke.

"Oh! I thought you don't like watching girls."

"I don't watch... I love to observe them."

"Wonderful, then what did you observe in me?"

"Everything."

"Everything?"

"Come on... How're your profits nowadays?"

"As usual, on average eight to twenty thousand daily."

"That's pretty cool profit, and how much investment?"

"Are you asking about the coffee shop or trading?"

"I meant the trading."

She thinks for a while and recollects her and replies.

"Till now, my investment is five lakhs and profits around twenty to thirty thousand a week."

Bobby took a bite of the Samosa and was thinking about her investments. He calculated a profit of one to two Lakhs from the coffee shop and not less than ten to fifty thousand from the trades per month. To his understanding, her investment should yield more than three lakhs a month from trading and the coffee shop. She should take care of her coffee shop rather than running with the stock market, he thought and moved his head. The shares he suggested were trading low, and he wanted to ask her how much she expected but did not. She waves her right hand before his eyes.

"Young man, what are you thinking? About me?"

She provoked him; he saw her and smiled. Her mobile started ringing; she excused herself and walked into the kitchen. She was convincing someone to meet her on Saturday; she was speaking in a low voice, yet her speech was audible. Bobby realized that maybe one of her boyfriends was to see her now, and she was avoiding him. Despite having many business friends, she's missing real, true friends, and he understands her loneliness. He presumed her age to be in her thirties and wanted to suggest her to get married and start a good family life. Nikitha walks into the living room and asks him.

"Bobby, if you wish to have a beer, it's in the refrigerator, chill man."

He hesitates, and she takes two beers, shows him, and asks.

"Do you need a glass, or straight from the bottle?"

She placed them on the table and sat beside him and gave him an opener. He opened two bottles, gave her one, and tossed. She took a large gulp, went into the kitchen, and returned with two plates with chicken pieces and onions and placed them on the table. He takes another gulp and tastes a small piece of chicken.

"I prepared, especially for you."

She said, smiling; he thanked her and observed her body movements. She moved aside on the sofa and supported her right elbow on the armrest. They were silent for a while, chewing the chicken pieces. Bobby received a message and a call from Sidhu. He excused himself, walked into the kitchen's balcony, and spoke. Meanwhile, she checked her messages and replied. She checked WhatsApp posts and was busy chatting with her friends. Bobby returned to the living room and sat opposite her. The spotlight from the ceiling was on her glowing beauty and gave a clear body outline through the transparent nightgown. She saw him watching her and raised her eyebrows. He feels irksome, smiles, and says,

"I never saw you so relaxed, Nikitha."

"You can call me Nikki."

She says and crosses her slender leg over the other and questions.

"Bobby, can I discuss and share a few things about my life? And promise me you'll never play or try to fool me with my lonely life."

"When you've decided to say something to me, it means that you trust me, ok?"

"Nowadays, I am very disturbed thinking about my life, marriage, and the new business."

"Are you into a new business other than the coffee shop?"

She stared at him for a while and continued,

"Yes, I am financing and taking a partnership in Karan's new die and mold industry. He wants to expand his ancillary, and I gave the surety with all my savings."

Nikitha told him about the meeting with a Mumbai partner, Anwar, and was anxiously explaining the turnover and profit. After discussing her future business, she told him about her wedding plan. He was shocked hearing her words and remained silent. She spoke of Karan and said he wasn't happy staying with his family and wanted a divorce. Praised his behavior and the business prospects. Calculated his net worth in crores and said she does not need a coffee shop now for her livelihood. She proudly called herself the wife of a wealthy businessperson and said she slogged as a slave serving useless customers. Later, she spoke about her dream of possessing gold, jewelry, and a big house in Jubilee Hills and wanted him to live with her. He realized her aspirations, dreams, and desires for the lifestyle of the upper echelon of an expensive society. After a few minutes, he clears his throat and questions.

"Nikki, are you serious about your marriage?"

"Yes! Why do you doubt it?"

"Think it over before you decide. Sometimes, life doesn't go with our dreams as we witness them with vague imaginations and desires."

"Why not Bobby? To my age, I think it's the right time, and with the right person of my choice, to get settled."

"Nikitha, are you in your senses; you are snatching away a husband and father? I don't understand, what made you fall for Karan."

He stops and rubs his chin and waits for her response. She looks surprised and he continues,

"Ok, tell me one thing now; if I propose to you, are you ready to get married to me?"

She takes a sip of her beer, peers at him, and replies,

"First, I'll have to check your earnings, bank balance, and affordability to fulfill my wishes. Later, I shall decide, and tell you."

She smiles and sits beside him. She tries to lean on him, but he avoids her, takes the empty bottles, and walks into the kitchen. She followed him and served the dinner with the second beer. They had dinner, and Bobby finished first. He went and sat on the sofa and closed his eyes. After a while, she returned from the kitchen and sat beside him. He moved aside, turned towards her, and spoke.

"Nikitha, do you remember the earlier days, when you were a sole proprietor, and your coffee shop was a favorite meeting place for youngsters? A quiet place for small businesspeople and an affordable eatery for low-budget guys like me, and besides, you took care of our choices as a perfect businesswoman does. I can never forget those moments."

"Yes, Bobby, you're right, and I think sometimes, something's going wrong and I am not able to point out the exact reason. And that's why I called you, my sweetheart."

Now, she feels uncertain about her dreams turning into reality, and tears appear in her eyes. The tears roll down her tender cheeks; he notices and tries to console her.

"Well, I never thought you'd be so casual and easy with your life. Nikki, I remembered you in a coffee shop in Chembur after an incident. A woman of your age, I assume, was taking care of the customers in her coffee shop. There was an issue with the bill, and her arrogance was intolerable. One of the students, while leaving the shop, tapped the sauce and ketchup bottles. The bottles rolled, fell on the floor, scattering all around, and splashed on some of the customers. A few customers called her, and she started yelling at the students and even at the customers who were complaining. Do you remember, one evening there was a similar issue here with the students; you convinced them and charged the bill as per their discounted price?"

"No, I don't remember."

She said it with a choked voice.

"When you can manage your business so well, then why do you want to take part in other people's financial matters, I don't understand? Your customer dealings, manners, and taste are impeccable; why do you want to leave the good business? Were you forced to accept the deal, or it's with your consent?"

"No, but the business prospects captivated me."

"Do you know how well you are doing with your business and with the stock trades? I believe you would be a well-established businesswoman in a few years from now. Nikitha, please don't get misconstrued with your wild dreams."

She stares at him and replies in a depressed tone.

"I don't want to enjoy my life after I get old, Bobby... To be frank, I need the money as quickly as possible and settle in my life."

"Listen... Now, let me explain my hectic job at my office. Do you know how I slog at my office from Monday to Friday? I am a scalper; every second and minute counts in lakhs for me. One miscalculation or delay in executing the orders and I have to struggle the whole day to regain the lost profit and minimize the losses. If I lose, my boss will kick me out."

Nikitha was watching him silently. He saw her and appreciated her confidence to discuss her personal life with him and with just a few acquaintances in her coffee shop. Thought of asking her about her family, but did not and realized, if she had a family, she would not have discussed it with him. He was feeling sorry for her marriage proposal to a married man and wanted to ask her to rethink her decision now, but it was too late.

She too was going with the same thoughts running inside her, as he did. Bobby is younger, and she was feeling ashamed revealing her marriage with him. Except for him, she has no one to talk to her now. She could not imagine how she convinced herself to have a word and take advise from this young man. Bobby was a better option for her to settle in life she felt. Karan may ignore her after the financial deal; being a married person, he would give a reason and can get rid of her. Besides, they could even face financial and legal issues. About Bobby, she assumed he's a sincere, loving person and imagined him in her drowsy dreams. She closed her eyes and leaned her head on the back of the sofa.

"Nikitha, I'd better leave now; it's getting late."

She opened her eyes, took his hand in her hands and smiled. He got up and said,

"I think your decision to marry a married man's something weird, and I can't imagine."

"I am in a fix now... Whom to choose Karan, or you?"

Bobby reacts instantly and replies,

"Hey! Leave me; I am not yet prepared for a woman."

"I'll train you to be my kind of man; come on."

"Be serious, Nikitha; it's your life, not mine."

"My life has been a mess. I have been sharing my lonely nights with Karan, and today, it doesn't make a difference taking you in my love. Genuinely, you are my true friend, and... I don't mind sharing my happiness with a young man."

She sings the song 'It's My Life,' grabs his T-shirt, and drags him into her bedroom.

'Mental balance was the need of the moment, and one wrong move might divert the paths of their lives.'

9. Nikitha's Weird Allurement

Karan was at the bank and received a call from Anwar; said he was at the airport and wanted to meet him and gave his hotel's address. Karan went to his unit, and in the afternoon returned to Nikitha coffee shop. Told her that Anwar had come to Hyderabad, and he was going to meet him at the hotel. Nikitha was uneasy speaking to him today, and he sensed that, and yet he asked her to accompany him. She bluntly excused herself and went into the washroom and observed herself in the mirror.

For the past few days, after becoming a business partner of Karan, she started living in a confused and deprived state of mind. She realized that to some extent her wish was fulfilled, but the future was still in no right direction to achieve her desired life. Her unstable thoughts about her assets, Karan's wealth, and Bobby's friendship were not allowing her to visualize a clear image of what the present is and what the future would be. The first choice was an independent business, then a posh house, and after the wish of gold ornaments with a handsome husband. Till now, only the dream of business was fulfilled, and the greed for more money eradicated the flourishing new idea for success, which was subsequently diminished.

'Her dreams and ambitions were stalled as an imaginary portrait in the sky rather than a reality. The unbalanced mind often plays to the wrong tunes. Now, Nikitha was in the sequel of her lifeline of the past, present, and future of time.'

She checked the time and returned to the cash counter. She politely said she was not feeling well and excused herself. He stared at her with disappointment and said he would return after meeting Anwar and left. She watched him leave the shop and waited until his car drove away into the traffic.

She called her manager, assigned the counter, and left. Karan met with Anwar; they discussed a few issues, and meanwhile, the drinks were served. Anwar showed the total investment and layout for the expansion of the unit. There was still a shortfall of a few lakhs and Anwar promised that he could arrange it in cash and continued,

"Karan, I think it's better if we pool the total money in your bank account and go with the process of other loan formalities. You're dealing with the bank process, right? So, you can handle the official work easily and in case you need me, just give me a call."

He agrees and questions him.

"Ok, Anwar, but if the collateral papers have to be signed before the bank officials, how many days are you staying in Hyderabad?"

"I'll be staying for another two days, and I have to visit a factory to lift the consignment."

"Well then, I'll try to arrange the formalities at the bank and the government offices tomorrow. If possible, we will complete the paperwork and place the order for the machinery."

"What about your friend; how's she?"

"She's ok."

"She's beautiful and a smart woman; I expected she was coming with you today, Karan."

"I asked her; she said she wasn't feeling well."

"So, let's wind up here. Chalo Yaar; let's go and meet her now."

Anwar said, and Karan was not interested in taking him to Nikitha's flat. But he could not avoid and they left the hotel. On the way, Anwar bought drinks, Hyderabad's famous Biryani, and talked about one of his friends in the old city. Karan thought of calling Nikitha but did not and decided to leave as early as possible. He realized that Anwar was more interested in Nikitha than the new project. He remembered Anwar's last visit; he was staring at Nikitha with a different view, and he could not tolerate him doing so. Thought she had to be careful with new people or strangers and wanted her to take care of herself. Later, he realized she was aware of the behavior and acts of the customers visiting her coffee shop. Was it an excuse, or a man's possessive version? Karan was not able to answer to himself. Nikitha refreshed herself and settled in the living room with a beer. She was checking her portfolio and found a profit of forty-five thousand on her one month's investment and remembered Bobby. In her imagination, now he was more attractive with a potential prospect than an establishing married man. A few months ago, she was a free and lively woman, and customers were trying to interact with her in one way or another. Now, she's feeling like a deceived woman with shattered dreams.

She enjoyed spending time with a married man and a young man and experienced no difference, but now, the decency of Bobby was more appreciable and loving than Karan's. Despite her weakness to explore the experience with him that night, he never spoke loose or behaved arrogantly as other men do but respected her. He called her before leaving and asked her not to be too insouciant, warning her to be alert and think twice before getting into any other legal matters. Though he was a few years younger than her, his suggestion was meaningful and sensible.

She finished her second beer and lay on the sofa, watching the US market news on the TV. At nine pm, Karan and Anwar reached Nikitha's flat. She unwillingly received them, spent some time with them, consumed half a beer, and excused herself for a while in her bedroom.
"Karan I am transferring the money to Nikitha's account."
"Anwar, I don't agree. The money has to be drawn for the payments, and I can't ask her for each payment."
"That's true, but depositing all the money in one account looks inappropriate anyway; I'd put some in your account and the rest in her account."

Nikitha heard their discussion and closed her eyes. Anwar thought that after the agreement and release of the loan amount from the bank, the infused personal money would be safely converted into legal. But if the money is mistaken as the loan amount and used for the expansion of the unit, then he cannot withdraw. So, he decided to transfer the money into Nikitha's account directly and believed it would be safer in her bank. He wants to meet in private and convince her. He assumed her to be easygoing, too friendly with wealthy businessmen than her usual customers.

After a while, Karan wanted to leave and asked his friend. Anwar said he would finish the last round and asked him to give some time. Anwar watched the TV for a few minutes and went to the washroom. He returned and saw Karan snoring, then he went into Nikitha's bedroom. She too was asleep with her hand spread beside her body. Her sleeping pose attracted and slowly approached her. When Karan was awake, Anwar was relaxing opposite him. Both men stood; Karan went to the washroom and, while returning, went into Nikitha's bedroom. He saw her sleeping with a blanket wrapped over her body. Karan locked her flat with a duplicate key, and they left.

The morning Nikitha smelled a strong odor on her body and thought it was Karan's new perfume. He loves perfumes, and a few days ago she presented him with an international brand. She smelled again: felt something was wrong, got off her bed, naked, and walked into the living room, and felt she depicted a disastrous and wrong pathway in her life. There were two plates with leftover Biryani, snacks, and empty bottles. She did not like last night's party and besides, she could not remember exactly what had happened. She knew he should be Karan but was not sure who she shared her bed with last night. The loan was sanctioned, and Karan spoke with the suppliers and finalized a meeting. Later, he met with Anwar, took the cheques, and deposited them in the company's account. Anwar said he had to stay for another day and asked him to meet him in the evening. Meanwhile, there was a call from the foreman, and Karan had to leave for his unit. Anwar called Nikitha and asked her to accompany him to the Charminar and said he wanted to buy a few clothes and bangles. Despite her attempts to avoid, Anwar's endearing and pleasant words persuaded her. She asked him to pick her up at three pm.

₹ $ £ €

In the meantime, Moin returns from the transporter's cargo godown with big tamper-proofed boxes to his house in the old city. Anwar meets with his friend and asks him to deposit the money after he confirms the date. He paid him some amount and appreciated his job. Later, they were busy with the accounts and the dates to deposit the money in the bank. Anwar took a snapshot of the paper on which he worked out the figures on his mobile and forwarded a copy to Moin.

Anwar left, and Moin brought three gunny bags, started counting the money, and made the bundles of rupees of ten lakhs each. It took him an hour to prepare the money to be deposited in the bank as per the date, He wrapped each bundle in a polythene bag, tagged each with a date, dumped the packets in the bags, and secured them in a secret place in his house. He lit a cigarette and was not able to understand why the money had to be deposited separately on different dates and in the same bank account. He did not bother to think further and was satisfied with the good commission he got for the job. He does odd jobs for his livelihood, but after meeting Anwar, and with the job of money transfer, he enjoyed working for him.

₹ $ £ €

Anwar and Nikitha visited the Charminar and Chudi Bazaar, and he bought the bangles for his wife and two daughters. Later, she selected dresses, dress material, Kashmir scarfs for his daughters, and kurtis for herself. She wanted to pay separately for her clothes, but he did not agree, and he paid.

57

She could not hide her greediness and selected one more Churidar dress, and that was also included in his bill. On the way, he told her about the money he wanted to deposit in her bank account. She did not understand, and he explained the rules of income tax. Very tactfully, he did not disclose that the surplus money in a sole account holder might cause unnecessary obligations from the income tax department. He behaved politely and generously and told her that she could liberally use the money if needed for her personal use. She was amazed, and her thoughts were faster than reality.

Nowadays, Nikitha is avoiding parties because she's not able to control her thirst for alcohol and her physical balance after the drink. So, she was feeling comfortable at home, especially with Karan. She called Karan, and he said there was a minor problem at the unit and said he would see her the next day. So, she was left with no choice and decided to meet Anwar alone.

She reached Anwar's hotel room; he welcomed her and ordered a few drinks. She took her drink in small sips, thinking that it may not influence her body quickly. But was wrong; the quality of imported malt whisky with soda was working faster than a large number of local brands. Anyhow, she managed and stopped taking her drink. The food was served, and both had their dinner. She was not feeling comfortable, and Anwar was ready to drop her and felt it would be safer for her to go with him than to travel alone to her flat.

He called a cab, and they reached her flat. She got off and said good night; he insisted he would walk her to the flat. Meanwhile, he received a call, said good night, and left. She was lying on her bed thinking about Anwar's money in her bank account. Remembered his words and thought of asking for a short loan for her house in Jubilee Hills. But she realized that he appeared something different from the earlier visits;

his behavior was reserved and short-spoken, but a wealthy look reflected on him with his attire. She was wondering, why she loved spending more time with married people than young men, remembered Bobby, and heard someone questioning.

Should one go with the person who fulfills wishes and choices and is satisfied with the money, or with the one who respects, cares for, and loves forever?

She couldn't judge who was the right person in her life now. One must think before accepting anyone in life and should not assume in a short time frame. She remembered a leftover beer in the refrigerator and opened it. After a few sips, she felt drowsy, placed the beer on the side table, and lay on the bed. Nikitha's weird allurement—was it for money, physical pleasure, or for a true-life partner?

There was a knock on the door; she woke up and opened the door. Anwar entered in and returned her purse that was left in the cab. She took it, thanked him, and she gave him a friendly hug. She thought that she needed more than a hug at these lonely moments. At once, realized her mistake and tried to move away from him, but she couldn't resist his strong perfume odor and from his arms.

10. Trial Run

Moin received a call from Anwar; he segregated the bundles of cash and deposited three of them in Nikitha's account in the Banjara Hills branch. He took a snap of the bank acknowledgement and sent it to Anwar. He went to his house and wrote a note of the amount he deposited in the bank. There was a message from his boss, and it mentioned another five bundles to be deposited after three days.

At five pm, Nikitha received a message from her bank showing the total balance available in the account. She was shocked and tried Anwar's number; meanwhile, she received a call from him, and he told her about the deposits.

"Nikitha, I have transferred the amount into your bank account. Please keep a note of the transactions, ok?"

"Ok, Anwar, but..."

Anwar interrupts and explains.

"Nikitha, keep this matter a secret, and don't tell Karan. I'll explain in detail when we meet."

Anwar told her how the working capital has to be utilized from the loan amount. He explained the procedure and the payments, but she did not bother to listen to him and enquired when he was coming to Hyderabad. He said next week and disconnected. She thought of asking him for a personal loan for her new house but decided to invite him alone to discuss and convince him. Moreover, she was anxious to show him the ready-built second-sale house in Jubilee Hills.

In the evening, she went to the broker at Banjara Hills, and he took her to the house. They met the owner, bargained, and negotiated a reasonable price. The owner was convinced, and they discussed the mode of payment. He said he wanted a part of the money from the bank loan and the rest in cash.

She agreed, and the broker said he would prepare the agreement and look into the registration process. Later, her broker dropped her at the coffee shop and left. Nikitha checked the total sales for the month and was surprised. The sales increased by fifteen percent with the reservation of the tables on the weekends and with corporate bookings. Believed it was a good sign and wanted to pay early and take the position of her dream house. She felt a positive vibe fanning her luck toward prosperity, and her second dream was to materialize shortly.

Nowadays, she is despised and shows no interest in taking care of customers in the shop. One of her waiters and a manager catered to the customers' requests and handled the cash counter successfully. She took the money from the counter and left. Karan called Nikitha and said he might not meet her; he was busy at the unit with a few minor machine line assembly problems. She was to tell him about the money, remembered Anwar's words, and did not speak of the fund transfer. Now, a dislike has developed in her, and she has the least interest in talking or going with him. Her intentions and mindset were recognizable only to the people who were close to her.

If she had been with her parents, then she could have been a different person with real values and morals in life. She started living alone from the age of ten after losing her parents in an accident in Chennai, and a distant grandmother brought her up. Now, after living single for many years, she lost the habit of listening to and hearing about the good deeds of others, which was something impossible for her. Her avaricious efforts motivated by a desire for money have also led to the loss of meaning in her relationships with friends, business associates, and herself. These characteristics had a significant impact on her mindset. Nikitha received a message from Bobby asking her not to invest the next day; he said he was missing her and might visit her, shortly. She replied and switched off her mobile, thinking he might call her again. After a while, she corrected herself and realized that she should not ignore an empathetic person, Bobby, and called him. He asked her to take a vacation and visit Mumbai for a change. She appreciated his idea and promised that she would see him after a few weeks.

After three days, her account displayed a credit with a new cash deposit. The total was rupees eighty-six lakhs. Later, she called the broker and asked about the property registration and miscellaneous charges, calculated the total amount, and included a rough estimate of the interior expenditure. She called Bobby.

"Hi, Bobby. How are you, darling?"

"Ooff, what a surprise, I am Bobby, not your Karan, mind you."

"Be serious, man. I want you to clarify a few doubts."

"Um, go on, madam."

"If I lend you some amount, for the short time investment, can you spin it for three or four times the investment within a month?"

He laughed at her words, and asked her,

"How much money do you want to invest... Lakhpathni Ma'am?"

She gets annoyed, speaks coolly, and tells him about the figure. Bobby was speechless and wondered at her words.

"Hello, Bobby? Ennachi da? Hello are you there?

She chuckles, and he comes to his senses and replies,

"Serious aa machi."

"Serious machaa."

"I am not confident in the present market behavior... Let me think it over Nikitha."

"Think it over, I am transferring the fund."

She disconnected the call. This was the first time they conversed in the Tamil language after meeting with each other. She reminds him of his college days and a naughty girl. Bobby's still unable to understand from where she got such a huge amount. After a few minutes, he receives a WhatsApp message,

'Bobby, I trust you, and you should be true to yourself and with me. I am badly in need of money, and you must help me, and for this favor... I am yours forever.'

He was in a dilemma; something was warning him to be thoughtful before promising to her. He texted the message and sent it to her.

'Nikitha, please don't pump in such a large amount in an unpredictable market. I suggest you go for an FD in a post office and the bank.'

The next moment, he received another text message, and it read,

'Bobby, it's not a one-night pleasure; I read you thoroughly and blindly trust you so don't insist me to go for the FDs in the bank. Keep in mind... It's strictly confidential between us and send your bank particulars. I can't let the time run out. Love you darling.'

'In the meantime, Bobby forgot that WhatsApp messages would also act as genuine proof.'

Bobby worked out the day's settlements and went to the restaurant, ordered a coffee, and was thinking of Nikitha's money and the investment in the market. He didn't believe she received such a huge amount by selling an old house in Chennai. However, it didn't matter to him; he was worried about the irrelevant trends of the indexes. There was a message on his mobile from Nikitha's number, again requesting bank details. Finally, he decided to try the market with her money and sent his bank account details. He returned to his flat, went through the market and index of the past few months, selected a few shares, and was busy for an hour studying the charts. The market collapsed and the index lost more than eight hundred and sixty points on average for three days. It showed an oversold of some and overbought of the other shares. He checked his mobile and a message from his bank displayed a total amount of rupees thirty-five lakhs in his account. Something was making him nervous, and he believed that hesitation sometimes predicts a good *cause* and *reason* before taking up a new task and would also make one cautious. He wanted to wait for a few more days before deploying her funds in the market.

The following day, the market was descending faster than he expected, and he checked the messages from his manager. He short-covered a few trades and sent the messages to his manager and MD. He suggested they should wait for closing; they too reciprocated the same. Now, it was a perfect time—fifteen minutes for the market to close. Bobby sold shares worth twenty-eight lakhs, though he plays with big capital daily, but today, he wasn't confident with Nikitha's money as the bait in his account.

'The incontinence and the unpredictable market indexes were confusing him today.'

Meanwhile, there was news of the amendment in the FDI and FPI policies and the index reversed with Bull's aggressive footing. He quickly squared off the open positions and settled with a profit of rupees three lakhs and sixty thousand. He calculated the earnings, copied them, and saved them in his pen drive. He mailed it to Nikitha and Sidhu to store as a record.

₹ $ £ €

The installation work was going on and within ten days, the major assembly was ready and waiting for a trial production. Karan took his wife and children out to a movie and had dinner at their favorite hotel. His wife was complaining that he was hardly spending time with the family. The school declared festival holidays and said she would spend some time with her parents. He was delighted and he too wanted to spend some time with Nikitha. In the morning, he visited the unit, and the engineers were waiting to run a final test. He called Anwar and he said that he was in the hotel in

Hyderabad and would be there in an hour. The arrangements were done and ready for trial production. He wants Nikitha to be present, but Anwar did not say a word about her and understands his religious practices. Thought Anwar did not want the women at these auspicious times. By the afternoon, the first round of trial production was going well, and the output was to the satisfaction of the engineers.

Anwar met Nikitha and she told him about the money she received. She told him about her house and said she wanted some financial assistance, a short loan from him. He was silent for a while and asked how much she required, and she gave him the figure. He was convinced and asked her to repay in a few days. Also mentioned the earlier deposits and asked her to transfer them into other accounts in short time intervals; she smiled and agreed.

Anwar left for Mumbai. Nikitha could not believe he would be convinced so easily for the short loan. She prayed and wished that Bobby would earn a good return on her investment. Fortunately, Bobby closed the transactions with profits and the earnings were more than his guess for the day. He calculated Nikitha's investment and profit and sent a message to her. She was thrilled to see her profits, called him, and said that she would be visiting Mumbai in a few days.

11. Nikitha's Murdered & Bobby's Trapped

Moin's half-brother, Abid, entered Nikitha's flat with a duplicate key. He searched the rooms and decided to hide the cash in the kitchen. The lower cabinet was filled with rags, junk, and empty bottles, and he placed the four small cotton bags inside. He called Moin and told him where he hid the bags and they decided to meet in the hotel at Madina, Hyderabad.

Anwar arrived in Hyderabad, met Moin, and found something different and suspicious in his strange behavior. Moin was busy with his phone calls rather than updating the information. Anwar took the total transaction and was surprised after hearing about the money in Nikitha's flat. Anwar wanted his money to be transferred legally into her bank account but knowing that eighty lakhs cash in Nikitha's flat pointed towards a disaster. It was like a weird dream after he had a drink at Moin's house. It took a few minutes to understand that Moin sensed his plan of conversion of the black money through the anonymous person's bank account. Anwar's act of money laundering was at bait in the hands of his cousin, Moin.

At once, Anwar called his office and asked not to send the money to Hyderabad and warned Moin to stay away for a while. Now, Anwar read his intention and wants to get rid of him and abort the money transfer for some time. Asked him to forget about the money that was placed in the flat and said that he could manage her. He gave him some money and asked him to leave the city. Hiding the cash in Nikitha's flat was disgusting and annoying, and it was not part of his plan. It was his foolishness in trusting him and depositing large sums in the bank. Anwar reached the hotel and worked out another plan to get the hidden money without her notice. He thought of calling Nikitha but did not and went to her coffee shop. They both had a cup of coffee and went to Necklace Road and asked her if she could rent her flat for a few days. She laughed at his words and asked him to be her guest. He could not explain his constraints; he requested if he could stay for three days, and she took his words for a joke.

They had packed the food, bought an Indri, a single malt whiskey, and reached Nikitha's flat. They finished the dinner by eleven thirty, and with a pretense of helping her with the dishes; Anwar tried to sneak and retrieve the hidden money from the kitchen cabinets. She asked him to leave the dishes, he had no choice and walked out of the kitchen.

₹ $ £ €

Anwar met Karan, and they visited the unit, gave a cheque, and asked him to deposit it in the company's account. They were satisfied with the trial production, and Anwar asked for a few sample pieces for the customers he was dealing with in Mumbai. Anwar funded the expansion by using the estimated escalated figure, despite the fact that the total estimate was a few lacs higher than expected. Karan appreciated Anwar for additional financial assistance and was glad that he had a good financial partner. He was not aware of the deceptive idea of his partner.

Later, he introduced a few customers, who visited his unit, and they discussed the orders, delivery, credit, and agreements. Karan asked him to meet at Nikitha's flat, but Anwar excused himself saying he had to attend an important meeting. Later, he called Nikitha and asked her to meet him, and she agreed. Karan noticed something different—an inconsistent attitude between both friends towards him. However, he was satisfied with his hard work, and his unit was successfully running two shifts a day with the new orders. One day, Nikitha meets Karan and expresses her unwillingness to spend time with him. After the dinner, she tells him that she decided not to be a partner any longer and wants to cease the partnership deed immediately. Karan stares at her and asks the reason, and she says it is due to personal reasons. When everything between them is open, then a personal reason was a vague excuse, he thought. Both were immersed in their thoughts, and Nikitha said she was tired and went into her room. Karan took the decision that it was not justified to continue the partnership deal if the partner was not interested, so he calculated her total investment. The next day, he used Anwar's additional funding, modified the partnership deed and got the documents registered. In the evening, he gave the cancelled partnership deed; a note of her amount, and left after fifteen minutes past eleven pm. Nikitha locked the door and went inside her bedroom. She saw a stranger before her and tried to scream, but his strong hand throttled and pushed her onto the bed.

₹ $ £ €

Gaikwad was busy with the bank statements, called Bobby thrice, and got clarification of the figures. After a while, Bobby received an email from his manager and a message from his MD from Mumbai to meet him at six pm. He closed all transactions and settled the accounts for the day. He went to Gaikwad's room, but he was not there; he placed a set of prints on his table and left. He hired a cab to his corporate office in Mumbai Central. Bobby's going to meet his MD after a few months, and he was in touch only with messages and emails. It took half an hour to reach the office, and he's asked to wait in the visitor's lounge.

After five minutes, he was ushered into the MD's chamber. His secretary entered with coffee and cookies, served them, and left. Sointhara took his coffee and waved his hand at Bobby to have his coffee. He was staring at his employee. Bobby finished his coffee, placed the cup on the table, and smiled at his boss.

"One should never be careless with the **easy** job and **money** in life. What do you say, Bobby?"

Sointhara spoke in a soft voice, and Bobby did not understand whom he was referring to or why he said it. He was thinking about his past month's profit and loss and about his manager checking his trading activities. Then he remembered about the two cheque payments of Gaikwad. If asked about the payments and discrepancies, he's prepared to reveal the issue to his MD. He was silent and wanted to hear from him first. Sointhara placed his cup aside and took some papers, read aloud, stared at Bobby, and said,

"Bobby, I am glad to hire you. Are you satisfied with your job and salary?

"Thank you, yes sir."

"I saw the discrepancies in the accounts and was confused about how one would save such a huge amount staying in one of the most expensive cities, in our country."

Bobby appreciated his soft opening of the topic. He guessed it's about Nikitha's fund in his account. Bobby thought of telling him about his friend and her money. However, even if explained, he might not believe the truth, as he was questioning about the savings and survival of a person. Unfortunately, he did not check his bank balance before coming, and Nikitha already transferred another fifty Lakhs into his account.

"Bobby, I still trust you, and if you feel the money doesn't belong to you then... You can transfer it back into the company's account. The dream of an overnight billionaire shall land one into many legal obligations and liabilities. I hope you understand. Take your time, but do it earlier, the best."

"Sir..."

"I know you are not like others; I do understand human errors. No need for excuses; now you can leave."

Bobby gets up, stares at his boss, and walks out of the chamber. He goes to the nearby restaurant and thinks of his MD's remarks. The situation was confusing, and he started recollecting every fact right from the day of his appointment. Nothing exactly points at him with either fraud or manipulation of the company's funds. Bobby was distressed; why and what made his MD speak as he was using his company's money? Later, he recollected, Gaikwad has been keeping an eye on his trading activities for the past few months. He was watching his every move and often asked him about his plans for the next day's trade. The two cheques were still a mystery, and he decided to get the information from the accountant.

Lately, he realized something was going beyond his knowledge. Now, Nikitha's money in his account was assumed to be the company's money. He opened his laptop and checked his bank account. It showed another three transfers into his account from Nikitha's bank. The latest total balance was one crore and fourteen lakhs. He called Nikitha, and she didn't answer his call. He left a message for her and went to his flat and went through the bank transactions of the past few months. Noted her transactions, investments, and gains through the market, except for a few thousand; everything was tallied, and the total money rightfully belonged to Nikitha. Now, he understood, it could be Gaikwad who took the bank statement of his account.

The breach of his personal bank account anguished him. He wanted to raise a complaint against the bank, but decided not to do so in the present circumstances, despite being honest; it would prove him guilty of fraud and crime. Hence, he abstains from the thought of the complaint. His company believed that he was misusing its money, and if he complained about cheating and fraud, he would be booked, and subsequently, Nikitha's money would be frozen until the case's settled in a court of law. He returned to his flat; it was half past eleven pm and again he called her; she didn't answer. He felt it was unsafe to keep her money in his account anymore; it might even involve her, and she would be co-accused with him. He called again, and now, her mobile was switched off. There was no way to contact her, so he transferred the money into his two accounts at the different banks. Bobby's frustration was racing with the anger; helplessness made him depressed and deprived of no other choice but to escape the situation. Eventually, now he was *legally trapped*.

12. The Fugitive

The local TV news reported the proprietress of a famous coffee shop in the SR Nagar locality was raped, and brutally murdered in her bedroom. The police were taking notes and suspected a burglar would have entered the flat and found the single woman asleep and raped her. When she resisted, he might have hit her with an empty beer bottle and escaped. Due to heavy bleeding from the temporal injury, she was believed to have succumbed in the early hours of the morning. Later, they collected the pieces of evidence—a broken beer bottle and a dirty waste cloth. The fingerprint experts were busy collecting the evidence.

Meanwhile, another news channel reported the ghastly accident on the PV Narasimha Rao's expressway at Shamshabad. The high-end model SUV was burnt to ashes, and the witnesses said that the car was hitting a top speed of 180 to 240 kmph. The driver lost control, the vehicle rammed against the divider, toppled, and landed on the other side of the road. The traffic was diverted onto another route for the people going to and coming from the RGIA—Rajeev Gandhi International Airport.

At three pm, Karan received a call from the police station. When he arrived at the coffee shop after leaving the unit, the news of the murder shocked him. He made a few calls. Meanwhile, there were three calls from the SR Nagar police station. He observed the manager at the cash counter was keeping an eye on him. Karan waved his hand at the manager and asked him about Nikitha. The manager said the police had left just half an hour before Karan's arrival, and they suspected of rape and murder. Karan was thinking about the police and the investigation. His reputation and his business were at stake. In fact, he never expected that his relationship would be exposed in such a *gruesome incident*. He went to his apartment and asked his wife and children to get ready, saying they were leaving Hyderabad. He told his wife that there was an accident at the unit, convinced her that the police interrogation may scare the children, and explained to her that he wanted them to stay away for a while. However, she didn't believe him; she packed a few clothes, and they left their house. On the way, he withdrew some money, gave it to his wife, and asked them to visit a holy place and offer a prayer for him. She asked him to drop her off at the railway station and told him that she would be visiting her parents. Later, he returned, took his passport, documents, and ID cards, and left.

₹ $ £ €

It was a weekly expiry, the market moved sideways, and the stock markets were to close on the next day on account of the festival. So, Bobby closed all the positions, left the prints on the Gaikwad's table, and left the office. He tried to withdraw some money from the ATM, but it did not dispense the notes. He tried three times, and there was a printout from the machine stating that his account had been blocked.

At this point, he was aware that his company might have filed a police report regarding fraud and cheating. Checked his wallet; there were five thousand and five hundred rupees in it. He booked a sleeper bus and hurried to his flat. Packed a few pairs, took his laptop, and called his friend, Sidhu. He boarded the bus and sent a message to Nikitha. After a few minutes, again he sent three messages. He opened his bank account, checked the credits for the past three months, and took a snapshot on his mobile. Remembered the two cheques, and scrolled the statement, but could not find any deposit through the cheques. Now he's aware, Gaikwad recorded the dubious entries on his name in the company account. He did not understand how he would use the company's cheque with his name and get the fund transferred into his account. It was no less than a *fool's conspiracy* to siphon off the other's money. Bobby reached Hyderabad, took a cab, reached the regular pub in Secunderabad, and was waiting for his friend to arrive. Sidhu met and was discussing the trends and markets, but Bobby was not interested and was preparing how to start the conversation.

"Bobby, you are a great man, in a short period you earned fifty percent profit. How did you play with the index and with such huge money? Any... Insider game?"

"No insider stuff bro and the money don't belong to me."

Bobby replied and told him about his MD's suspecting him of fraud and assumed Nikitha's money was the company's fund. He said that his bank account was blocked, wanted to meet Nikitha and explain to her the misconception the company has about her money in his account.

They were silent for a few minutes and Bobby asked,

"Sid, can you lend me some amount bro?"

"Sure bro, how much?"

"One lakh."

"Ok, and what's your plan?"

"First, I have to run away from here... Then meet Nikitha and explain the situation at my office... Later, I have to transfer her money from my account to her bank."

"Ok, let's go; I'll draw the money and give it to you."

"No Sidhu, better you go alone and get the money; I think by this time the police would be searching for me to arrest."

Sidhu moves his head, has his beer, and walks out of the pub. Bobby paid the bill and was waiting for his friend. Sidhu returned and showed a carry bag containing the five hundred notes in it. Meanwhile, he saw the news on the TV and waved his hand at the TV behind Bobby. He turned around and saw his photo and a report from a business channel mentioning Bobby's fraudulent money transfers from a corporate account. The reporter was briefing Bobby's trading skills besides, mentioning his fraudulent practices with a reputed construction company. Sidhu expressed a startled look and was staring at his friend. Bobby wiped the sweat on his face;

Sidhu said he was ready to help and suggested that he should not go online and stop using his mobile for a few days. Bobby promised that he would not get him into any legal matters and asked him not to reveal this matter to the other friends. Bobby went to his house, collected his backpack and laptop, and took a cab to Kacheguda railway station. He's prepared not to go by public transport; there were chances of being caught with the cash red handed but he forgot about the CCTVs in the railway stations. He went to the helpdesk and enquired about the trains that were ready to depart within half an hour. He had no loose cash and did not want to use his credit card. He went to the washroom, took half the notes from the carry bag, and secured them in his shirt pocket. Later, he tucked a few more notes into his jean's pockets, dropped the carry bag back in his backpack, and returned to the ticket counter.

The Howrah Express was ready to depart; he bought a ticket to Kolkata. Did not know why he was traveling to Kolkata and had no one known to him there. He convinced himself to leave Hyderabad and Mumbai for a few months to escape from the police. He's desperate to meet Nikitha and wants to ask her to prove his innocence to the police and claim her money back. He received an SMS from Sidhu, read and deleted it, and switched off his mobile.

Was his decision, right? The future may proclaim the truth and his honesty, but the present time might get him caught red-handed for reported fraud.'

He was often watching the hung CCTV; he did not see any news reporting of fraud. Yet he was scared at the sight of the railway police moving around on the platform. The train started moving. He ran, got in, and climbed onto the upper berth. Adjusted his backpack under his head and lay with wild thoughts. After a short while, he took his laptop, opened the trade journal in an Excel sheet, and scrolled through the dates and trades. Now, the total investment was one crore and fourteen lakhs, and the approximate profit was thirty-nine Lakhs on all closed trades. It was just four months after he met Nikitha, and her investment earned more than forty percent. The remaining balance was his salary and his personal trade profits.

A final total was approximately more than two crores in his bank accounts. He wants to transfer the total fund into Nikitha's account. She told him that she was a business partner and in love with her friend. None would believe that a business partner would trust and give her such huge money. If her friend Karan, could manage the finances by himself then, there was no question of taking her as a partner. He was feeling a mild headache, shut his laptop and slept.

After a few hours, the train stopped; Bobby heard some voices and saw the passengers speaking loudly. He got down and enquired with the co-passenger and knew the train had stopped for the past half an hour. He said someone snatched two gold chains from a woman's neck and pulled the chain to stop the train. Later, the chain snatcher jumped out and ran into the fields in the darkness. Thought of switching his mobile on but did not want to disclose his location.

Bobby reached Vishakhapatnam and checked the late-evening trains to Kolkata. Want to take another train to avoid his movements being tracked by the police. Two trains were available in the evening and left the railway station. Now, he could not walk steadily; his footsteps were unstable after starving for hours. He bought tea and biscuits from a street tea stall and enquired about the nearby Temples.

He took an auto and reached the Shree Hanuman temple in the Gajuwaka locality. He prayed and dropped a couple of notes in the donation box and smiled to himself for his unmindful act. Was he bribing Lord Hanuman, maybe to prove his innocence and honesty? Later, Bobby chose a roadside eatery, had a meal, spoke to the waiter, and requested his mobile. He gave a tip, and the waiter gave him his mobile. He searched for the next stop after the Vishakhapatnam railway station. He returned to the temple, selected a clean place under a big tree, and his fatigue made him take a nap. Bobby reached the highway and waved his hand.

A truck stopped, and he requested the driver, saying he missed his train at Vishakhapatnam main station. The driver agreed and after an hour, the driver stopped at Palasa bypass road and asked him to take an auto to reach the railway station. Bobby took some money to give him, but the driver politely refused and drew away. Bobby took an auto and reached the railway station. He observed the CCTV cameras, found an alternate way from beside the cargo office, and bought a ticket to Kolkata. Cautiously, he left the station and was waiting for the train to arrive. The train arrived, and after the second whistle, he ran into the station and got on the train.

After a while, the train stopped for signal clearance, and he saw a few men smoking beside the track. Bobby got off the train, and the steps of the compartment were three to four feet above the ground. He walked along the track ballast and stood on plain ground a few feet away from his compartment. He was watching a shimmering red light at a distance and felt relaxed observing the dark and silent environment all around.

He was born and brought up in the city, and except for a few cities, he never visited a remote place or a village. He enjoyed the fresh air and serene surroundings. For a few minutes, he forgot he was on the run, a fugitive running away from the police and his company. Meanwhile, he heard the whistle and turned around; the train started moving and was picking up speed. He did not recognize the compartment he was in and tried running along the moving train. It was a dangerous task, and finally, he got hold of the lower edge of the handlebar beside the door and stood on the lower step of the compartment.

Now, he experienced how difficult it is to board a running train without an even and leveled platform. The train was taking a sharp curve and the door was locked from inside. He struggled to open it but couldn't, and gradually, he was losing his hand grip and leaning out. Suddenly, something hit the back of his head, and he lost his grip. Later, he was lying on the wet soil and listening to the horn and the rail squeal of the train moving away from him. He heard someone singing folklore in a different language on the elevated railway track.

'The stars are bright,
The sky is dark.
Eyes are blurred.
And the mind is off...'
Bobby's eyes closed involuntarily.

13. Bobby in Cuttack & Gaikwad's Fired

Bobby opened his eyes, saw the tiled roof above, and turned his head. He was on a coconut coir woven cot and with a white blanket over his body. Saw an older woman in the front yard of the house. Assumed her age to be in her forties, she finished cooking on the Indian traditional outdoor cooking stove. The burnt smell of wood and dung was entering inside the house. She went to the water tub; brought a mug full of water, sprinkled and doused the fire.

She came inside the house, and before Bobby could say anything. she asked him to get up carefully and gave him the water in an aluminum glass. She returned with a plate with three Jowar—Sorghum rotis and a small quantity of rice. The dal and curd were served in small steel bowls. She asked him to have his lunch and went out. It was like a dream for Bobby; he didn't recognize the place or the elderly woman. She was speaking a different language which, he hadn't heard before.

He felt a mild pain in his neck and forehead. Placed his hand over his head; felt the bandage around his head. Now, he remembered the last night, the train, and something struck on his head. Had she been aware of him as a fugitive, she would have immediately called the police and handed him over to the police. He could not speak her language, and thought it's better for him to pretend to be a dumb; he took the plate and completed his lunch. The woman returned and gave him tablets and a glass of buttermilk. He had the medicine, felt drowsy, and turned to another side and was sleeping. The woman called her husband and told him that he had his food, and she gave him the medicine. Her husband's in his mid-fifties with grey hair and a bushy mustache. Bobby heard their conversation; they were speaking with an accent of Bengali and Odia. The man called his wife, Laxmi and asked her to cover him with a blanket. They were having lunch together, discussing the bank loan from an agricultural co-operative bank.

Bobby woke up at four pm. The old man introduced himself as Swamy Das in Oriya language and asked him how he was feeling. Bobby waved his right hand, signaling to Swamy that everything was well. The doctor at the Village Government Hospital sutured his wound and asked him to take care for three days. After he was discharged from the hospital, Swamy Das brought him to his house. It's the second day, and Bobby was trying to recall what exactly happened. He asked him in sign language. Who admitted him to the hospital? Swamy understood, spoke in Hindi, and told him that he was lying in the pool of blood in his field with a head injury. He said that he thought him to be dead from the train accident; after checking his breath, and with the help of other farmers, they took him to the hospital.

Subsequently, Swamy Das narrated about a similar incident that occurred a month prior in which a thief had leaped from a moving train, crashed into an electrical pole, and died. Bobby tried to smile and, with his strange sign language, asked him how he knew that he was not a thief. Swamy got up, went into another room, and returned with a rusted tin box. He opened it and gave it to him. The box contained his wallet, his company ID, and money, and his mobile was missing. The moment he saw the company id, he was upset and tried to get up. But Swamy convinced him that the doctor asked him to take rest for another few days. He folded his hands, greeted Namaste, and apologized for using his money to get the medicines. Bobby felt ashamed for his deceptive behavior toward an honest man. An elder man asking him to excuse him for using his money without his knowledge hurt him. He proved the compassion and selfless helping nature of the village people. He never witnessed such a true person until now, and he tried to touch Swamy Das's feet with his hand to pay his respect. But, at once, Swamy withdrew his both legs back, took Bobby's hands into his hands, and smiled. He said that educated people should not touch the feet of an uneducated village farmer. Now, Bobby could not hide his emotions, and tears were flowing from the eyes for his love and respect. He waved at him to come close and hugged him. In fact, Bobby wanted to speak to him and explain about the consequences he faced but did not, as the news may alert the local police. He was feeling guilty for taking advantage of the elderly couple and hiding in disguise at their house. Decided to leave as early as possible and checked the money. His laptop, cell phone, and the remaining fifty-six thousand, eight hundred rupees were all lost in the accident.

₹ $ £ €

On the third day, Bobby's able to walk but could not stand for a long time. He told Swamy that he would go to the field with him and wanted to see the place where he met with an accident. Swamy said it's one kilometer away near the railway track and said he should get well and fit to walk such a long distance. Bobby said he was alright and got ready with him. The next morning at four am, they left the house, and on the way, Swamy told him about his three acres field, the methods of the village's farming, and about the local markets. Spoke of the major crop and the loss they incur when there's no right price for the yield.

They reached the field, and Swamy went to the other side and switched on the water pump. The red light of the railway signal was shimmering on the flowing water in the field. Later, Swamy took him to the place and pointed at an electrical pole and a signal post beside and on the twenty feet-elevated railway track. They climbed up towards the track, and Swamy said that numerous individuals had been struck by the pole when they tried to look outside or stood on the footsteps of the moving train. He explained the train's swing on the sharp curve and said that the poles are five feet away and leaning inward towards the tracks. While the train is maneuvering the curve and by the swing, the passengers at the door would swing out of the compartment and would lose control of their grip, fall, and get their heads hit by the signal post or else, by the electrical pole.

Swamy said that he had been informed a few months ago at the railway station and they said they were in the process of acquiring a part of his field for expansion of the additional track. Bobby saw the depressed look on Swamy's face; he said he has to forgo a part of his field for railway track expansion. Bobby was silent for a while and decided to help the poor farmer when he had the money, but when? He went to the pole to watch for the blood marks. He smiled at his crazy thought, sat on one of the tracks, and told him that he lost his belonging in the sign language. He was enjoying the silence and the pleasant weather of the dawn.

After a few minutes, they heard a train's horn. Swamy at once took Bobby's hand, and they started descending over a roughly dug two feet width walkway down from the track. Meanwhile, a goods train was passing behind them. It was a strange and lovely experience for Bobby, as Swamy was holding his hand and taking him down to the field. They sat on the tied heap of dried grass, and Bobby asked in his sign language about his family. He said his son was married and staying with his in-laws looking after their business in Bhubaneswar. Bobby realized and did not continue the topic. At seven am, they returned to the house, and Bobby had a breakfast of Jowar—sorghum rotis, potato curry, raw onion and a cup of curd. He loved the potato curry and the curd, and enjoyed the village atmosphere. He took the medicines, and they induced him to sleep for hours. In the evening after dinner, he told Swamy that he would be leaving for Kolkata. Swamy and his wife requested him to stay until his head injury heals. Bobby smiles and gestures about his job, saying that he will take care of himself. He decided to leave at midnight without saying goodbye. He placed twenty thousand rupees in the box with a letter written in Hindi expressing his gratitude for their love and care and left the village of Rathipur, Bhubaneswar, Odisha. On the way, he promised himself that he would revisit and help the old couple.

₹ $ £ €

In Mumbai.

There was an urgent meeting in the office of the Medusaa constructions. Sointhara, Fulkeery, and Gaikwad were present; half an hour passed in accounts scrutiny. Sointhara did not believe that Gaikwad adopted such an absurd mindset and misused the company's money. Fulkeery nervously explained to his friend about his idea of defeating him in the game of trade in the stock market, and he admitted his fault, apologized, and promised that he would help with the financial assistance.

Gaikwad's candid acceptance of his involvement in fraud with the company's money and also with Fulkeery's funds convinced both friends. After getting a confirmation report from the accounts manager, Sointhara got annoyed and decided to get rid of Gaikwad from the company. He instructed his secretary to settle the accounts of Gaikwad immediately. Later, he turned to Fulkeery, stared at him, and thanked him for help. He could not believe his friend's involvement in his business affairs with a fraudster.

Gaikwad apologized and promised Sointhara that he would return the money he earned from the company's investment and begged not to hand him over to the police. He wept and asked them to have mercy, citing the condition of his wife's health. The total money payable to Gaikwad was around fourteen lakhs, and the fraud money was adjusted against his retirement benefits. The final payment is hardly two lakhs after the deduction; the accounts manager gave the cheque to Gaikwad. Gaikwad's frustration and a fire of revenge were igniting an evil idea to end the young and smart trader, who's on the run. He went to his house and saw his wife sleeping on the floor of the portico with the children's books spread all around her. He kicked on her back to wake up; she got up and stared at him in anger. Nowadays, his anger was uncontrollable, and he was physically torturing his wife. He called a cab, took his wife, and admitted her to the mental hospital. He signed the papers and the declaration and submitted the letter issued by a doctor declaring her mental instability and returned home. He called his friends to his house and arranged a party. He said detailed about Bobby and his money in the bank and asked a favor with one of the notorious men of his locality.

The next day, Gaikwad went to the bank and deposited his cheque. He met with the teller clerk and enquired about Bobby's account balance. The clerk told him that the account was ceased and under the surveillance of the investigation department. He asked for a statement of Bobby's account; the clerk hesitated, and after an assurance from the Gaikwad that he would not disclose the matter with others. The clerk pretended as if were dealing with the case of an international scam account. He knew the clerk was expecting something in return, and Gaikwad took out a few notes and pushed them toward him. The clerk picked it up and placed it in his lunch bag and asked him to wait.

After ten minutes, the clerk returned with a piece of paper and gave him; the figures were handwritten with the dates of the money credits and debits. The clerk excused himself and said he could only have a view of the account and had no permission to get a print of the frozen account. Gaikwad left the bank and went to the tea stall, met with a person, gave a Xerox copy of the paper, and asked him to find Bobby within the shortest time. Sointhara re-checked the prints of account statements. He lately realized that Bobby was honest with his job, though his personal trading was against the company's rules and regulations. He remembered the money from Bobby's account and still was in doubt about clarifying whether it belonged to his company or his own. He called his accountant and asked him to re-check the statements. The accounts manager told him that the investment and the cash were tallied with the company's financial statements. So, there was no reason to accuse him as a fraudster when the company did not find any discrepancy or misappropriation in the company accounts. He was thinking of the company's reputation and his fame. If Bobby's proved correct, then he would lose his respect in society for the false accusation of an honest employee. At once, he sent a letter citing the withdrawal of the case and mentioned the facts for closure of the fraud case filed at the police station.

After a while, he called his friend, one of the senior investigating officers, who is due to retire in a few days. Later, he met him in person, told him about Bobby and his activities in the office, and said that his company would now mollify by retaining him in the office with respect. First, the officer did not believe him and asked how he allowed him to use the company's money. Sointhara explained to him about Bobby's trade through EPTC— Employee's Personal Trading Compliance, the agreement and they are waiting for him to return. He said the company wants him to clarify the whole issue before him and the investigating officers.

He spoke of his appointment and showed him prints of how Bobby was devoted to his job and with honesty. After the officer went through the last sheet that explained the balanced accounts, he asked for a copy of it to cite the reason for closing the case. Later, Sointhara told him about the Gaikwad's speculation and misuse of the company's funds. The officer asked why he didn't hand him over to the police. He explained to him of his wife's illness and said he deliberately left him on the compassionate ground. Sointhara offered the retiring officer a job as a liaison officer in his company. But he said he would be leaving the country to stay with his son in Europe. He asked him to recommend a good officer like him if any such issue arises in the future. The officer thought for a few minutes and asked if he could afford to hire a US investigating officer. He said an officer wants to retire and settle in India with his daughter, who runs a school in Mumbai. At once, he agreed, and the officer nodded and said he would send a mail to his friend in the USA and confirm. Sointhara thanked him and left the crime branch office.

14 Edward & Police Investigation

The police sent Nikitha's dead body for autopsy. One of the officers enquired with the watchman, and he told him about her alcohol addiction. He complained that he often saw her drunk and out of her senses, coming late at night. He also said in a low voice that she was regularly seen with men till late hours and named two men by verifying the visitors register. One of her neighbors told the officers that she was a good woman, but a few men were frequently visiting her. A teenage girl said that she was going to get married shortly. A woman was cursing her for her negligent and shameless life. Some residents raised the issue of her character and started telling different stories.

Since the steel almirah had been unlocked with the keys, the officer assumed the thief had taken the money and jewelry. The bathroom floor was littered with used bath towels, and the kitchen was untidy. Searched the bed and a pillow covers; inside was a bank-sealed ten-thousand-rupee bundle. The officer approached SR Nagar Bank and requested the clerk to check for the transaction in their records. The clerk confirmed that there was no withdrawal of ten thousand rupees. Instead, the clerk confirmed a withdrawal of five lakhs and fifty thousand with a self-cheque. The officer took the rupees bundle, a Xerox copy of the cheque, and transaction details and noted down her mobile number. Her bank account was with a few lakhs of rupees, and the last debit was on the day she was murdered. Later, the bank gave a detailed official bank statement to the police, and Bobby Shacal's name surfaced as the only beneficiary and mentioned his bank account and mobile number. The multiple *cash credits* and *online debits* from her accounts were suspicious, and the objective was not yet known to the investigators. Meanwhile, the police found a mobile from the car that was almost burnt after the accident on the PV Narasimha Rao's expressway. A few parts of the burnt car were still holding the clues, as the metal of the car's body was of strong and standard make. There were hardly any fingerprints and, surprisingly, a piece of vital evidence—a mobile was in the burnt and shrunk glove box of the car.

₹ $ £ €

Mrs. Sofia George chaired the proceedings of the Special Review Committee along with three other officers from the DEA Field Division, Texas. They charged Edward John Barrata, Detective, with thirty years of service. He's been charged with numerous counts for his lapses while, on duty. He was suspended, and his case was handed over to the Internal Departmental Inquiry for negligence and irresponsible attitude. A month ago, during the raid, a shootout on a highway resulted in three deaths and one was injured. Edward confronted the drug dealers, shot three of them, and left one injured on the sidewalk for an hour without access to medical care. He was also charged for his adamant and verbal abuse. His chief suspended him for ignoring his order to recover a stolen car and the jewelry. Edward tried to convince officers by saying that he had to use abusive language, threaten the offenders with authority, restrain the culprits from any further action, and importantly, try to avoid unexpected incidents. Sophia George questions Edward.

"So, you frame the new law, dictate your rule, and display your authority to stop drug peddlers by your abusive and threatening style."

Edward turns to her with clasped hands and speaks in a low tone.

"Sofia, you have to understand the repercussions; if I didn't intercept them, that night you can imagine. You have to consider looking at it from my side. I am sorry for my abusive language, and besides, I still remember my oath and respect the law."

One of the officers' claps and frowns at his words, while another officer takes a sheet and reads the notes.

"*Point one*, you deliberately ignored the injured victim. *Two*, you didn't inform the control room or the paramedic immediately after the shootout. *Three*, injured victim's statements declare your irresponsible and life-threatening behavior."

Edward tries to control his anger, and another officer mocks at his idea of offering water to the injured person and questions him.

"Ah, well, Edward... Since when did you become a savior by offering water to the injured defaulters rather than getting help from the doctors? *Evidently, and eventually, who stands decorated with the badge of honor... You? Or the offender?*"

Edward's frustration was visible on his face now, he closed his eyes and controlled his rising blood pressure. After a while, he deliberately accepted and told the committee that he had to display his official power to intimidate the street criminals. Later, he explained that his act saved many in a few incidents. However, the committee unwillingly acknowledged the issue of saving the injured and the act of self-defense. They did not get convinced of his negligence and irresponsibility for leaving an injured person to suffer for hours. The committee members deliberately ignored and didn't take note of the paramedic's delay caused by their vehicle breaking down.

Edward remembers that after the incident, his blood pressure was rising and he had to take medicines, so he went to the nearby medical shop and bought his tablets. To cover up the health issue, he had lied and said he brought a bottle of drinking water for the injured. His words did not convince, them and that was the vague reason, so his case was marked for a Special Review Committee. Edward's behavior was not the major offense after the huge package of drugs recovered by special officers from the gangsters, and it surprised the department and the committee. But the committee and the chief's office disliked his arrogant and provocative attitude. After the arguments, they decided to transfer him from the Crime Division. The authority found a valid reason to transfer him to the financial division that deals with stock market irregularities for the second time in three years. Edward returned from the office, took a shower, settled in his living room with a beer, and checked his messages. His ticket to India was confirmed, and his boss was glad that he got rid of him from his team.

Edward's fifty-nine years old, with thirty years of service in the special Crime Division and narcotics and fourteen transfers did not bother him. Edward is physically fit with an average height and weight. Has a crooked nose and a large scar on his left eyebrow. A well-built body, strong arms, and a cruel look in his eyes distinguish him to be a street-beaten cop. Always anger expressed in his words, and a few cases of domestic violence settled off the record by his authoritative behavior. He believes in an amicable settlement than without the involvement of the police and the courts.

His style of dealing with the gangsters surprised his partners and the other officers. He was often posted to investigate the messed up and slogging cases where he worked alone and enjoyed his job. His age was often discussed for his witty and sexy topics and discussions. He never cared for the rules at the time of distress, rescue, and help, and the best results fetched star entries in his record for his perilous rendezvous. Everyone disliked him, except one young female officer, whom he taught the techniques to solve, and the tactics to deal with the tough cases.

Edward went to his new office, gave a letter of resignation, surrendered all the departmental belongings he possessed, and asked for the account settlement. He was asked to wait till the department gets approval and a confirmation letter for his resignation. The next morning, he called one of his friends, said goodbye, and took a flight to India. Now, he felt a new inspiration and joy as he was going to spend his life as a civilian in India, along with his daughter.

₹ $ £ €

The police officer interrogated the staff of Nikitha's coffee shop. The manager told them about Karan and his regular visits to the coffee shop. Told him that he used to manage the cash counter when Nikitha and Karan went out together. And also mentioned about a regular customer, who used to visit the coffee shop in the morning and evening. He said that he used to write something on tissue paper and throw the tissues in the dustbin, and after a few days, his madam started collecting the tissues and kept them with her. The officer questioned him about writings on the tissues, and he could not give them the right answer. Collecting the used and thrown tissue papers was a weird and strange act, and the officer wondered what would have been written on the used tissue. Was the person an extremist, sleeper, or agent passing the vital information?

The crime investigating officers and the local police were ordered to conduct separate investigations, one on murder and the other on the car accident. According to a report, Anwar hired the SUV, and Nikitha was the owner of the cell phone discovered in the glove box of the burned car. The Assistant Commissioner wanted both cases to be taken up following the clues they found till now. Besides, it was a better idea to compare the links that might relate to both incidents. Two new officers took charge of the cases and started going through the facts recorded earlier. Was Nikitha using two mobiles then? what about Anwar's mobile? The officers started working with the service providers. Meanwhile, Karan's wife, Amala Karan filed a missing complaint against her husband and mentioned that he did not return for the last two days. Now, her complaint was another new story for the police. Surprisingly, her complaint was viewed as a second case; the priority has been given to the murder and the car accident. One officer left for the hospital and the other for the police station at Mehdipatnam. The officer collected Nikitha's medical report; it mentioned that there were two traces of semen found on the night she was murdered. It declared the death was around eleven and a half past midnight by strangulation. There were no fingerprints around her neck or on any part of her body. The report highlighted the presence of a high alcohol level in her body and that she was asleep when assaulted. The officer took the report, went to his office, and compared it with the FIR. It states there was no weapon of assault found near or around the victim or in her flat except, the broken pieces of a beer bottle. The asphyxia without the fingerprints and the head injury with a beer bottle in no way matched the FIR and the latest reports of the investigators.

Usually, a rope or a cloth should be used in such cases, but none were present at the crime scene. The mention of an open lower kitchen cabinet was something unusual. He took note of the lower cabinet opening and the gas cylinder on the floor. Later, the officer went to Nikitha's flat. The flat emitted a foul smell; he kept the door open for a while and went into the kitchen. The lower cabinet was open; he bent and saw the round rust marks of the gas cylinder, which indicated it had moved away from the original place. Was it an attempt to blow up the flat? He returned to the bedroom and saw the wardrobe, drawers, and the attached bathroom. He walked into the balcony and viewed the surroundings. It was easy for anyone to get in the flat by adjoining five feet of common walls between the balconies. Now, Karan and Anwar were the main suspects under the purview of the police. The police could not find Karan in Hyderabad, and his team was closely watching for him. The mobile service provider gave the second name, Anwar, and his call records. They tracked the mobile calls for the past month and found a new number. There were a few calls in a month, but one number displayed a longer duration, especially in the late hours, and that intrigued enough to include another suspect's involvement in the murder case. The officer noted a few assumptive points and returned to his office. The second officer who is investigating the car accident re-read the report, and it mentioned that a sari and a nylon rope were burned to ashes in the car. The link between the victim's mobile, sari, and nylon rope in Anwar's car was a perfect lead to the murder. But the mystery was going deeper; how could the offender leave the dead body in the flat and the belongings in the burnt car? Both the officers returned and were waiting in the Commissioner's office.

Meanwhile, they observed a hefty man walking into the Commissioner's room. Hameed met the Commissioner and the two investigating officers were ushered in, and the officers asked him a few questions about Anwar. The two officers said that they wanted to talk in detail. Hameed agreed, signed the legal formalities, and gave them the address of the hotel where he was staying and left. Later, he attended a meeting with one of his suppliers in Banjara Hills and returned in the evening. He was expecting the officers, but none visited, and he left for the airport. The officers decided to crack the case; they wanted the information from Mumbai about Anwar, and later, they wanted to patch up the missing information directly from Hameed. One of the Crime Branch officers from Hyderabad was returning from Mumbai; the Commissioner's office called him and sent an email. The received an email from the officer of Crime Division, Mumbai to the Commissioner's office in Hyderabad.

The officers collected the copies of the report. One officer found a lead that Karan was just a pawn to initiate the process of black money conversion to white, and Anwar's other business activities and his relationship with Nikitha were yet to be confirmed. The other officer was going through the report of Hameed and his multi-business profile.

15. Edward Tracks Gaikwad

Mrs. Amala Karan Reddy was nervous about the officer's questions; he noticed her unwillingness to answer his questions.

"Madam, can you show me the latest documents or the legal paper that proves you are the working partner of your husband, Karan Reddy."

"Yes sir,"

Without a hesitation, she enters the other room; the officer looks closely at the new Xerox papers on the newspaper and tries to take them. Meanwhile, she returns and gives him the partnership deed. He goes through the pages and notices the registration was done a day before murder. Ram Reddy, aged mid-twenties, enters in with the set of papers, and she introduces him as her younger brother, and he wishes the officer.

"Don't mind, does your husband have an extramarital affair, madam?"

"No sir, my brother-in-law is a work-oriented man, and how could he go with the affairs when my beautiful sister is with him?"

Ram Reddy replied, and smiled looking at his sister

The officer took note of his pretense rather than the surprise or confusion. Amala was muted by her brother's words and the officer observed her.

"Mr. Ram Reddy, then why is he absconding now?"

The officer questioned and collected takes a set of the Xerox copies of the partnership deed and told them that he would visit again in case, if he had to and warned them not to leave the city without prior notice.

'Sometimes, obedience, uncalled sincerity, and undue influence are the acts to conceal an apprehension or hideous crimes.'

Edward John Barrata arrives at Mumbai Airport, India. His daughter Helen received him, and they reached the MIG colony, Kurla West. Helen, aged thirty-five, is divorced, a certified instructor of Yoga and Meditation, and also runs a school of Arts and Crafts for schoolchildren.

Edward reported to the MPL—Medussa Associates Limited office in Chembur and met Sointhara. They shook hands and introduced themselves, and after the coffee, Sointhara briefed him on the story of the stock trades of Bobby as a scalper. He emphasized Gaikwad's illegal involvement in business and how Bobby was framed for the fraud. Edward takes the file, excuses himself, and sits in one corner. He reads the details, returns after a few minutes, and sits opposite Sointhara.

"Edward, how did you like Mumbai, my country?"

He smiles, moves his head, and replies,

"Wonderful and beautiful city. My daughter took me on a tour whenever I visited India. We explored the city and suburbs and I am familiar with a few streets, roads, and localities. I love the Pav Bhaj, Paani Pori, and the mimbaities..."

"Mumbaikars..."

Sointhara smiles and corrects him.

"Yes! Mr. Sointhara... Mombykars."

They smile at each other and Soithara asks,

"I am surprised, how do you converse, speak, or understand the Marathi language?"

Edward takes his latest iPhone, shows it to him and says,

"My phone has the language translator App, which can be used for almost all foreign languages. I select the language, speak to it and it reproduces the meaning and words of the desired language."

"Wow, wonderful, if you still require any assistance from my office, feel free to ask."

"I appreciate it, but right now, I don't think so. Let me first handle the case from my side."

"Ok, all the best."

Sointhara takes an envelope and gives it to Edward. He takes the envelope and leaves the office. Meanwhile, Gaikwad meets one of his friends who lives in the posh locality of Juhu, Mumbai. He requested his friend to allow him to stay in his flat for a few days. His friend asked him to stay, but with the condition that he must share fifty percent of the rent for the flat. He agrees, as he's with the idea of staying in Juhu until he gets Bobby's money transferred into his account. He's frustrated and annoyed by his company's MD, Sointhara, and for his kindness. His boss did not book a cheating or fraud case yet; he has developed a vengeance for firing him from the job. In his view, he deserves the right to get a share of the company's profit and feels self-esteemed for lending his service to the company. He forgot and disregarded his employer's kindness and mercy, and he now intends to go straight after Sointhara.

'Some people cannot tolerate other's judgment or futuristic view of them, and Gaikwad's mind was pushing him to fulfill his revenge for gratitude.'

Gaikwad, along with his friend, traveled to Chembur and met with Bobby's flat owner and convinced him that they were on an official search for the company's official papers. The owner frowned, did not trust them, and unwillingly gave the keys and sent one of his men to watch them. Gaikwad and his friend searched the rooms and found an envelope containing some papers and also found a personal file containing his certificates. Later, Gaikwad returned to the flat in Juhu and searched the envelope and the personal file, but in vain; he did not find any important paper to blackmail or a cheque to extort the money from his account. There was nothing useful, Gaikwad decided to burn the certificates and tossed the file in the dustbin. After the drink, he called his friend, and they went to the beach restaurant and had their drinks and dinner. Then, as usual, they decided to have some fun with the cheap entertainers of the by-lanes and returned late at midnight. Surprisingly, they found the flat's door ajar, and Gaikwad did not bother and thought one of them had opened the door. The fact was realized the next morning.

Edward goes to the beach restaurant in Juhu and waits for Gaikwad and his friend. As he guessed, they arrived in the afternoon and finished their drink and lunch with a serious discussion. Edward smiled to himself, knowing why they were disturbed. Then, the waiter presented the bill along with the file containing Bobby's certificates—in duplicate. The waiter told them that they had forgotten the file last night. The brightness over the face of Gaikwad revealed that he was relaxed; he thanked the waiter and left the restaurant. Later, the waiter approached Edward and collected his check with a good tip.

Surprisingly, it took one day for Edward to get familiar with the habits and routine of Gaikwad. Now, deliberately allowed Gaikwad for a while to track his movements. Edward meets Sointhara and gives the file containing Bobby's certificates and the latest bank statement. All educational certificates had a stamp of excellence and distinction right from the school and from the University of Hyderabad. He noted the names and addresses of educational institutions in Hyderabad. Sointhara watches the certificates and bank statements.

"Mr. Sointhara, it seems that Bobby's not aware of what was happening behind him, poor guy."

"Yes, Edward, I am aware of it, but still we need him to clarify, and testify to whom the money belongs. What do you say?"

"Yeah, as per the law, he has to testify before the magistrate. So, what do you want me to do, sir?"

"You tell me, Edward... What should we do now?"

He stares at Sointhara for a while, tightens his fists, and thinks. Later, he comes up with an idea.

"Sir, if Bobby's not guilty of any illegal activity, by your company's financial statement, then, I believe Gaikwad is taking leverage of Bobby's absconding. I'll grab him to my hell of justice."

"Edward, be careful; it's not the USA; here we have a different set of rules for the investigating officers and private detectives. Just keep that in mind; I believe you got me."

"Yup."

"Edward, one more thing; I have come to know that Gaikwad had been torturing his wife, and now, she's admitted to a mental hospital. Take care, and we don't want to hurt her in the process of nabbing him. Here's the address of the mental hospital."

"Um... He shall be charged with intimidation, physiological emotion, and with a complete chapter DV—Domestic Violence too. Don't worry, I'll take care of her, sir."

₹ $ £ €

In the evening, he talks about Gaikwad's wife's tragedy and asks her to accompany him to meet her. She agrees and they visit the mental hospital. Edward feels tired, looks at his daughter and said,

"Helen, why am I always assigned with domestic violence, sexual abuse, children and elders... and with street punks? Sometimes, I am tired of doing such a kinda job. Can I handle such cases now?"

She stares at him, holds his hand, and replies,

"Dad, you're better than the others; do you remember what Mama once said? We are a family in our house, and outside you are responsible for the underprivileged families. They need you, everywhere and in any country. So, you must take care of yourself and take your medicines regularly."

He watches his daughter and feels proud of her, nods, and walks into the mental hospital. They meet with the Doctor, and he instructs them not to speak or discuss the children. The Doctor said she was suffering from a mental disorder and was unattended for a long time. He briefed them about

CBT, therapies, and counseling. Edward and Helen are ushered into the lounge, where Mrs. Saritha Gaikwad sat. They approach and sit beside her; at once she gets up and occupies the other chair away from them. Helen takes out a children's book and starts drawing the alphabet and numbers. Saritha watches her and sits next to her; takes the book and the pen from her and asks her to hold the pen right. Helen takes the pen; Saritha holds her hand, makes her write the alphabet, and asks her to repeat the word after her.

They spent a few minutes, and Edward introduced himself as an NGO working for the welfare and betterment of orphan children. Her deep sunk eyes were brightened with happiness. Her body language expressed her happiness when he spoke of the children of the streets. He discussed their education and the institutions where they study and told her about the government's fund for orphanages in the USA. She's quite surprised when a foreigner works for the motherless children in India. She expressed her love for the children and told him that she could not conceive and laughed to herself thinking about her husband. They understood her depression and assured her that they would take her with them. She was happy and asked when he would take her out of the mental hospital. Helen convinced her that she would take her shortly and walked her into the ward.

Later, a nurse brings the juice and tablets, and Saritha has the juice and the tablets happily. Meanwhile, the visiting time was over and a psychologist asked Edward to meet him in his room. He met the doctor and spoke of the rules and the terms and signed a letter of consent.

16. Court Summons

Edward collected copies of the life insurance certificates of Mrs. Saritha Gaikwad from the insurance company. A few months ago, one policy matured, and she has not yet claimed the eight lakhs. The next day, he visited her bank, met the manager, explained her medical condition, and wanted to stop any unauthorized withdrawal of her money. The manager checked her account; her husband was a joint account holder. He asked him to produce the legal papers to stop her husband from drawing the money. He insisted on getting a certificate from the mental health institution, her presence, and her consent with witnesses.

He told Helen about the insurance policy, and one of her student's fathers was an advocate. Edward and Helen met with the student's father, who practices law at Mumbai High Court. He prepared the papers, gave a date, and asked them to get her to the court along with the Doctor's prescriptions and the medical reports. Edward met Saritha and showed her the images of the children and other students at his daughter's school of arts and crafts on his mobile. She was impressed and imagined herself to be the mother of one of the children. Now, she was speaking of how to take care while giving a bath to the baby and the effects of a cold and cough. The nurse patiently heard, said she was going to have a baby after a few months, and gave her the medicine after dinner. She asked her to take care, said goodnight, and slept murmuring a lullaby.

After three days, Gaikwad received a letter from the advocate, and it ordered him to meet and mentioned the date and time. He was surprised at how the advocate got his new address and could not guess why he had to meet him. The illegal search of Bobby's flat might be the reason he thought and called his friend. He answered and said he was at a party in Lonavala. He decided not to meet the lawyer; he would tactfully try to convince and drag him into the case and prove him as a defaulter. He was thinking of running away from Mumbai for a while but could not, as his friend was not a trustworthy person; in his absence, he would reveal about the search they did in Bobby's flat.

Meanwhile, Edward met Bobby's flat owner, who runs a hardware shop, and introduced himself as an advocate's assistant. He asked about the rent and agreement. The owner was annoyed and said he would not return any amount for the unoccupied flat as it was mentioned in the agreement. Said Gaikwad introduced Bobby, and he is one of the witnesses who signed the rent agreement. He also said about the Gaikwad and his friend's visit. Edward took the help of the shop's salesman who knew English, asked him to translate, told him the purpose of his visit, and requested that he explain it to his employer. The salesman explained to his employer; the shop owner stared at Edward. He asked him to take care of the customers and took Edward into a private room.

Edward gave him a set of papers and said the papers entitled Gaikwad to take occupancy for six months until Bobby's rental agreement ceases. The flat owner did not understand, so Edward explained to him through the translator that Bobby left the company. And said, as per the documents, Gaikwad could use the flat and wanted him to call and give him the flat keys. The flat owner thinks for a while and makes a call from Edward's mobile. The call was in conference with Helen, and they spoke in Marathi and were also recording the call, as he did not understand the language. The call was for three minutes duration; the flat owner said Gaikwad was coming in half an hour. Edward gave him the documents, asked him to get the papers signed by Gaikwad, and left. Gaikwad met the flat owner at his shop; they had a discussion and surprised, and said he did not know that the witness too had a right to use the flat in the absence of the original applicant—the tenant. He said that the witnesses are always to witness the *bad ending of the story* and never the beneficiary. His thought was correct, but his alcoholic mind blinded him, and he did not bother to read the full contents of the documents.

After Gaikwad left, Edward thanked the flat owner, collected the signed documents, and asked him not to worry about his flat. The documents signed by Sunil Gaikwad were not only the rent agreement but also contained a No Objection Certificate to convert the joint account to a single account permitting his wife to operate as a sole applicant.

₹ $ £ €

Edward, Helen, Saritha Gaikwad, and a nurse attended the court. Sunil Gaikwad did not attend the court, and the case proceeded and took note of the mental health of the petitioner. Edward provided the CBT reports, and the nurse clarified the symptoms and treatment of CBT—Cognitive Behavioral Therapy for childless women. The court ordered them to obtain the MHA—Mental Health Assessment as her divorce petition could not be granted and insisted on medical evidence. Besides, the ailing petitioner requires a guardian to safeguard her life, earnings, and assets, as she has no relatives known to her knowledge and lives in a state of solitude and illness.

Therefore, the court approved Helen's request to take up her responsibility. She volunteered, took an oath, and signed the legal documents. The contempt of court held Sunil Gaikwad liable to be punished for irresponsibility and disrespecting the dignity of the judiciary, and Saritha Gaikwad was directed to report to the psychiatrist for further medical examination. Edward met the superintendent of the mental hospital, and Helen signed an undertaking agreement. Edward and Helen met Saritha and took her along with them. She spent some time with the students at the school. In the evening, they dropped her back to her ward. After a week, the mental and physical examinations were completed by the authorized government psychiatrist. Later, on the date, a doctor appeared in court with Saritha and the MHA reports. The court examined medical prescriptions issued before admitting her to the mental hospital and compared them with the recent psychiatrist's report. Finally, the honorable court was satisfied and considered a *plenary guardianship* of Saritha to Helen.

Gaikwad was found guilty of false accusation, physical abuse, and the deliberate act of leaving his wife at the mental hospital. The documents of the rent agreement further proved that he's living separately in the rented flat in Chembur, in Mumbai. After, ascertaining, the fact of his addiction to alcohol, the court granted the sole rights to Mrs. Saritha Gaikwad to operate her bank account with any one of the two witnesses. One was Helen, Saritha's guardian, and the other was one of her colleagues.

The court issued an arrest warrant for Mr. Sunil Gaikwad. Mrs. Saritha Gaikwad was discharged from the hospital, and Helen accommodated her in her independent house.

17. Misleading Clues

The police officer returned from Mumbai and submitted a report of Bobby and Nikitha's transactions and their relationship. An officer took note of Bobby's friends and went to the bank where Sidhu holds his salary account and collected the statement for the past six months. Similarly, he obtained the other two friend's statements too. He noted their local and permanent addresses.

The officer met Sidhu and told him the story of Bobby's involvement in Nikitha's murder. Sidhu was speechless.

"Sidhu, for how long do you know your friend, Bobby?"

"Sir, we are childhood friends."

"How was he with the women?"

"He was an introvert, shy, and never had any girlfriend."

"But now, he's involved in a woman's murder case. Do you know Nikitha?"

Sidhu said he only heard him talking about her but never met. He said that Bobby used to give her tips on shares, and she owns a coffee shop and did not know they had an affair.

After hearing the story of her murder, he disagreed and told the officer that his friend was true and sincere. He said Bobby would never go to the extent of murdering a woman just for the sake of money and explained his trading skills, investment ideas, and profit-earning strategies. Later, he said that Bobby was trading with Nikitha's money, but with her consent, and earning her thousands of rupees without taking any commission. His sincere service was for free and convinced the officer that he helped her and the other investors who lost in the stock market. Detailed how he gave perfect tips on intraday trading for a few investors who took losses in the past. The officer was surprised when Sidhu showed them the exchange of messages, the share tips, and the profit of the successful trades on his mobile. Then, he explained to the officer that earning profit in the stock markets was not his idea, but winning over the market trends was his hobby and an ecstatic joy. The officer questioned Sidhu.

"What made him transfer the money into his other bank accounts?"

"Sir, none of us were aware of the murder. Bobby thought his money was misunderstood as the company's fund and presumed they might book a case on him."

"Well, then there was no reason to run away, if he had nothing to do with Nikitha's murder, and he could have explained the facts to his company."

"Sir... Just imagine his plight. He was in the breaking news, and the TV channel reported him as an accused in a company's fraud case. He was tactfully framed and booked a case with the false allegations by his company."

Sidhu briefed him about their last meeting, took his mobile, showed the latest messages he had received, and continued,

"He intended to return the invested money to Nikitha before he's caught. With the huge amount in his single account, he felt that he'd be a prime suspect behind the murder. He had no money, his account was ceased, and... I gave him a loan for his daily expenses."

He gives concise replies to the officer, yet he's unsatisfied and doubts all his friend's involvement. Before leaving, the officer asked him to co-operate with him in the investigation. Sidhu called his friends and told them of the police investigation and warned them to be mindful and cautious while answering. The officer met the other two friends of Bobby and visited the hotel where Anwar stayed before the accident. The receptionist recognized Nikitha's photograph and said they checked out in the evening. He referred to the reservation chart and told the officer that the suite was booked for three days and left the hotel after one day. The officer takes note of Anwar's recent visits, check-ins and check-outs, and payment prints.

Mrs. Amala Karan Reddy received a call from the police; she said she was at the unit and asked him to meet her at her residence. At five pm, the officer went to Amala Karan's house. The officer asked her about Karan's activities for the past few months. She said he was busy with the expansion work of the ancillary and said a Mumbai-based partner provided the financial assistance. She appreciated his ambition to grow his business, besides expressing concern about the huge loans. She told them that she was with her parents in Vijayawada, and from the next day, she could not contact him. When she called, his mobile was switched off and showed the messages on her mobile.

One of the two officers observed her; she did not speak of Nikitha's murder at any point. He understood that she was not aware of the *husband's affair* with the decedent or deliberately covering up issues after the murder. He asked her to show the loan papers and bank statements of her husband's accounts. She showed them the documents, the partnership agreement, and loan details, and the banks provided the financial assistance. Nikitha's name was not mentioned on any of the documents. But the foreman at the unit told him that Nikitha was a financial partner assisting him in the expansion works.

The officer enquired about the partner, and she said her husband would rarely speak of his business matters at home. She started weeping and said her children had been worried from the day he went missing and pleaded with the officer to find him. The other officer convinced her and assured her that they were trying to locate him and they left. Now, the case was further leading to different angles, the officer decided to check on Amala Karan, and her brother's activities and wanted to meet with the children in her absence. After Nikitha's *murder*, Bobby's on the *run*, Karan *escaped*, and the *death* of Anwar, the new male business partner from Mumbai, was in no way related to any information he gathered in the last few days. The officers have no new lead to proceed and could not prove anything useful with the clues they have on the records.

₹ $ £ €

Sidhu met his friends Naveen and Vinay at the pub over the weekend. They were discussing their missing friend; they did not know where he was hiding. Each one told their stories about the police officer's inquiry and was worried about their jobs and further interrogations. After an hour, they left the pub.

Edward arrived at the pub where Sointhara said that he first saw Bobby and his friends when his car broke down in Secunderabad when he came to attend the manufacturers' meeting. Sidhu was going to the parking lot and saw a foreigner, a fair man with brown hair who gave a crooked smile calling him. He approached and introduced himself as Detective Edward and said he wanted to talk to him. Sidhu stared at his short hair and well-built physique. By his accent and body language, he did not appear to be a detective but a retired army man from another country. He was wondering how he got his name. Later, he realizes that the bank might have given his details and believed not only him but also the names and addresses of all of them

Edward said he wanted to talk to him about his friend Bobby. He placed his strong arm on Sidhu's shoulder and walked him into the pub. He ordered beers, despite Sidhu's refusal. He took his scribbling pad and read a few lines about Bobby, his job activities, and the money transfers to the other accounts. Sidhu questioned him about his credentials, and Edward gave him his visiting card and showed an authorization letter from the company. He recognized the company that employed Bobby, Edward spoke about his job as a private investigator and spoke of his career and retirement in the USA. He said that one of the commissioners of the crime branch was a good friend, who recommended him to investigate the company's fraud. Later, he briefed Bobby and his fraudulent manager, Gaikwad who framed his friend. After a few gulps; he convinced Sidhu that he would not drag him into any controversy and wanted to get the true nature of his friend.

"Thank you, Sidhu, and I appreciate your co-operation, now, please tell me how they met and whether the money belongs to Nikitha."

"Sir..."

He abruptly stops him and says,

"You better call me by my name, and feel free to talk to me."

"Ok Edward, we used to meet in this pub and discuss the stock markets and bet on the indexes and shares. He's brilliant, used to guess the market's next move, and always won the bet. He spent more time in her coffee shop analyzing the stocks."

"So, he met her in her coffee shop, right? Now I got you; she might have asked him to trade with her money... That's clear now."

He notes down a few lines and asks,

"When did you meet Nikitha last time? Do you know how much she lent him for trading and now, how would he meet and return her money?"

Sidhu stared at him for a short while and said,

"Edward, I never met her; I only heard of her through Bobby. Now Nikitha's no more, dead... Brutally murdered and that's the reason he ran away."

"What? Nikitha's murdered... Oh, God?"

Edward looks at him, places his pen on the table, moves his head sideways, and continues,

"I am sorry to hear that; I was unaware of it. How and when did it happen?"

Sidhu narrated the story of Bobby's trading activity and about the murder. He said Bobby would never murder a person for money and explained his trading strategies, research, and free tips for investors who lost their money in the stock market. He also showed a few messages and the trades with Nikitha's fund. He repeated similar words that he told the police officer. Later, Sidhu speaks in a pleasing tone.

"Bobby couldn't have transferred her money... Now his company had filed a fraud case... And he was desperate, as the company would claim her money, believing it to be the company fund and so he had to escape."

"Now, the case turns to a deadly conspiracy, and ironically, Bobby squeezed himself into the legal trap. So, Bobby's unaware of the death of his girlfriend Nikitha?"

Edward said, sighs said and stares at Sidhu.

"Perhaps, yes, I assume so."

Edward moves his head sideways, has a sip, and continues,

"He should've returned her capital and clarified it with the company, but he didn't do so, and now, you and the other friends can also be booked for aiding and abetting. I think I can't help now... Have to find the facts behind her murder."

Edward's remarks annoyed Sidhu, who was also irritated that he had accused them and his friends. Sidhu again explained his friend's job offer as a scalper, a self-taught trading technique, and asked him to check Bobby's trading history for the past few months. Edward took out the copies of the transactions and another set of papers from his folder and observed. It confirmed Bobby's personal bank account reflected the figures he received from Nikitha's bank and the company's money in another account. Edward realized Gaikwad had eluded himself through the fraud and Bobby was forced into the well-planned ambush. Sidhu said Bobby was suspicious and spoke about the manager's unnecessary intervention while he was busy in the trading sessions. Edward analyzed that trading, and murder could not interlink as he was trading in Mumbai while the murder took place in Hyderabad, Telangana. Later, Edward thanked him, said he would meet him again if necessary, and asked him to relax.

The next morning, Edward went to Nikitha's coffee shop and met the manager, who's managing it with the permission of the commissioner of labor. The hotel association's president obtained permission, stating that it's a steadily running business and wanted to retain the employees and their jobs. Edward inquired about daily sales and financial management. The manager showed the receipts and the remittance of the money to the coffee shop's account after it was scrutinized by a government-authorized official.

Edward heard the story of how Bobby and Nikitha met and the visits of Karan and Anwar. He asked for the address of the bank and the police station. He met with the SHO, police station and gave his introduction letters that were issued by the Company and the Commissioner of Police in Chembur, Maharashtra. He registered his request for investigation and signed the paper. A police constable was assigned to assist him, but he politely thanked and left.

On the way, he went to the private bank where the Nikitha coffee shop's current account was and met with the manager. They just showed the transactions on the screen and rejected his request for a hard copy, citing the customer's privacy policy. He returned to the coffee shop and finished his lunch. Later, he called Sidhu and they went to the Nationalized Bank at Balkampet, where Nikitha held her personal savings account. They met the Branch Manager and detailed his investigation. The manager insisted on getting an authorization letter and Edward showed the letter. He read and asked him to get a legal order, which entitles him to inquire about his bank's customer. They went to the DGP office and obtained the permission letter. Yet, the manager was unconvinced to give the transaction statements and mentioned her safe deposit locker. Sidhu asked him about the legal procedures to search the safe deposit locker. The manager sarcastically says that it was the duty of the police, not of a foreign detective, and that has to do with the

Magistrate's order. Edward was angry and controlled his hypertension. He anticipated this could happen and knew how stingy and miserable the banks are while dealing with such matters. Finally, the manager gave him a list of documents and asked him to get them approved to open the safe vault.

Edward and Sidhu went to the coffee shop and asked the manager about Nikitha's parents and relatives. He said that she was from Chennai and received a bequeath after her parents passed away; said she never mentioned any of her cousins or relatives. Edward thanked Sidhu and told him that now he believes Bobby was not guilty of murder and he's determined to find and help him out of the legal issue. He asked him to try to contact Bobby and tell him that he shall be proven not guilty if he surrenders and testifies before the court of law.

Now, Edward knew the motive behind Nikitha's murder and assumed someone else framed Bobby for this crime. It's a wonder how she trusted her boyfriend to such an extent that obliged her to give away all her money was yet an unanswered question. Why did she have such confidence in her boyfriend? Was she in love with him? If so, why did not she tell or inform him if something happened to her or the business? Who shall be the sole beneficiary if any unforeseen incident takes place? Edward has a doubt, that Nikitha might have left a will, a successor certificate in Bobby's name, in the bank.

18. Nikitha's Will

Edward met the manager of the bank, and he was asked to wait for SM, the Senior Manager. Meanwhile, he called Sidhu and asked if he knew anyone in the DIG's office and said he may need a lawyer too. After ten minutes, Sidhu messaged that he could arrange a lawyer. The Senior Manager walked into the room. Edward introduced himself, told him the story of Nikitha's murder, and showed the relevant documents. The SM called his clerk and asked for the transaction of Nikitha's account. He said her account was not operated for the past two months with a zero balance, and her rent for the safe deposit locker was due.

Edward assumed there might be some personal or vital information in the bank's safe deposit locker. He asked about the procedures to open and view the locker. SM called one of his staff, and Edward was ushered into the other cabin. The clerk explained to him the legal procedures and a few sections of the Banking Regulatory Act, 1949, and the Banking Companies Rules, 1985. He thanked him and returned to his hotel. He searched the legal procedures to access the dead person's safe deposit contents. The rules were similar to those of the US and India, except for a few clauses and sections.

The job was completed, he found the transaction, and the figures tallied, but something was knocking him that he was overlooking or missing a clue. The eagerness was mocking him and felt his research's incomplete; if solved successfully, it would be a superfluous attempt and praiseworthy. Meanwhile, he received a call from Helen; she told him Saritha was admitted to the hospital with a knee injury. She asked him not to worry and said she fell while playing with the children. He called Sidhu and told him he would be leaving and asked him to try to find the whereabouts of his friend. Edward arrived in Chembur, called Helen, went to the hospital, and met Saritha. She's on the bed with the belt around her knee and is glad to see father and daughter. Helen spoke to the doctor, and he told them to take her after two days. They spent some time, and Edward saw an exciting look in her beautiful round eyes. He spoke to her, and she thanked him and said she would recover fast with their presence.

Edward went to his office and met with Sointhara, briefed him about his findings, and said he would prepare a report after the final round-up. Later, he asked the receptionist and collected the mail sent from his former office, USA. He left the building and again walked inside and asked the receptionist whether there was any mail for Bobby. She said a few days ago, there was a registered letter; the postman tried to deliver it twice and said that he would return it to the sender with the unsuccessful delivery remarks. He thanked her and asked her when the postman enquired; she told him it was after a few days after Bobby left the company.

At once, Edward went to the Chembur post office and inquired about the registered letter. A postman came from the sorting section with a list and showed him the returned date, sender name, and address. When Edward asked about the procedure, the postman told him that the unsuccessful delivery would be returned to the HPO and later to the sender's address. He returned home, and after dinner, told his daughter that he had to leave for Hyderabad. She was annoyed and asked him to take a break for a while; he smiled and promised that he would after the case's solved.

The next day, Helen dropped her father at the bus stand; he boarded a sleeper coach bus and reached Hyderabad at eleven am and called Sidhu. He did not get an answer, and later, he received a text message from Sidhu stating that he was in a meeting. He went to Nikitha's coffee shop, finished his breakfast, and got her residential address from the manager. He went to Nikitha's apartment and met the security officer; he showed his ID and letter and enquired about her mailbox. The security said he does not keep the keys in the security office and asked him to meet the secretary of the housing society. Meanwhile, he received a call and walked towards the gate. There's no CC camera coverage; Edward searched for her name and found it on the third row. There he saw an envelope in Nikitha's metal letterbox; he slid his Swiss knife into the keyhole and turned it clockwise. The rusted box opened, took the two letters, locked it, and left the apartment.

He reached his hotel and opened the letters; both were addressed to Bobby and were posted a few days before her murder. The post offices stamped the two letters and returned them with the notation, 'Return to Sender.' He carefully opened the first letter, which detailed her total investment and her assets. Edward spread the letter on the table and took a snap on his mobile. He took a piece of paper and wrote the figures she invested in the stock market. He came to know that she had purchased a house in the prime locality of Jubilee Hills in Hyderabad.

He searched for the prevailing price on the internet and noted the approximate value. The coffee shop was on annual rent with a fifteen percent increase every following year. He calculated the total investment and the average return. Earlier, he worked on a few fraud and trade speculation cases. Therefore, it did not take him long to understand the motive of her investment through Bobby's account. He appreciated her brilliant idea; the tax liability was on Bobby's account, and unknowingly, he would also pay the income tax for her money. Yet, something was convincing him not to blame her and he took her fear and apprehension into account for a clear picture of the murder. Later, he opened the second letter; it was a copy of a Will, and the successor was none other than her boyfriend, Bobby Shacal.

Sidhu and Edward are at the coffee shop and after a while, Edward asks,

"Sidhu, do you have any idea how much Nikitha invested through Bobby's account?"

Sidhu showed him the messages, and emails; wrote them on the tissue and gave them to him. Edward gave a paper that shows the total transactions and date-wise trades. Sidhu compared the figures and there was a small difference of about a few thousand.

"Edward, where did you get these figures?"

He smiled and showed him Nikitha's letter. Sidhu took the letter, read it, and asked.

"Edward, is the money still in Bobby's account? Did he transfer it into Nikitha's bank?"

"His bank accounts are ceased; I think he could not have transferred the money."

The intriguing issues, incidents, and daunting task made them restless.

19. Chameli & Bobby – 1

Bobby rolled the empty beer bottle aside and leaned on the tree trunk behind him. It's eleven pm and a car stops; the back door opens, and a woman's pushed out from inside. She fell on the pavement. Then, her purse flew out of the window and landed on the road. She got up, picked a stone from the ground, and hurled it at the moving car. Bobby was shocked and ran towards her. She saw him approaching her, took another stone, and was ready to hit him. He stopped and said,

"It's ok, I'm not going to hurt you, ma'am."

In the faint light, he could not see her face but saw her right hand in the air with a sharp granite piece. The blood was dripping from the right elbow. Her sari was torn, and her purse was a few feet away on the road. The purse was open, and a few notes were partly visible. He slowly reached, picked up her purse, and saw her. She was watching him; he pushed the notes inside and gave her. She did not move; did not try to take it. He took a few steps slowly, placed the purse on the pavement, and turned around.

He expected a hit on the back of his head, but nothing so happened, turned around and saw her taking her purse and running away. He returned to his place, leaned against the tree, spread his legs on the grass, and closed his eyes. After a short while, he heard footsteps—someone approaching from the other side of the road. She's the same woman walking towards him. She stopped before him, took a note from her purse, gave him, and said,

"Take this man. I am thankful for your concern and *help*."

"Save it. I did nothing and better hurry up, ma'am; it's too late. Good night."

She's of medium height with a beautiful face. He noticed the smudged makeup and the spread of black marks of Kajal around her eyes. Her slender figure made him assume she's in her late twenties. She stared at him, placed the note beside him, and walked away. It was like a dream for Bobby; a scared woman returns and pays her gratitude after the ghastly incident. Who was she—really a woman or a ghost? He took the note and observed, that it was a real five hundred rupee note and was desperate to have another beer, but the shops were closed.

His mind was consumed with memories of his friends in Hyderabad. None of them were as generous as Sidhu, who always had the willingness to pay the bill despite other having the money in their wallets. Now, a woman has given him a tip just for returning her purse. He acknowledged her kindness, pocketed the note, and headed to the bar, where he works as a waiter for the evening shifts. The night security recognized him and allowed him in, and he proceeded to sleep on an empty table in the hall.

In the morning, he went to his single room on the first floor. The owner's son, Ajay asked him why he did not return last night. He said he slept in the bar, and it was too late to return. Ajay said he had another key to the gate and gave it to him. He thanked the kid and went to his room. There was a knock on the door. Bobby opened the door and saw the kid standing with a cup of tea and biscuits in the tray.

"Mom sent tea and biscuits for you."

"Oh! Ajay, say thanks to your mother."

"Yeah, I'll, and I want your help, bro."

"Ok, what's it, bro?"

"I need some information for my project."

"Sure, let me see, get your papers."

Ajay is an intermediate student; he goes down and brings partly prepared project papers. Bobby read and scribbled some notes about the concept, structure, and present capital market scenario. Later, he explained the macroeconomics, about the investment, and a few points of the domestic and international investment. Bobby asks him to feel free to clear his doubts any time, and Ajay thanks him and leaves. While going to the bar, he went to the shopping mall, bought a pair of cheap dresses for himself, and bought two second-hand books on money, banking, stock market, and investment from the street vendor. At the time of closing hours, there was a group of five youngsters who ordered a few more beers and non-vegetarian snacks. After the third serving, one of them stared at Bobby while he was attending to other customers. Bobby returned, said there are closing, and asked for the next order. A hefty and medium figure lit a cigarette and asked,

"Where were you last night, man?"

Bobby stared at him and said,

"I was serving you, sir."

"Bastard, I meant after your shit job of waiting here."

Bobby was annoyed, but controlled his anger and replied,

"I went to the park and stayed till midnight."

"Yes! Yes, I told you guys, he was there when we kicked that bitch out of the car. I saw him while taking a turn."

"Forget it mottu, finish let's go hunting."

Said one of his friends, and while leaving, the hefty figure stared at him. Bobby was scared, remembering the last night's incident. She runs, then returns and gives him a five hundred note. His mind was flashing with a few questions, and he asked himself.

"Oh God, is she dead? Did they murder her? And am I an eyewitness?"

Later, the bar closed and the waiters pooled their tips and distributed them among themselves. Meanwhile, Bobby had a few drinks and asked them to adjust his tips for his drinks and left.

₹ $ £ €

Bobby took a bath and settled with the newspaper in the morning. He remembered the night and the incident that took place two days ago. So, these were the guys in the car who threw her out that night? Does she know them, and why didn't she bother to book a complaint with the police? Who was she, and what was her job? He guessed and did not like calling her a prostitute; he termed her profession as a public business. Bobby opened the cupboard and took the five hundred rupee note she gave him, stared at it, and then replaced it at the same place under the old newspapers and lay on his bed. In the afternoon, locked his room and went to the railway canteen. Had a meal and went to an Internet cafe. Browsed for an hour and checked the shares and index. Later, he searched for restaurants and bars in Cuttack City and found one, and it's four kilometers from his locality. It's at the commercial center; he went and met with the cashier. He spoke with his employer, and he asked Bobby to join after three days.

On the way back to his room, he saw a beautiful woman crossing the road and who resembled the woman he saw a few days ago. She's walking a few feet away from him and enters a shopping mall. She was carrying a new grey handbag in her left hand. There was a bandage around her right elbow, but he could not notice; she covered it with her sari. Her sexy walk and swing of her slim waist attracted him. Bobby decided to find out about her and followed her into the shopping mall.

He found her in the female garments section, with a pair of white Salwar and Churidar. Then, she bought bread and pastries from the bakery and left. He was strolling and watching her from a few feet away. In the meantime, there was a collision and a fight between the drivers of the two cars, and he had to wait. He saw her taking a right turn, briskly walked, and took a turn, but did not find her. It was two pm in the afternoon, stood there for a few minutes in the hot sun and returned to his room. Bobby was reflecting on his previous job and his passion for trading on behalf of others. He realized that he had become involved in fraud, and despite his sincerity and honesty, he was defamed as a fraudster. If he were to be discovered, the entire issue would backfire on him, resulting in major stock market fraud, speculation, and the misuse of company funds. He feels unfulfilled, and his life lost its charm after he distances himself from the market and trading. His peculiar addiction could be described as a 'Tradadict' as he consistently succeeds in the market regardless of the trend, and it remains a mystery to himself.

He believes it's important to focus on the trend rather than making vague guesses about the equity or index. Inexperienced traders often lose money due to emotions, frustration, and overestimating or underestimating trades, as they disregard the market trend. Consequently, some traders illogically try to recover their losses by averaging their trades or by relying on the idea of short covering, but this approach is often unsuccessful.

Bobby was never attracted to or trapped by any *emotional trade* on any stock or index and his *flexibility* to use the right strategies for a quick recovery. The money's not the criteria, but winning the trades was his ambition. The ability to grasp and capture the minutes of market moves fetched him his good fortune. His trading legacy may or may not continue, but his confidence in predicting the movement of the index and share price proved him correct until now.

Others may think of a new day with the same sunrise and sunset, but for Bobby, it's new and different every morning and night. The basics of his scalping and trades are to earn *little money* and gain most of the *experience from the markets. And* he feels the money in the bank or in the safe vault gets devalued with time. Moreover, it's true for a brilliant mind and a smart business. He never blamed the market for losses or got excited with the profits; he believed the investors and traders must take care of the risk and save their capital. His concept was simple; hold until the target is achieved and exit with small profits. In day-to-day trade, strict financial discipline is a basic rule, and he believes it. Success does not need applause; it's a personal satisfaction for the rightful action, and it gives inspiration and self-respect. A span of time was the essential remedy needed, and he was waiting for a way to get restarted again.

₹ $ £ €

In the morning, while, returning from the library, again Bobby saw the same ghost woman coming out of a temple. It's five days after he first saw her in the same locality, and today she was beautiful in her light blue sari and black blouse. Her face flashed a new and pretty look that he could not stop staring at her. She held a carry bag in her right hand, and with her left hand, held the frills of the sari. He followed her deliberately; she took a turn, and he almost ran and saw her entering a double-story building.

He walked casually, and after a few seconds, she appeared on the first floor and stopped at the second door beside the staircase. The stairway's in the middle with two flats on either side. After a while, he entered the building, reached the first floor, and stopped at the second door. The moment he raised his hand to press the doorbell, suddenly, the door opened, and she was before him.

"Yes! Whom do you want?"

Bobby tried to look inside; she moved the curtain, blocked his view, and asked in a harsh voice.

"Hello! Mister, I am talking to you."

"Sorry. I came to the wrong address."

"No, if you're true to your heart, you have come to the right person, but at the wrong time and place."

"What?"

"Never mind, meet me at seven pm. At the park where you returned my purse."

She said and slammed the door in his face. He was surprised; she recognized him and was aware of him following her. He reached his room, gulped some water from the bottle, and lay on his bed. Her words made him feel guilty and ashamed for his mindless behavior.

'True to the heart, right person, wrong time and place.'

Yes, he should be true to himself about why he followed her to her house. Was it love or lust? He's yet to decide. The right person, so that night when he saw and assumed her to be a *public businesswoman* was true. Agreed it was the wrong time because it was the afternoon, resting time. Her house was the wrong place for her business. Therefore, she does not entertain her customers in the afternoons or entertain them at her house. It's unusual, but it's a sensible social discipline she practices. He appreciated her wise thought, and in fact, it also restricted her exposure to the neighborhood. Unfortunately, not everyone in the neighborhood was kind enough to accept and understand that her work was her livelihood.

Bobby took permission from the manager and reached the park a few minutes early. It was with a few visitors, and he went to the other end, where the road leads to another locality, to the industrial area. The setting sun, the shade under the huge tree, and swinging branches displayed a beautiful picture he never witnessed. Sometimes, a *happy mind* and a *painful heart* may perceive the same place in nature differently. He sat on the grass, leaning against the tree.

After a while, she appeared on the road; he stood and waved his hand. She waved her hand and walked towards him. Her slender body, dressed in a white sleeveless blouse and a pink sari, gave her a glamorous look. The light perfume fragrance was a perfect match for the evening. She placed her purse beside her and asked him to sit. He was confused. Was he dating a pro or meeting a new girlfriend? He sat opposite her and smiled. She observed him for a short while and then introduced herself.

"Well, I am Chameli."

She said and extended her hand. He took her hand and said, "I am Bobby."

"You are really like the hero of the movie, Bobby."

She referred him to a movie hero, and he thought it was a good act of pursuance. Her tactics are now exposing her profession and her tight-fitting transparent dress to attract her customers was annoying him and she stared at him and said,

"Bobby, how much can you pay?"

"What?"

"I mean, I charge more for rich brats, it's a fair price for my tough job, but I'll charge you a little less."

Bobby smiled at her words, a wonderful woman with a dirty job, and offering a generous discount. Stared at her and said,

"How do I look, a rich brat or poor man?"

"I know you are a middle-class boy, and I can't expect more from you, so your place or any hotel?"

"Let me be clear ma'am, I am in no way to afford you; I just thought you were beautiful and followed, and I have no other intention."

"I know the intentions of men, be honest to yourself, young man, the time's running out."

"I am sorry if I am wasting your time, but I want to return your five hundred rupees, that's all."

Now, she looks into his innocent eyes and says,

"Well, you have come to just to return the money, it's weird. What do you do? Are you employed? Have a family? What makes you come to me? I am confused, and why do you want to return the money?"

Her voice changed to a soft questioning tone. He takes out a five hundred rupee note, places it in her hand, and asks,

"How's your right elbow?"

She drops her sari from her right shoulder and raises her right elbow. The wound is still healing, and a round band-aid is placed over it. He glances at her transparent blouse and, at once, turns his head away, but could not escape the eagerness to have a look at her shapely body. She smiled, covered her shoulder with the sari, and loved his innocence and care. She holds his hand and says,

"Bobby, you are the first person in my life to care, at least ask about my injury. I am thankful to you."

Bobby saw a film of tears in her eyes. He slowly withdrew his hand and replied.

"Chameli, I know what you are. Can't you take up any other job than this body business? You can get a good office job. What's your qualification? I shall try to help you if I can."

She wipes her tears and looks into his eyes. He could not see her eye to eye now.

"What job can you offer me? Do you act as a pimp for my body business?"

She said and smiled. He was angry but hid his temper and spoke.

"You should try for an office job, then this dirty work?"

"Do you call it a dirty job? Don't you see, people throw money for this dirt and enjoy a woman's body. Where are you living, my innocent baby? And even our great emperors, sages, and Gods couldn't escape from the female scent, if I'm not wrong."

"You are right, but we do have other jobs too. Why don't you try."

There were a few minutes of silence; a wave of cool breeze flew her hair from behind her ear. She tucked them back with her tender fingers and spoke.

"My profession is my *choice*, it's my business, and I can't leave it just for your kind and caring words. Thank you."

"Great, you call your job a profession? A business, I am surprised!"

"I pity your naïve survival, and it shows you lack knowledge of ancient history."

"That's not my subject, although, I truly agree, I am not aware of the subject."

"So, don't ever suggest anything until you read or know better. Anyway, what's your subject?"

"Never mind, forget it... I am not here to discuss the subjects."

"That's right, even I am not interested in debating about the centuries' old respectable tradition."

She says, gets up, pushes the note into his shirt pocket, and starts walking away. He walks along with her; she stops, turns around, and speaks out in frustration.

"Bobby, what is it now? What do you want from me?"

He takes out the five hundred rupees note and gives it to her; she does not accept it and says suggestively,

"Never refuse the money, Bobby, maybe someday. It might be helpful in the future. Don't get bewildered by my profession. It taught me to respect my beautiful body and me. I have to earn now for my *disgusting life* and save it for the *dreadful future*. Goodbye."

20. Chameli & Bobby – 2

Bobby starts after his lunch at the railway canteen, spends an hour at the library, and takes a bus to the city center. He has his dinner at the bar and returns late at midnight. It's the second week for Bobby at the new restaurant and bar in Cuttack City. He did not vacate his room and searched for a single-room accommodation near his bar. He felt his hardship was bearable for an unknown happiness and with a momentary mental satisfaction seeing Chameli from a distance. Later, he took a loan from his employer and rented a single room. However, the rent was higher than what he paid for his earlier accommodation. He has an idea of getting a roommate to share his lonely life. Was not confident but determined to persuade Chameli to stay with him. Is it a favor? No now, it's a desire of a woman; he could not justify it and speaks to himself.

"I am a Scalper; I should play any position either in the market or with a woman, and with the same rule."

Chameli visits the temple in the morning every Saturday and returns in the afternoon after the shopping. Bobby was determined to talk to her, convince her and take her to his flat and was waiting at the temple. After eleven am, she appeared from a lane beside the crossroad. She was in a white cotton sari, her purse in her right hand and her left hand holding her mobile. She crosses the road, goes to the coconut vendor, and purchases the coconut and flowers. Takes a jasmine from the carry bag and tucks it in her loosely tied hair. Bobby walks to her and says hello, and she smiles; she gives him the carry bag and takes her purse to pay the vendor. He said he would pay, but she ignored him, paid the vendor, and both started walking into the temple. It was a new and wonderful experience for him; he remembered his mother, and she used to take him to the temple every Tuesday and Friday. The tears blinded his sight, and she noticed and said,

"Do you remember your mother?"

"Yes. I do."

"A human's life's nothing but a memory, good or bad. It teaches us a way to live, and leads our life to witness the uncertain tomorrow."

Her words were exactly as his mother said once. He was surprised and saw her; she was not more than thirty, but now, her behavior was more of an elderly woman. After offering the prayers, they went to a cement bench and sat in the shade. She was observing the small plants and the flowers beside the walkway. She showed a plant and said she planted it a month ago. There are three small roses on the plant. He asked her if she wanted the rose, and she moved her head sideways and said the flowers are adored for their beauty on the plants rather than as a useless decoration on people.

After a while, they left the temple and reached the road. He bought a soft drink and offered her. She stared at him, took the pet bottle, had a sip, and questioned him.

"Bobby... I don't understand. What makes you come to a whore?"

Her words hurt him, looked around and saw her. She wrapped her sari over her head and said,

"I think you heard me, gentleman."

They started walking and reached her regular shopping mall. She asked,

"Bobby, are you scared to reply? If you are, I won't insist, and please don't follow me. My character's unbearable and untouchable for the good people."

"I don't know, but I want to help you, Chameli. I am a scalper and have to play all positions."

"Why, and who's a Scalper?"

"Don't ask me; I don't know."

"Do you live with your parents?"

"No, my parents are dead; I live alone."

"My guess was correct; the moment I saw tears in your eyes in the temple, I knew you were alone and missing someone. One has to live for oneself and survive... Anyway, it's a *tough rule* we have to obey. I am glad for your kind words, but my life's different, and it doesn't go with an innocent boy like you."

He did not speak, and she bought groceries, the daily needs, and both walked out of the mall. She turned to him and said,

"Nice meeting you, Bobby, and I am thankful for your concern. Goodbye."

He stood there until she disappeared into a lane on the other side of the road. The next Saturday, Bobby was ten minutes early and waited for Chameli. There are many women, who do their kind of job and earn a better living. Her job's the worst job ever; any woman would hardly prefer it. One does not have to use her body for money; any small job could get her the money, maybe less than what she earns now. He wanted to know what made her choose that kind of life. What was her education and her family? He could not think further, as he had never met any such women in the past.

She appears to be happy with her life; can a woman stay happy with a disgusting and dangerous life? He knew she was pretending, disgraced with her sorrowful life. Yet he could not find the right reason to convince and take her into his life. Although it's a tough decision as well as a delicate issue to debate, and none would dare to listen or express their thoughts in public. Despite a miserable life, she imagines a beautiful view of herself by crushing her feelings inside. If she's really happy and satisfied with the way she lives, then why would she agree to live in companionship with him? He questions himself. The obvious behavior of a prostitute, glamorous body display, and sexy expressions were intolerable to Bobby. However, the way she looks into his eyes and turns her head sideways while talking fascinates him. When he spoke, she stared at him and looked from the corner of her eyes at something new that he didn't observe in Nikitha. Her shapely body and soft voice do not suit her profession, *but she has to attract, attract to lure, lure to earn was her equation for living*. Unknowingly, fifteen minutes passed away, and he was tired of the frustration.

"She has to come, it's a Saturday."

He said it aloud, but she did not promise or say that she's a regular devotee to visit the temple. He went to the tea stall, had tea, and sat on a chair. Now, half an hour has passed. Thought of asking the flower vendor about her, if she had come and left before he came, but it was not appropriate to enquire. He spent another ten minutes and later, went to the railway canteen for lunch.

₹ $ £ €

On the fourth day, Bobby could not control his worried thoughts. He remembered the incident of throwing her out of a car and imagined her to be raped, stabbed, and thrown at an isolated place. Alternatively, at a hospital or in prison or her customer captivated by her charm and kidnapped. Now, Chameli's hardship was unbearable to him, and he was eager to see her in good shape.

Now, he could not wait anymore, walked into the lane, and searched for her house. He recognized the house with grey paint and the staircase in the middle. Took the stairs and reached her flat. The door was locked; observed the lane below and could not dare to ask anyone about her. Sat on the third step of the stairs leading to the second floor. After a short while, he heard the sound of bangles and slapping the footwear. He stood and peeped; Chameli was reaching the first floor. He moved aside from the steps; she saw him and stopped. He smiled; she did not, took her sari and wiped the sweat from her forehead and cheeks, and went to her flat. She unlocked, entered, and immediately locked the door. Her unwelcoming behavior annoyed him and pushed the calling button. A melodious chime rang for a few seconds; she opened the door, stared at him in despair, and unwillingly invited him inside. It's a single bedroom with a small living room and kitchen, and the washroom was behind the main door. Bobby sat on a chair; she went to the refrigerator, took a water bottle gives it to him, and sat on a dirty couch facing him. She bent her head backward, her face facing the ceiling, and closed her eyes. He saw a bandage on the left side of her waist that extended towards her navel and another bandage around her left index finger. Except for the humming of the ceiling fan, there was a kind of hush filled in the room. She was taking deep breaths; he thought she might have met with an accident—or *another professional hazard?*

"Chameli, what happened?"

She did not answer. He sits beside her and speaks.

"Chameli, did you meet with an accident?"

She opened her eyes, turned her head, and replied,

"My life is an accident, an inevitable disaster."

He had no words and did not know what to say. Sometimes, a woman's grief cannot be guessed and understood easily.

"Bobby, you shouldn't have come here."

She said and closed her eyes. Meanwhile, there was a chime; she went and opened the door. A man and woman in her late fifties speak rudely to her. Chameli pleaded with them; the old man was silent, but the woman was stubborn and harsh, and asked her to vacate the flat. And also warned her that she would complain to the police station if she didn't. They warned her twice and left. She closed the door and returned to the couch, dropped her head in her palms, and started weeping. It was an unexpected situation for him, and he was feeling guilty for coming here. A few minutes passed in silence, and then he asked her,

"Chameli, how long have you been staying here?"

"Now, it doesn't make any sense."

"They're not supposed to talk like that to a tenant."

"How should they speak? If you were in their place, how would you speak? Now, please leave me alone. Please."

Chameli started sobbing again, and he could not bear seeing her in tears. He took a piece of paper from the small table, wrote a telephone number, and placed it beside her. He walked to the door and saw her, but she didn't look at him, and he left. Bobby used to feel proud of his astute ability as a scalper in the markets, but now, it proved him wrong with real-life experience.

₹ $ £ €

At ten pm, Bobby asked the cashier, and he said there was no call for him. He bought packed food, reached Chameli's flat, and pushed the calling button. She opened the door; her tired look and tears dried eyes were uninviting. He stepped inside, closed the door behind him, and asked her.

"Chameli, pack your belongings, you're going with me to my flat."

He went into the kitchen, brought a plate, and unpacked the food. She watched him serve while her tears rolled down her cheeks. He took the plate and asked,

"Do you want me to feed you?"

Suddenly, she cries out loud, and he sits beside her. She leaned on him, wept for a while, and he asked her to finish her dinner. He went into her bedroom and packed a few things he felt she required.

"Bobby, you had enough trouble, and still, you want me to stay with you?"

"Take it as a yes and come with me."

"No, you are still young; have a good future... You're unaware of society... And no respectable person invites me to live with."

"Chameli, I am aware; I don't want you to bear this insult and don't want you to do the dirty body business. Think again; how can one live with this torture daily, and how can you bear the insult and humiliation? I can't tolerate it. I know it's a compulsion for you, but not till I am here with you."

"How I live is my life, and it's good and suits me. Why should you bother when it's none of your business?"

"Everyone has social concerns about it, but many people ignore it. In addition, people like you do not ask for help when you can correct yourself and alter your lifestyle."

"It's not fair, Bobby, helping a desperate woman and insulting her for her survival? Unreasonably, some may not like my survival. You tell me? What should I do live, or die?"

He clasps his hands and requests her.

"Please, Chameli, don't argue now."

He apologized and said he has no right to force her to live with him. He convinced her that she could stay with him as long as she would, and it was up to her choice. He requested her to stay for a few days till she got well. She stared at him and thought he was overly mature for his age. Asked him to give her some time to decide, he nods and leaves.

The next morning Bobby goes to get Chameli, and the owner said she vacated last night. He asked about her forwarding address. The old man smiled and sarcastically said that *a bitch does not have a real name and the correct address* and closed the door. Bobby felt heartbroken and had no idea what to do or where to search for her.

21. Damayanthi & Bobby – 3

Bobby returned to his room by eleven pm and was thinking about Chameli. He heard the people yelling at one another; he walked to the single window and saw a woman surrounded by a group of people on the street. At once, he recognized her in the faint light and ran down the stairs. She was weeping, and her elbow was bleeding, her cheeks bruised, and her hair pulled out of the braid. Her Dupatta was torn, and two men were pulling her. Bobby called her name and pushed away the mob. A man stopped him and said he wanted her first. Bobby explained to him that she was not such a woman; convinced them that she was on medication and that knocked out of her senses. One of them grabbed and pulled Chameli towards him. The situation was getting worse and out of control. Bobby stood watching her and the people helplessly.

Meanwhile, a car stopped, and a man walked to Bobby, Shaahil his former landlord. Then, his wife and son, Ajay got out of the car. They recognized Bobby and observed Chameli. Shaahil and his wife spoke to the people and convinced them not to get involved in a family dispute. An elderly man came forward and spoke in Odia, asked the people to get away, and pushed a few drunken men away. Still, a few did not agree and started an argument. Shaahil asked his wife and son to take her away and he spoke with people.

A police patrol car was passing by and the mob quietly dispersed. Bobby approached Shaahil's family and thanked them. Ajay innocently asked Bobby and Chameli to go with them and stay the night in their house. Shaahil and his wife exchanged looks and Bobby said he rented a room nearby, thanked them again, and said goodnight. Shaahil asked Bobby to meet him the next day and drew away. Bobby took Chameli and her single suitcase to his room and made her lie on the bed. She looked pale and tired and after a few minutes, she was snoring.

The next morning, He reached the railway station, had a cup of coffee, and later went to the temple. He prayed, spent the time, and went to meet Shaahil. They welcomed him and offered breakfast and tea. Bobby told them the complete story and expressed his idea of helping Chameli. At first, they were surprised and annoyed, asked him to leave the woman at once, and spoke of the society. Despite this reality, Bobby didn't agree and said he would try to change her way of life and provide employment. They realized Bobby's love for her and did not further speak of her. Later, he requested a loan from Shaahil's bank under the self-employment scheme; he said he would try to arrange it and asked him to get her educational certificates and apply for a woman's unemployment scheme. He also suggested that she should get herself enrolled in some institute for a short-term course to avail herself of the facility of the bank loan.

While returning, Shaahil paid him the remaining balance from the advance amount he paid for his room and thanked him for helping his son with his subjects and exams. Bobby smiled and said he did nothing and politely refused the money. Mrs. Shaahil forced him to accept; he could not say no and took the money. He tried to touch her feet with respect, but she moved away, blessed him, and asked him to take care of himself. On the way back, he called Chameli from a local landline phone, but she did not answer.

Now, he understood how helpless he was, despite having money in the bank account and his inability to draw and use it. Until now, he has not used his ATM card, as it could give a lead to the police about his present location. He had rupees thirty thousand after leaving the Swamy Das's house and he was left with little money only to buy a square meal for a person in a day. Now has to be prepared to feed another person who's living with him. He returned to his room; she was not there and found a note in English, saying she was going to visit the Amareshwar temple in Durga Bazaar. He appreciated her English and thought of going to the temple that was half a kilometer from his room.

Now, he's scared to go out with her after the last night's incident on the street. He realized the embarrassment and dignity and remembered Mrs. Shaahil's words. He laughed at his dignity and self-respect and decided not to get discouraged. Determined to get her corrected, make her walk with pride, and if possible, take her away from this city to another place. He wants to teach her the art of trading and educate her for regular earnings without leaving her house, from his room.

In the corner beside the door was her suitcase partly opened, and a dress was out of it. He went, unzipped, and pushed it inside, and saw a personal file and a few tablets with the clothes. His anxiousness made him look inside. A file has her school, intermediate, graduation, an NCC certificate, and a state-level participant certificate. Her real name was 'Damayanthi,' now, her age is thirty-two, and her mother tongue is Marathi.

His assumption of Chameli led to a stalemate at this juncture and forced him to review her with more respect and dignity than before. He wanted her to refrain from her past life and change her ideology. Now, with confused thoughts and a disturbed mind, he leaned onto the wall and closed his eyes. He did not notice her; she stood watching him for a while and later walked into the washroom silently. He felt guilty for checking her personal belongings and replaced the file inside the suitcase. She observed him, and he didn't dare to look at her and left. After a long time, she remembered her alcohol-addicted husband. A pimp and a worthless person. He disliked her for being an educated woman; insulted and used her until she left him. She assumed that even Bobby had the same mindset.

Bobby returned with the food, fruits, and juice. He placed a plate with egg-fried noodles and a juice bottle beside her and said,

"Damayanthi, come, let's have lunch together."

It's been a long time since she heard someone addressing her by her real name. They finished their lunch in silence; it was the moment to make a decision for them. A time to reschedule their lives and plan the right path for their future. He finished first, asked her to be ready, and said he wanted her to go to a temple with him and left.

She did not know what to do. To leave or stay with him? Staying with him would be insulting and torturing his innocent life. Earlier, she had no restrictions; none opposed her lifestyle, and now he's helping and, besides, controlling her free movements and freedom. Despite her freedom being restricted, she aspires to live a new life with a new identity and with his help. She took her mobile, took a selfie, and viewed herself. Her pale face, with sunken eyes and bruises on her left cheek, criticized her existence. For the first time, she saw herself in tears.

No person can hold or control tears for a long time when in despair. There was a knock on the door; she wiped her tears and opened the door. Bobby entered with bags in his hands, gave her, and asked her to get ready in ten minutes. She took the sari; he smiled and asked her if she wanted him to help her wrap. She did not like his closeness and was nervous about his approach.

They visited Amareshwar temple and later, went to Maa Chandi temple at Tulasipur colony. Both were preoccupied with their thoughts and hardly spoke a word. He took her to a restaurant, but she refused and said she would cook at home. Later, she took him to a local market, bought a refillable, ready-to-use gas stove, groceries, and the vegetables, and paid the bill with her mobile.

₹ $ £ €

Bobby met with Shaahil at his bank, took the application forms, and returned to his room. He signed as a guarantor, gave her the application, and asked her to fill in the rest. She read and asked why she had to take a loan and how she could repay such a big loan. He told her that he wanted to buy the latest version of a new laptop and open a new trading account. She did not understand, and he explained to her the investment and online trading. It's a new subject to her; besides, she was worried about the repayment of the loan.

She heard about the stock market and hardly had any knowledge of trading. Said he would teach her to trade and said it's a new business and she has to learn on the new laptop. He took her certificates; she stopped and asked him to be careful with them. He smiled, promised, and went to the bank. While returning to the railway station, someone called him from behind, stopped, and was waiting for him to approach.

"Bobby Bhai... Armaan..."

He remembered him, and they shook hands.

"Armaan... How come, you are here man?"

"I have come to file a tender." He folds his hands, says namaste, and speaks.

"Bobby, by the grace of your hard work and wishes, now I run a good business, deal with the government and local housing projects, and provide the electrical lighting and LED installation through the tenders."

They went to a teashop, and Bobby told him his story and said that he was going to Mumbai, shortly. Armaan asked where he would be staying, and unwillingly, Bobby said that he and his wife were trying for an apartment in Colaba. At once, he mentioned his apartment and said they could stay as long as they wished to stay. He thought, now he could repay his gratitude for helping him in his hard times. He asked for the mobile number, and Bobby gave Damayanthi's number. A message was received with the details of the flat and the address on her mobile.

While leaving Armaan's eyes were wet with tears, Bobby noticed, hugged him, and said,

"It's your willpower buddy; stand strong and believe in yourself. I did nothing, but I may need your help in a few days. Please, try to help me."

"Sure Bhai, Jaan Hazir Hai yaar tere liye. By the way, I will be staying for a few days in Mumbai and would love to meet you and Bhabhi."

"I'll call you Armaan, take care... Goodbye."

A cheque for rupees one lakh was received by Chameli, and she deposited it in her bank. Later, she gave her cheque and passbook and said,

"Bobby, this is my dirty earnings; if you wish to use them, please don't hesitate."

He took the passbook; it has rupees five lakhs and forty-nine thousand, and he saw her. He placed his hand over his head and confessed.

"Oh! I should have discussed this with you before taking the bank loan. It's my mistake."

He should have told her about his plan before going to the bank; he was frustrated with the blunder he committed, and that made her accountable for the unnecessary loan and repayment. Now, he learned that *one should not assume and act unsolicited, however noble a good deed may be, especially for others.* Today, he's responsible for his haste and ignorant act. She observed him, placed her hand on his shoulder, and said,

"Never mind, my dear Bobby boy, if you can still use it for a good use and I'll be glad, please accept."

A new laptop and the printer were delivered, and her trading account was active. Damayanthi lit a lamp and completed her pooja. Bobby asked her to log into the trading platform. Showed her the process of trading shares and explained to her about the buy and sell transactions. Later, asked her to watch and left her with the laptop. At half past twelve, she said she had to cook and began preparing the lunch. It was a long time since he watched the Nifty, Nifty Bank, and Sensex, and the indexes. He was tempted to take a trade, then realized the impending disaster that was already with him, and it may also shadow her in the future.

After lunch, he explained to her the basics, and the process of buying and selling, and how the orders are executed. He asked her to place a buy order without a stop loss for delivery. At once, the order was executed for one hundred shares. He showed her how to check the intraday orders, execution, portfolio, and available cash margin before and after the trade. She raised a few questions, he coolly answered, and she asked him how to withdraw the money. Showed her the pay-in and pay-out process and he said,

"Well, it's very easy, isn't it, and not tougher than selling one's body?"

Her frustrated look made him guilty and at once he took her hands and apologized to her.

"Sorry, I am sorry Damayanthi, a slip of my dirty tongue."

"No Bobby, you're correct... One can't hide the feelings for a longer time... For the sake of politeness, pretense is normal. In one way or another, it flushes out your inner mind, your true self. It's a human tendency... I can understand; I studied society's behavior, especially men, and I don't find fault with you."

In the evening, she went shopping, bought a new Smartphone, and registered it in his name. While returning from the bar after his shift, Bobby bought four beers and non-vegetarian snacks and food. Damayanthi saw him with bags, took them, and placed them in the kitchen.

He refreshed and sat on the floor. She gave him a box and asked him to open it. He saw the gift-wrapped box and placed it aside. She said she bought a new mobile for him and he was silent. He asked her to keep it for herself, and she said,

"If someone gives a gift, it's a traditional respect to humbly accept and it should be presented only to the person to whom it's being bought."

"You have answers for everything, but ignored the good answers of your life in the past. Now, I need you Chameli, oh... Sorry... Damayanthi. Now, Damayanthi reforms her life for a better future."

Bobby lowers his head in shame. She sits beside him, places her index finger below his chin, and raises his head. Looks into his eyes and coolly speaks.

"Now, did you realize? What I said a few minutes ago, the pretense, inner mind, human tendency, and of the society, remember... My young man."

"Ok, you're very stubborn, Chameli alias Damayanthi. Some time ago, Chameli was a good friend of mine, and now, let me be the best man of my Damayanthi, forever."

He smiles, takes the gift, and salutes, and she too salutes him in return. Later, he gets the beers, and she serves the food and sits opposite to him. He opened a beer and gave her. She hesitated, understood his feelings, and took the bottle. He opened, tapped her bottle, and drained half of the beer in one go.

She was observing him; however, it didn't surprise her, but his intentions were different today. After half an hour, they finished dinner and retired on the single bed.

22. Damayanthi & Bobby – 4

Damayanthi returned from the temple and smiled to herself, seeing Bobby sleeping like a child. She finished her kitchen work and woke him with a hot cup of coffee. He had his coffee, had a bath, and left. Neither of them spoke a word and Bobby went to the Amareshwar temple.

She opened her trading account; she saw the shares Bobby marked for the day trade and placed the order worth rupees six thousand. She's excited looking at the profit and the market further moved up. It was cool and tireless earnings on her investment; she remembered Bobby's words and booked the profit. She was fascinated to buy again, but she didn't dare and logged out. It was her first step toward the future of her investment business; in fact, it was a good start and better learning for her.

Bobby sat beside a stone pillar in the temple Has been living a lonely life for the past year; he hardly spoke to anyone in days and today it was a wonderful feeling. But has a guilty feeling and was not able to judge his male chauvinistic act of the last night. He's ashamed of his callous behavior; he felt like he disrespected her. She fed him as a wife does and eventually, fulfilled his physical desire too. Now, he was appalled but knew it was not only from one side, but both of them needed one another. Accepting a man was not new to her, but his ideology and the rule of ethics were subdued and ignored.

Bobby saw an old priest approaching him; he smiled at him, stared and pointed his right index figure to his head, and waved it towards the idol in the temple. It meant to leave all your worries to the almighty, the infinity. Bobby folded his hands and said namaste; he placed his hand on Bobby's forehead and closed his eyes for a few seconds. The soft touch of the priest made him feel relaxed, and a firm assertion gave him confidence. Now, his remorseful heart was not feeling guilty anymore. On the way, he called one of his friends from a pay phone, asked him to call, and gave Damayanthi's mobile number. Bobby and Damayanthi had dinner, and he was silent and could not start the conversation. She observed him, said there was no need for an excuse, and said she loved him as an honest man. There was a call on her mobile; she answered and gave it to him. He spoke to his friend and asked him for the money, and said he would meet him in a few days. Her mobile received a message of an online transfer of three lakhs in her bank account after ten minutes. By the time, she returned from the kitchen, he was asleep in his chair. She asked him to sleep on the bed and spread a bed sheet for her on the floor. He refused and said he was comfortable on the chair and slept.

Now, day trading is a full-time job for Damayanthi, while Bobby researches and gives trade suggestions for her the next day. One day, the markets fell more than three hundred points after the USA rate cut news, and she lost five thousand rupees in panic. Later, he explained the behavior of the trending markets and asked her to be patient, focused, and steady in such situations. She was in tears, asked her to stay calm and encouraged her by saying,

"What you deserve shall always reach you, while what you don't will leave, no matter how hard you try to save or hold it."

The obvious and true meaning in his words obliged her. The daily ups and downs were routine in her day trades, and now she's well acquainted with a few basics and trading strategies. One month passed away with the gains and losses strengthening her confidence to trade alone and safely with the ever-dancing indexes of the stock markets. There was a registered letter in her name, an offer letter from the stock broking house in Mumbai. She was surprised; she did not apply for any such job. After Bobby returned late at night, she showed him her appointment letter. He smiled and checked the mail and asked her to be ready by eight in the morning and said they were leaving for Mumbai. It was like a dream for her, a job from a broking house in Mumbai. Bobby explained to her about her at the new office and showed the email of his friend's recommendation. Said she had to stay alone for some time in his friend's flat until she got a good flat near the office. She did not agree to go alone; in fact, she didn't want to leave him and felt like she was once again deliberately left on the road, for the customers. Asked him why he didn't want to accompany her to Mumbai. He was silent, took a beer, and settled on the chair. After a short while, he lay on his bed. She goes, sits beside him, places her hand on his chest, and questions him.

"Bobby, are you satisfied with this bitch?"

"Please don't use such language, and I never viewed you so."

"Then, why do you want me to accept the job and stay away from you?"

"Because you have a right to your bright future."

She sarcastically smiles and repeats his words.

"Right and bright future, and what about yours?"

Bobby stares at her, walks, and occupies the chair. She goes and sits beside his chair on the floor and leans her chin on his knee. He could not bear the intensity of her inquisitive look; he sat beside her and told her about his job, the fraud, and getting him trapped by his manager at the Mumbai office, and now he was running for his life. He told her about his obsession with intraday trade and passion for winning the market every day in the past. She was skeptical about him and could not believe him and his present job as a waiter at the bar. It was like fiction, a thriller movie, and she decided to clear her doubts before leaving him and taking up a new job. Later, he confessed his sordid deals and told her how he managed the trades with the time-sensitive precision of a scalper. He elaborated on how his manager duped both companies and made him a scapegoat in the process. Said he hated him and was ready to play dirty with revengeful play through the stock market. She could not understand the exact meaning of his words but guessed he was up to something big and dreadful and advised him to be calm with patience. Finally, she learned and appreciated his motive, which is not solely for the money.

Bobby woke up at three thirty am, checked the flights to Mumbai, and booked an economy class with her bank account. The ticket was confirmed and checked in online on the airline's web portal. Later, he lay beside her; she turned toward him, and the dawn cast a happy day for them. The next day, they reached Bhubaneshwar airport; he gave her a few tips and gave her his new number. Said he would activate it after four days; gave her fifty thousand cash and kissed her on the cheek. She loved his unexpected act in public and happily walked through the entry of the domestic terminal.

₹ $ £ €

Damayanthi reached the address and called Bobby's friend. He asked her to take a taxi, then he asked her to give her mobile to the driver and he spoke to him. After fifteen minutes, she was before the twelve-story apartment. The security gave her the keys and guided her to the lift. It's a well-furnished double bedroom, neat and clean. She checked the bedrooms and assumed none had used the kitchen for the past few days. She chose the east side bedroom and unpacked her single baggage. She refreshed and was waiting for Bobby's friend.

Meanwhile, she remembered the folder Bobby gave her at the airport. She opened it, and there were nine papers, and each had the figures, all in lakhs and three pages showed the figures in crores. She was confused and counted the figures and decimals. At the end of the file, there were handwritten user IDs and passwords and sticky notes. She found a separate paper showing the map and distance between the flat and her new office from the central railway terminal and bus stand. It was like a spy's execution plan in the movies, and he requested her to keep the file safe in a bank locker and mentioned a private bank. Lastly, he requested her not to call or speak from her office phones.

At six pm, Armaan Bhatia visited the flat, met her, and introduced himself as one of Bobby's close friends. He took her to the Hotel Taj in his car, and they had dinner. He also briefed her about the location of her office and the locality of the flat where she's now staying. Later, he suggested she take public transport while commuting from her flat to the office. He pointed out the traffic jams and exorbitant rates the taxi and private carriers charge. At nine-thirty, he dropped her at the flat and said he would be staying for a few days and gave her his mobile number. Asked her not to hesitate for any help, and while leaving said,
"Goodnight, Bhabhi."

She was glad to hear him addressing her as Bhabhi and waiting for the elevator. Meanwhile, she heard him speaking in Marathi with the security and told him that she was the owner of Flat No. 1005. She was surprised; Bobby said she had to share the flat, and now his friend informed the security as the owner. She did not understand and wanted to ask Armaan but did not and went to flat on the tenth floor. She changed into a nightgown and came out of the flat. Each floor has eight flats and her flat, was third right from the first elevator on the East Block. Meanwhile, there was a hum of an elevator approaching the floor; she returned to her flat and locked the door. She made her bed and retired alone on the luxurious double bed. The next morning, she woke early and was offered prayers to the photo frame of the deity she brought along with her. Someone rang the doorbell; she opened the door and there was no one, then she saw the milk packets and newspaper in the bag hanging beside the door.

At eight am, she started from her flat in Colaba to her new office on Dalal Street, near the Bombay Stock Exchange. Took the bus and reached the office after enquiring with fellow commuters. She's received by a woman in her mid-forties; she introduced herself and ushered her to the manager. Introduced her as Mrs. Damayanthi from Cuttack and she was happy to hear her original name. After a brief talk, she was shown her seat in the record room. The single room was eight by ten feet with racks filled with files and shelves with the books of the stock market. Later, the receptionist took the joining letter, explained her job, wrote a few files, user IDs, and passwords on a piece of paper, and asked her to enter the figures in the pre-prepared Excel format.

By lunchtime, Damayanthi learned and become accustomed to her new job. There are four women and two men in the office. The staff shared their lunch with her and the men left for the smoke while women were chit-chatting. In the evening, Damayanthi ordered coffee and snacks for her colleagues. Now, that routine was marked, she took the extra lunch box and shared it with her officemates, and gradually, she transformed into a new personality called 'Damayanthi madam.' She loved her new identity and woman's status as Mrs. Damayanthi and as the wife of Bobby Shacal. When her colleagues enquired about her husband, she told them he was still working in Cuttack and would shift in a month. Except for her flat and the office, she hardly visited any place in Colaba.

Earlier, she never liked her name as it reminded her of the myth that the princess of the Vidarbha kingdom married the king Nala of the Nishadha kingdom, a gifted charioteer who was fond of disc games and often gambled. Kali Purusha felt insulted and angry with Queen Damayanthi for not choosing him in the Swayamvar. With a vengeance, he diverted and persuaded Nala to play the disc game, and subsequently, Nala gambled away all his wealth and kingdom, lost them, and later separated from his beloved wife. Now, even though her name, myth, and history were defamed, she loved being called by her true name and the great character of mythology. After the office, she shopped for a few grocery items at the mall and started cooking at home. On the fifth day, she called Bobby's number at late hours, and it rang for a few minutes, but he did not answer. She was upset and thought of calling Armaan, but did not want to bother him for the mere reason of not taking a call.

₹ $ £ €

One day, while returning from her office, she noticed a man was following her. The next day, the same man was watching from behind his car. With the idea of escaping him, she went into the shopping mall that was behind her apartment. She selected a few face creams and moisturizers and strolled around the store for a while, secretly watching him. Suddenly, an old man appeared from behind her and asked,

"Excuse me, madam, are you Chameli?"

Damayanthi was shocked and tried to move away from him and entered the other section of the mall. He followed and tried to speak to her in Hindi. His short peering eyes with a forced smile and thin mustache frightened her. The expensive yellow suit and brown shoes were peculiar. The person who followed her was in his forties, and this man appeared elderly.

Now, the forgotten past of Chameli's memories was haunting. Her second and original personality— 'Damayanthi,' was easily noticed by one of her earlier customers, and she did not know how to pretend and disguise. He noticed her confusion and the irksome gestures on her body and excused himself.

"Sorry ma'am, if I bothered you. You resemble a person whom I have known for a long time. Please excuse me."

He walked into the next section. She took her items and followed the old man. It was the liquor section; he selected three varieties of liquor and returned to the cash counter. She briskly walked away and followed the queue at another cash counter. Later, she walked into an ice cream parlor and sat in a corner. Meanwhile, the old man walked out of the shopping mall and went to his car. The driver was the same person who had been following her for the last few days. She felt lonely, and helpless without Bobby by her side and called Bobby's number.

Bobby expressed his happiness and appreciated her for keeping his word; she thanked him for the motivation for a new and decent life. He said he would be meeting her in Colaba. She said she was missing him and was scared of staying alone in an unknown place. Thought of telling him of her daunting experience and about the person who was following her, but she didn't want to rake up her past and make him upset now. He requested her to stay for a few more days and promised he would return shortly. She was silent; he said he would call her later and disconnected.

She lately realized, that dependence for some sometimes results in *incapability* in their lives, and now she has no alternative but to depend on Bobby for her survival. Damayanthi receives a courier, a pack of four beautiful saris from Bobby, and realizes it's his first experience of presenting an expensive gift to a loved woman.

23. Case Dropped & Muthu Arrives

Bobby called Damayanthi and asked her to take a taxi and meet him. She received a message; she took an auto and reached the restaurant. Bobby was waiting for her in a restaurant beside the engineering college. The moment she saw him, she ran, hugged him, and her tears were wetting his cotton shirt. A few students saw them, clapped, and showed them thumbs up. He smiled at them and forcibly got separated from her. He sat beside her; she leaned over him and spent a few moments, and it lightened her heart. Her eyes were dripping the love tears; Bobby took his handkerchief and wiped them.

Five months passed away with moments of happiness and joy, and now, where is the direction of destiny leading to another unknown passage of fate? None was sure. They had Pav Bhaji and fruit juice. Bobby took out an envelope and gave it to her.

"What is in the envelope?"

"It has valuable information, and I want you to keep it with you and in a safe place."

She stared at him, and he took her hand and smiled. He asked about her new job; they spoke for half an hour and said he had to catch a bus. She said she would drop him on her way; Bobby was glad and joked, saying he could take care of himself. Her beautiful and complete smile was obvious to him, and it displayed that she was living a normal, confident, and self-respected life. He kissed her hand and asked her to leave as it was getting dark, and he went to the bus stop and boarded his reserved sleeper couch. The bus started; after a journey of ten minutes, the bus attendant asked the passengers to get themselves relieved and buy the snacks, as there was a roadblock after the accident. Bobby got down, walked behind the bus, and started checking his mobile. He saw a pillion rider, Gaikwad, sitting on a grey-colored old scooter and speaking loudly to the driver. At Acharya Atre Chowk it takes a turn. Bobby speaks to the driver, takes his shoulder bag, and leaves the bus. He runs a few feet and turns into the broad lane, but he does not find Gaikwad or the grey-colored scooter. He looks around, returns to the main road, and takes an auto to Gaikwad's house.

Bobby gets down a few feet away from the Gaikwad's house. The portico is illuminated by the dim light inside the house, and only one light is on in the kitchen, and the door is locked. He goes around the house and finds the kitchen door partly open. Suddenly, a dog runs away from beside him, he carefully pushes the door, and it opens with a squeaking noise; enters and observes the hall, single bedroom, and a rectangular living room.

The house was disarray with the foul odor of the stale food. The dining table is with empty bottles, snacks, and unwashed dishes. Walks into the hall, switches his mobile's flash, and focuses on the small table beside the worn-out and deformed cough. He looks at the blank letterheads of the Medussa Associates Limited, signed and stamped by the Sointhara. He did not understand why the official papers were in Gaikwad's house. did he planned to use the letters to frame him and get away with the fraudulent money? He collects the letterhead and the other official papers.

He searches for single-room hotels and lodges in the locality, selects one, checks in for a night stay, and pays through cash. He has his dinner and takes out his former company's blank letterhead and papers. A letter was addressed to the SHO, Chembur, police station, Mumbai, about the withdrawal of the case of fraud and theft. It requested the police department to consider the apology for unnecessarily involving them. It also mentioned that the company regrets the miscalculation of the internal accounts. He could not understand why the company did not mention Gaikwad's name; now, he was infuriated and developed a grudge against Sointhara and decided to avenge him for the defamation.

Bobby works out a plan, checks over the internet, and downloads the requisition formats of NOC, a letter requesting the police authority. This will declare him free, and the case registered against him will be dropped from their records. A personal letter appealing to the police authority to fulfill the request for appearing in the competitive exams. Bobby left the hotel, took an auto, and reached the Chembur police station. On the way, he gets the copies of relevant documents. Meets with the Circle Inspector and gives him a copy of the company's letter, his requisition letter, and NOC format. CI questions him, sitting on the edge of the desk with the papers in his hand.

"So, you want to register a case on the in-charge of the police station."

"No sir... how can I dare to do so? I have a competitive exam and need a letter from your esteemed office."

The CI observes his beard, crumpled cotton shirt, and shoulder bag. Looks at his slippers and says,

"Ok, let me speak to my higher officer, you better come tomorrow morning."

Bobby folds his hands and pleads with him.

"Sir, it's very urgent, and my career depends on your favor; if you want me to wait, I shall wait here."

"Um... let me try."

The CI looks at his wristwatch and calls his officer.

"Jai Hind sir, sorry to disturb you..."

"Jai Hind, what's the matter?"

"Sir, do you remember the fraud case of Medussa Associates? The accused, Bobby from Hyderabad..."

"So, come to the point."

The officer at the other end cuts him short. The CI taps his head and continues,

"He had come asking for a letter mentioning that we must give him a letter stating he is not found guilty, and he said he has an exam tomorrow. . ."

"Ah, yeah, the case of false accusation of fraud and cheating by the company... um, the case was already closed."

"Yes sir."

"He was terminated from the job, and what does he want?"

Bobby asks for the mobile from CI and requests him. CI speaks to his officer and gives his mobile.

"Namaste, sir, I am Bobby, and tomorrow I have a civil competitive exam. Sir, I need a letter stating I have no legal case pending..."

The officer on the other end asks him to give the mobile to CI. The CI nods three times and disconnects the call. Meanwhile, Bobby opens his laptop and searches for his previous hall tickets. Luckily, he finds one, but it's a past year's hall permit; he copies it on the PDF writer, changes the day and the date, and shows it to the officer. The officer checks the name, date, and center and feels satisfied.

"Did you get the requisition letter, or should I write it for you?"

"I have bought the letter."

Bobby takes out the letters and gives them to the CI; he takes and reads them. He goes to the other table, stamps, and returns them to him.

"Pai laagoo sirji,"

Bobby tries to touch his feet; he moves away and says,

"All the best."

Bobby thanks him, goes to his hotel, and checks out. It's half past eleven; checks for private buses leaving for Hyderabad, and books a single ticket. The boarding is at Matunga at midnight; he calls Damayanthi and at once disconnects the call; he didn't want to disturb her at this hour.

The new mobile was not easily accessible for Muthu Raja, aged twenty-five, a college dropout from Chennai. He took the SIM and inserted it into his old mobile and the old messages started popping up one by one. There were four messages, and he opened one after another, and the fourth had some important information. Nikitha's number was saved as Niki Akka, and the message startled him. He goes to his room in Jafarkhanpet, packs two pairs, and asks his friend to drop him at the Koyambedu bus stand. He told his friend he had a job offer at Hyderabad and boards a state-run interstate bus.

Muthu Raja arrived in Hyderabad, took a local bus, and reached the address mentioned in the message. He changes his SIM from the old mobile, inserts it in the new mobile, tracks the location, and reaches the apartment. He speaks to the security in Tamil and the new security does not understand; besides, he's also not aware of the Nikitha's murder. Muthu entered his name and address in Tamil language and reached the flat. He observes the other flats on the floor for a while and gets on the four-foot wall and starts climbing up, holding the water and sewage pipes.

Usually, open-to-sky ducts in the apartment premises are deliberately left open for ventilation and for the plumbing work. He reaches the outer unit of the AC of Nikitha's flat and pulls out a dirty and wet cloth bag. It has a few sheets of newspapers wrapped in the form of a rectangular packet. He hangs the bag on his shoulder, and it has the address printed in the Tamil language along with an image of the famous temple in Chennai.

He carefully slides down and continues, till he reaches the ground floor. His shirt and jeans get soiled with the dirty water; he jumps off the small wall and walks toward the other side of the apartment. Meanwhile, the security walks to the elevator and waits for it. Muthu briskly walks away from the second gate and takes a sharing auto to Ameerpet. He walks to SR Nagar, stands a few feet away, and watches Nikitha's coffee shop. Wanted to go in, but looking at his attire, he decides not to meet her and remembers the fourth message that also asks him not to visit her and her coffee shop after collecting the papers and the money.

Now, he is undecided about where to go. To Jafarkhanpet, Chennai? Or to Udupi, Karnataka, where his elder sister stays. He missed his dinner last night and he asks the tea stall vendor, goes to mess nearby, and finishes his meals. Muthu goes to Kacheguda railway station and buys a ticket to Mangaluru.

24. Gaikwad's Disappeared & Armaan Past

Edward waits in the lane that leads to Gaikwad's house. After midnight, he returns and within minutes, he hurriedly leaves without locking his house. At the crossroads, a bike arrives, he takes the pillion seat, and they drive away. Edward follows the bike, and at the Chatrapathi Shivaji Maharaj Chow, the bike skids under the flyover and slides towards the heavy truck, maneuvering a wide turn. The truck suddenly stopped, and a car hit the bike from behind. Gaikwad falls a few feet away and tries to get up.

At once, Edward stops his daughter's scooter in the middle of the road, stands, raises his arms, sideways, and waves his hands in the air appealing to the commuters to slow down. Then, he runs toward Gaikwad, helps him to sit supporting the footpath railing, and runs back to check the bike rider; he's crushed under the rear tires of the truck. Meanwhile, one of the bikers calls the ambulance and the injured Gaikwad is taken to the nearby hospital. A policeman arrives and starts inquiring about the accident. A few people answer and some leave coolly, and Edward goes to him and briefs him about the accident.

Edward sees a mobile on the footpath; he briskly walks and picks up the mobile, which's intact, and drives away to the hospital. He visits the ICU ward and speaks to the receptionist; she asks him to come in the morning, as the patient's still unconscious with a head injury. On the way, he stops at a tea stall, has a cup of tea, and goes through the old model mobile without a screen lock. He finds a new message, name, and address in the Navy colony, Colaba. Later, he returns to his house, has a few beers, and completes his dinner with Helen. He's exhausted and sleeps on the couch in the living room; his daughter tucks a blanket and watches him remembering her mother. Meanwhile, the mobile rings in the dining hall; she finds a new mobile, and by the time she answers, the call gets disconnected.

One of the ICU ward attendants was busy searching for the missing patient, Sunil Gaikwad, in the morning. Edward realized he might have escaped and was planning a hideout. He leaves the hospital and checks the call list of the mobile he found at the accident site. It has three calls, the caller listed as Giri, and a message asking Gaikwad to meet him at the Parel railway station. Edward opens maps on his mobile and navigates the route to reach the railway station. With the morning crowd, it's impossible to find a single and an unknown person. An idea struck him and he requested a passenger to text a message in Marathi asking Giri to meet him at the Higgin Bottoms bookstall, beside the coffee vending machine.

After a few minutes, a tall, slim man in jeans and a white T-shirt walks and stands waiting for Gaikwad. Edward walks close to him, holds his elbow, and walks him out of the railway station. They reach a tea stall on the opposite road; Edward orders the tea, and they walk a few feet away from the other people. Edward shows his ID, speaks in a broken dialect from the translator, and waits for his reaction.

"Giri, I am a friend of Gaikwad; last night he met with an accident, and he's in the hospital."

"Kya? Kaise?"

Giri asks in surprise. He throws the empty teacup, wipes his lips, and lights a cigarette. He looks at Edward and requests him in English.

"Sir, I don't know what Gaikwad was unto; I run a small business of making rubber stamps and nameplates for office and residential purposes."

He takes two self-inking rubber stamps from his pocket and gives them to Edward. He takes them and stamps one on the wall poster, and it display someone's signature. Edward takes a two hundred rupee note from his wallet and gives it to him, but he refuses and briskly walks away. Edward returns to his house, meets Saritha, and shows her the contact list of the Gaikwad's mobile.

"Ma'am, I found this mobile on the road at your house; do you recognize any of these numbers?"

She takes it, scrolls up and down, stops at one name, and shows him. He takes the mobile, stares at the name and the number, and questions her.

"How do you know him?"

"He calls me Saritha Thai.'

"I didn't understand. What's Thai?"

"Dad, he calls her an elder sister, in Marathi."

"Thee barobar aahe. She is right."

Saritha smiles and looks at them, and Edward questions her.

"When did you meet him, Saritha?"

"One day, I was unwell and tried to contact my husband, and I couldn't get him. Then, I called him and told him about my sickness. He asked for the prescription and bought the tablets. He waited till... I had my dinner, gave my tablets, and left. Such a kind person is my brother."

Helen and Edward watch her in surprise, and Helen asks, "Who's he Saritha?"

"Don't you know? He works with my husband, Bobby."

Now, Edward understood the whole story—the perfect criminal conspiracy. But to prove Bobby's innocence, he has to get Gaikwad and present him before Sointhara and in the court of law.

₹ $ £ €

Bobby opens his new laptop and tries to log into his bank account. He gets a message asking him to contact the branch. He has a copy of the letter from his old workplace asking for his bank accounts that were discovered in Gaikwad's home to be reactivated. Later, he takes a print of it, a personal requisition letter, and a copy of the letter issued by SHO,

158

Chambur. Bobby visits the bank to submit the letters to activate his ceased bank accounts. One of the notices displayed the instructions for activation and updating of KYC with the latest mobile number. His Aadhaar and PAN card were lost after the accident, and he returned to the flat.

Armaan called Bobby and said that he was in Mumbai and going to visit them. Bobby remembers Armaan, his mischievous acts, and his marriage with his girlfriend. Damayanthi returned after taking a bath and saw Bobby snoring on the sofa. She takes a cushion, and gently replaced it under his head. At once he woke up, yawned, and said Armaan was visiting them. She gave a surprised look and asked what she had to cook. He asked her not to bother and said he would order the food. He took a bath and returned to the living room. And saw Aarman and Damayanthi discussing over the issue of Mumbai traffic; walked to him, shook hands, and settled on the sofa.

"Bobby Bhai, what's this? A lot of issues took place, and at least for once, you should've told me."

"It's nothing, Armaan Bhai, just a part of the game of my life, that's all."

Armaan turns towards Damayanthi and exclaims in surprise,

"Damayanthi Bhabhi, we were close friends right from our college days; each of us knows well, and still, he doesn't want to speak about his trouble. Bhabhi did he say anything about him or you're also like me, unaware of his habits?"

She smiles, and Bobby points with his index finger at the package. Armaan takes the wrapped gift and presents it to his beloved friend. Bobby unwraps, finds the single malt whiskey, Johnny Walker, and looks at her.

"I believe it's your college-time favorite drink, enjoy, I'll get the glasses."

She said and walked into the kitchen and brought a chilled water bottle and two glasses. Armaan takes the bottle and prepares the drink. He looks at her and speaks,

"Damayanthi Bhabhi, where's your glass?"

She smiles and moves her head sideways, saying, no.

"Bobby, should I tell her about the girl who chased you?"

Bobby stares at him for a while and smiles; she pretends as if she's unheard, gets the plates, and serves the non-vegetarian dishes for them. Armaan takes a wine bottle and offers it to her; she stares at Bobby, and he asks her to get the wine glass. Three toss and relax with the old and new experiences they had in their lives. Armaan Bhatia was a one-year junior and spent most of the time with Bobby and his classmates. After his father's elder brother's demise, Armaan's father had to look after the export and import business and shifted to Mumbai. Armaan had to stay back in Hyderabad to complete his final year.

Six months after Armaan's wedding, his father passed away from a heart stroke, and being the only son, he took up the business. Later, there were family issues, and his wife started living with her parents. His wife issued a divorce notice stating that her dowry, money, and jewelry were sold for his business. And his mother was diagnosed with cancer, hospitalized, and one after the other; the issues were mounting tension over him. After three months, he lost his mother, got divorced, and paid huge alimony, and his business was ceased for the non-payment of loans.

Subsequently, he was hospitalized for hypertension and an irregular heartbeat. His company's insurance too was delayed. The loans were unpaid, and default notices were issued to him for the recovery. After some time, his relatives, friends, community, and society boycotted him. In his community, if a person defaults on the repayments, he would be banned and alienated for the rest of his life. Mostly, the loans and money matters are agreed upon verbally, and no legal documents are used; trust and belief are taken into account before the elders and experienced businesspersons. If one defaults with the non-payment of the loan, then he's dealt with a strict repayment process. Also, they might even dissolve or transfer the business to other interested entrepreneurs and settle the dues. After the settlement of the loans and takeover by another businessman, he was left with only a few lakhs and was undecided on how to start a new business.

One day, Armaan spoke to Sidhu, told him about his business loss, and expressed his helplessness. Sidhu, in return, spoke to Bobby and convinced him to trade with Armaan's money. Unwillingly, he agreed, and fortunately, the market's directional trends proved an advantage. And within three months, the money was doubled. Bobby traded only with futures and options, and the trade journal displayed a loss of thirty-two and a profit of seventy-eight percent. Bobby created a portfolio of a few blue-chip shares in his account and asked Armaan to open a trading account in his name. After a few days, he transferred the portfolio and the total fund into his account. He appreciated and wanted to pay him some money, but Bobby strictly warned him and requested not to disturb him in the future.

Armaan left Mumbai, relocated to Gurugram, and started a new partnership business of manufacturing and exporting domestic and industrial LED lamps and accessories. His luck turned positive and his business into good profits. After a while, he took up a small manufacturing unit and ran independently and obtained local contracts with the government and builders. One day, one of his friends from Mumbai told him about a fully furnished apartment for sale in Colaba. The prices of the apartments declined after the COVID wave. He negotiated the fair deal and finalized it, and registration of the apartment was done within a short time. It was vacant until Damayanthi's arrival.

Damayanthi was returning from her office Damayanthi when saw Maanik at the Crawford Market, now; it's called Mahatma Jyothiba Phule Mandi. The owner of the famous furniture showroom in Haridaspur, Cuttack, regularly supplied the interiors and furniture to his Mumbai customers. He was in love with her, and once, he requested that she stay as his mistress and promised that he would keep their affair a secret. Now, she's scared of going out alone, and while going and returning from the office, sometimes she takes different routes to avoid him. She told Bobby that someone was following her regularly from the office and decided not to reveal about Maanik.

Bobby understood she was feeling insecure and losing her self-confidence. He thought for a while, booked a ticket and asked Damayanthi to pack her belongings.

25. The Delivery

Muthu Raja helped Nikitha find a better deal for her ancestral property, and she promised him a good commission. However, after opening her coffee shop at SR Nagar, she never returned to Jafferkhanpet, Chennai. Recently, she called and asked him to collect money hidden in a safe place. At first, he was scared and questioned why she had to give him the money in secret. Later, she sent a message saying that she was scared for her life. She even left a letter for Muthu to deliver, providing the name and address. It took him sometime to believe her, but he eventually planned to meet and help her. He was hurt when she asked him not to visit her coffee shop, and he realized that he didn't fit into her society. Despite this, he was determined to meet her after delivering the letter. Till today, he's unaware that Nikitha was murdered in Hyderabad.

Muthu alights at Udupi railway station and walks to his sister's house, just a few meters away from the City Center Mall. While waiting for her, he carefully removes a few five hundred bundles from the packet, takes two bundles of cash, and hides them behind a large money plant. Later, he wraps all the bundles with newspaper and places them in a cotton bag.

After a while, Mani arrives with her daughter from school in an auto. She's surprised to see her younger brother after a long time, and her daughter smiles. After serving lunch, they have a brief discussion. Mani asks him to take care of her daughter and says that she will finish the paper correction at her school and return. She works as a primary teacher in a small private school, and her husband works in a retail clothing showroom. In the evening, Muthu takes his sister and niece to the new shopping mall, where he buys a sari for his sister, a T-shirt for his brother-in-law, and a frock for his niece. He also gets Biryani and soft drinks before returning home. After his brother-in-law returns, they all have dinner and retire for the night. Muthu decides to give some money to his sister as a gift and plans to use the rest to open a shop.

The next morning, he gives the money as a gift to his sister and gives her another packet, asking her to keep it safe. The remaining cash was packed separately in a cotton bag. He reached the bus stand, took a private bus, and arrived in Chennai after a thirteen-hour journey. Upon exiting the bus station, he bought a soft drink and noticed a police constable approaching him. He quickly escaped into a nearby lane, but the constable chased and caught him as he tried to board an auto. The constable then took him to the police station, where they frisked him and found cash worth two lakhs and forty thousand rupees, as well as a sealed, thick envelope.

During the Circle Inspector's interrogation, Muthu is appalled by their questions and was unable to provide the correct response regarding the source of the money. It was the time of local elections; the officer suspected it to be a money laundering case and detained the suspect for inquiry without being arrested. Later, he gave his sister's mobile number; Mani answered and told them that she gave him the money for his new business. The officer asked her to come down and produce a receipt or a legal document. She took the help of Head Master; he prepared a promissory note in Tamil language stating that her husband was paying Muthu two lakhs and fifty thousand and asked her to get it signed by an authorized notary.

She arrives in Chennai and meets the SHO. He was convinced; he takes a letter and copy of the notarized papers and asks her to take him. Later, Muthu takes his sister to his room, and they have lunch. In the evening, while leaving, she instructed him not to go out carrying the money. He smiled and went to the police station where he was detained. Meets the Sub Inspector and requests the envelope they found in his moneybag. After a lazy search, he threw the letter on his face.

Muthu meets a shop owner in his locality. The general store was not running well, and the shop owner wanted to sublet a small portion of it on rent. They spoke, the deal was finalized, and Muthu returned to his room. He called his sister, thanked her, and detailed his new business, saying that he wanted to sell coconuts, flowers, and other pooja items. Since there were three temples in the proximity of five hundred meters, and only three such stores were present. She liked his idea and advised him to also sell fruits and small bronze items used in the process of pooja in the temples. Later, he bought new jeans and T-shirts and booked an Ac sleeper ticket on a luxury bus.

₹ $ £ €

Muthu arrives in Hyderabad, reaches the address, and knocks the door. A woman opens the door and questions in the Telugu language.

"Evaroo."

Muthu shows her the name and address on the envelope and speaks in the Tamil language.

"Bobby? Irkka raa?"

"Eleaye, nee, yaar thambi?"

"The delivery."

Damayanthi takes the crumpled envelope and asks for the sender's name and address, but there's none. She turns to look for the person who handed it to her, but he has already left. He didn't seem like a delivery boy; his face showed innocence and nervousness. Furthermore, he did not ask for her signature upon delivering the package. She looked around the lane, but he was nowhere to be found. The thick envelope weighed about half a kilogram. As she felt it with her fingers, she sensed something solid, perhaps a mobile phone, inside. She thought of opening it and wanted to call Bobby but refrained from doing so. She has been staying in Bobby's house in Madhura Nagar for the last three days at his request. The grocery store owner gave her the key after confirming with Bobby. She loved staying in his independent two-bedroom house. Imagined herself as the owner of the house and decorated it as per her choice. Went to the shopping mall at the Ameerpet and bought the new bed sheets, curtains, and cutlery sets. She has been avoiding the grocery store thinking the owner might ask about their relationship.

One day, while returning home, Damayanthi noticed a man with short hair was watching her standing at the pan shop with a mobile and a few papers in his hands. Her sharp eyes were trained to read people's looks, and she realized that he must be a plainclothes police officer. She pretended to linger at the house, then entered and locked the door. She went straight to the bedroom window and observed him.

He paused, checks his papers twice, and walked away, speaking over his mobile. Later, she sends an email to Bobby with the details and PDF copies of his Aadhar, PAN card, and voter ID. She messaged, mentioning that a police officer in mufti was watching her and the house.

₹ $ £ €

Karan Reddy had his dinner at the small restaurant and returned to the house in Maharani Peta. He's staying in Sreenu's small house in Gajuwaka. Late at night, he called Sreenu, one of his loyal employees, and learned that his wife was managing the unit with the help of the foreman. He enquired about Nikitha's murder and was told that no one had been arrested. Karan has been receiving financial assistance from his younger brother, who lives in the UAE. His brother transferred money to Sreenu's account, and then he transferred the funds into his wife's account. Later, she withdrew the money and gave it to Karan for his daily expenses. Now, he was tired of his refugee life and thought he should surrender to the police and tell them the facts, but he decided to wait for some more time because the situation was not right. Even if he tells the truth, no one will believe him. Surprisingly, he did not see any news of his disappearance in the newspapers or on the TV.

Karan was pondering the events that transpired after he left Nikitha's apartment and believed that someone was following them. He wondered if it was Anwar or his associates. If Anwar was following them, then who could have killed him? How did the accident happen, and was he really dead or faked his death? He recalled modifying the partnership deed and paying the amount after Nikitha declined to be a partner. After leaving her apartment, he never saw her again. Meanwhile, he observed Anwar and Nikitha's behavior and realized that they were avoiding him. He suspected that they were attempting to manipulate his money and were involved in some sort of scheme.

At ten pm, there was a knock on the door. Karan opened it, and a young man handed him some documents. Now, Karan has a new identity as a contracted laborer on a cargo vessel that is set to depart from India the next day with a load of wheat.

26. Muthu & Damayanthi's Interrogation

Edward traveled by train and booked his stay in the hotel opposite the Secunderabad railway station. In the afternoon, he visited Nikitha's coffee shop and spent some time. The manager recognized the foreigner and recommended a fresh croissant, sandwich, and black coffee. Edward was obliged and wanted to try; besides it had been a long time since he had it.

At the table next to the entrance, Muthu was with the menu and ordered a filtered coffee and Samosas. He asked for the bill, went to the counter, and asked for Nikitha in English and the cashier was shocked and observed him for a while. He told him about her murder that took place a few months ago. Now, Muthu was astonished to hear the news of her murder, paid the bill, and hired an auto to the Secunderabad railway station. He bought a soft drink and was watching the display of the train timings.

The investigating officer follows him and tries to get into the conversation in Tamil language by showing Nikitha's photograph. Muthu stares at the photo and the officer; the officer asks him to go with him. Meanwhile, there was an announcement of the departure of the train bound for Chennai. Muthu requests him, saying that he doesn't know anything about the Nikitha and told him about the delivery of the envelope to Bobby's address. The officer tells him that he knows about the delivery and wants to find some information about the murder. Muthu was scared, and the officer took him into the first-class lounge and asked him to sit. Muthu narrates the story and convinces him that he's in no way connected to the murder. There was a call; the officer answered, waved one hand at him, asking him to wait, and took a few steps away. It was the right time; Muthu got up, ran outside the waiting lounge, and reached the platform, but the train already left. He at once, ran out of the railway station and crossed the road. He sees the hoarding of the hotel welcoming the guests; he walks a few steps up, sits beside the step, and hides from the officer.

Surprisingly, a hand lifts him and asks him to accompany him into the hotel with sign language. Now, Muthu was trembling with shock, and Edward dragged him into his room. He looks at the foreigner and thinks he needs a companion to fulfill his physical desire. He places his palms together, saying namaste, and pleads in English. Edwards asks him to calm down and says,
"Do you speak English?"
"Yes... Simple... English,"
"Good, I am Edward, a private detective investigating the case of Mr. Bobby Shack, sorry, Shacal, and don't try to lie to me, ok? I saw you at Bobby's house."
Edward gives a photograph of Bobby and asks him to identify him. Muthu takes the photo and gives it back, waving his head sideways saying he doesn't recognize him.
"Now, tell me, who are you and what were you doing at Bobby's house?"
"The delivery,"
"What delivery?"
"A letter and a woman takes it?"
"A woman... who's she?"
"Oru akkaa. A lady,"
"Ok, who wanted you to deliver the letter, and was Bobby in the house?"

Muthu wiped his sweat with his sleeve and stared at Edward. He tells him about Nikitha's request to deliver it to the address and takes his mobile from his pants. He carefully selects a message and shows him the messages written in Tamil language. Edward checks the message, takes a snapshot with his mobile, and translates it into English. It said he had to give the letter as early as possible and did not mention anything about his commission money. He nods, takes a snap of him, notes his mobile number, and throws a notepad. Muthu gives his phone number and writes down his address. Edward asks him to answer his call, when he calls and Muthu leaves.

Now, Edward has two questions; What was the letter that Muthu delivered, and what is the significance of the letter? Who murdered Nikitha, and what is the motive behind the murder?

₹ $ £ €

Damayanthi gets dressed in a Salwar and Kameez, packs her clothes, and leaves the house. She takes a cab, reaches the RGI Airport, Hyderabad, sends a message, and changes the SIM of her mobile. She walks towards the boarding queue. Suddenly, she's stopped by a tall man with a Walkie-talkie and he introduces himself.

"I am Xavier from the Crime Branch; please come with me."

"Sir, I have to board a flight."

"Please, follow us."

He waved his hand at the woman constable standing a few feet behind Damayanthi. The police Jeep reaches the Commissioner's office. She's taken into the interrogation room, and there are two officers; one is male and the other is a middle-aged woman. She shows the chair, and Damayanthi sits and places her shoulder bag and purse on the table.

"Can we check your passport and IDs, ma'am?"

She takes her passport and IDs and gives it to the officer sitting before her. He observes them and passes them to the next officer. She goes through and questions,

"Damayanthi? A good old name. Are you a graduate, and what do you do for leaving?"

Damayanthi stares at her, adjusts herself, and replies,

"Ma'am, I am a housekeeping maid."

The officers observe her confidence in her tone.

"Do you know whose house you're staying in. I mean housekeeping?"

"Yes ma'am."

They exchange their looks, and the male officer speaks.

"Do you know who owns that house?"

"Yes sir, I was told that some person by the name Bobby owns it."

"Well, then you might also be aware of his involvement in Nikitha's murder?"

Damayanthi was bewildered hearing the news. She did not know of the murder until now, and Bobby too might be unaware of his friend being murdered here. Bobby told her that he was falsely implicated in a financial fraud by his company and that the money used belonged to Nikitha. The male officer accused him of the murder and said he still had her money in his bank account. It was confusing; if he were aware why would Bobby tell her that the fund has to be transferred at once, as soon as his trading and bank accounts get activated?

Now, she was certain that Bobby did not know about the murder. The officers were observing her; she composed herself to a cool state of mind, and they knew she was hiding something from them. After a minute, she folds her hands and speaks in a low voice.

"Yes sir, my employer told me about the death of a woman and also warned me not to speak of it with anyone here."

Xavier speaks from behind,

"Sir, one of our officers reported that she was staying for the past three days and a parcel was delivered to her the other day."

Damayanthi was nervous, leaned back, took a few deep breaths, and tried guessing about the next question. She remembered Muthu and decided not to mention him. The woman officer took her turn and questioned.

"Damayanthi, what is your job, to be precise? Can you brief it?"

It was an unexpected question, and she looked at the officers.

"Lady, tell us about you coming here, staying, and suddenly leaving Hyderabad. If you're involved and found guilty, then you would be booked on numerous charges, and there's no way to get you out."

The officers saw the tears in her eyes, and Xavier moved his chair aside and spoke to her.

"You can tell them the whole story, and that might save you to some extent; think it over madam and take your time."

There was silence in the room, and she could hear her breath. She read the officers' false instinct and eagerness to solve and close the case. After a short while, she takes a folder from her shoulder bag, removes a few documents, and gives them to the officers. The lady officer takes the file and reads the lease agreement till the last page. Later, she goes through a recommendation letter stating her financial status and the urgency for an immediate job. The next officer too goes through the papers and drops them on the table.

"Ma'am, my employer rents the properties for travelers and tourists for a couple of days for a comfortable homestay. And I visit, stay, and redo the house for the next guests."

She stops and observes them and continues,

"I have two loans to repay. So, I chose this job, and that's all. I shouldn't have taken up this housekeeping contract."

The male officer moves forward and stares at her, and she avoids his look. Then, he asks,

"Well, the agreement's dated a year ago and the house was vacant for a long time. Then, why didn't your employer assign the job of cleaning earlier? And what made him send you now, to Hyderabad all of a sudden after Nikitha's murder?"

"Damayanthi what was in the parcel you received, and tell us where's Bobby hiding now?"

"The letter was the final notice, stating the financer shall auction my eighty square yards vacant plot. I was anguished, tore it into pieces, and threw it away. I don't know about Bobby. Now, I am least bothered by my job. Ma'am, will you please let me go."

The officers are surprised by her stubborn reply, while the male officer was playing with his pen and watching her *fake emotions*. An officer entered the room and handed over her mobile phone to the officer. He said he checked the call records and the messages and could hardly find any useful information. Meanwhile, a call disrupted the proceedings, and the officers took Damayanthi to the Commissioner's chamber.

The Commissioner walks towards Damayanthi, stares at her for a while, and asks his officers what evidence she has. All the officers were silent; he looked at each of them. Since they did not get a piece of strong evidence, he ordered the officers to leave her.

27. Bobby & EPTC

Bobby submits his credentials at the bank, and returns and uploads copies of his Aadhar and Pan Card on the trading platforms and waits for Damayanthi to arrive. He's disturbed after hearing the news of Nikitha's death. He remembered her conversation and the messages she sent to him; the messages were written evidence to prove the money genuinely belonged to her.

Bobby went to a small mobile repair shop and asked him how to get his friend's SIM activated. The shopkeeper calls Bobby's lost mobile number and moves his head sideways. He requests Bobby to wait and attends to the other customer. Again, he asked what happened, nodded, and called some number. After speaking for a few minutes, he said that there was some fraud, and the company blocked the number. Bobby asks him how to get the number, or the call records and messages. He said that only the owner of the SIM can give a request to the service provider. Bobby thanked him and was thinking about how to retrieve his lost mobile number again. Bobby thanked him and was waiting at the lane's corner for Damayanthi. He went to the general store, purchased a jute bag, bought a couple of beer cans, took the parcel of Hyderabadi Chicken Biryani, and returned to the flat.

He refreshed and could not wait anymore for her, took a beer can, switched on the TV, and was watching the stock market channel. An idea struck him, and he was concentrating on the commodities and currencies. The Russia-Ukraine war was mounting pressure over the crude and the Dollar. In contrast, even the Israel and Gaza strip was also fueling the tension, demand, and supply with the blockades and disruptions of the gas pipelines. Natural Gas was trading sideways, and WPI, Brent, and Indian Crude mini and Futures were moving unpredictably. He noticed the Dollar appeared strong compared to the Indian Rupee while Japan's Yen appeared with crazy highs and lows. The British pound was hardly moving with low volumes, and later, he noted down the facts of an interview, lied on the sofa, and dosed off.

After an hour, he heard someone washing the dishes in the kitchen; the TV was switched off and saw the mobile, shoulder bag, and purse on the corner table. Bobby gets up and goes into the kitchen; gets excited seeing Damayanthi, approaches her from behind and turns her around. He kisses her, takes her into the living room, drops her gently on the floor, and hugs her compactly, and she gasps for her breath. He releases and they sit on the sofa. He opens a beer can, takes his half-consumed beer, and gives a toss. They have a few sips, and she goes into the kitchen and returns with worm Chicken 65 pieces on a plate and offers him. They have a few gulps, and she tells him about her interrogation by the police officers in Hyderabad. She deliberately did not discuss Nikitha's murder. Later, they have lunch and retire in the bedroom; the naughty words and moans fill the room.

In the evening, Damayanthi asked Bobby to take her to the Ram temple in Wadala, Dadar. They hired a taxi and had darshan of the Lord Rama, Mata Sita Devi, and Laxmana and spent some time in peace. At eight pm, Bobby opened the remaining beer cans and sat waiting for her to return from the kitchen. She appears in a night gown and joins him. He clicks his laptop to sleep mode and observes her shapely body in the dimmed LED lamp. After a couple of sips, he asks him,
"What are you looking at... my big man?"
"A beautiful, faithful young woman in my life now."
She stares at him; he still has the child's innocence and is waiting for him to ask her to be his wife. Later, she

remembers his first love, his friend Nikitha, and raises her eyebrows and he questions.

"What?"

"I was just wondering, don't you want to know about your first love?"

"First love?"

"About Nikitha,"

Damayanthi says and walks into the kitchen. Bobby was disturbed; he did not like her speaking so casually because he had a special affection— maybe it was love, but he didn't distinguish it earlier. Now, her speaking about Nikitha was not on a good note. However, he still feels guilty for not saving her and for the repayment. He doubts Karan and another partner from Mumbai for the murder. Unfortunately, his fate points at him as a fraudster and murderer; he leans back and closes his eyes. She returns with salt and pepper sprinkled boiled egg slices, places them on the table, and sits opposite him. He opens his eyes, looks at the plate and she said,

"Take a slice; it goes well with beer."

"Now, tell me about Nikitha; I am prepared."

She leans back, crosses one leg over the other, and folds her hands. Tells him what she heard of Nikitha, her brutal murder, and mentions Muthu's delivery. Later, she spoke of the interrogation. She thanked him for sending the lease agreement and the letter on time. He smiles, opens another can, and gives it her, she refuses; and he has a gulp and sits in silence.

"What could be in the envelope?"

"I don't know, was checking the sender's name, and meanwhile he just disappeared."

They were silent for a while; Bobby appeared tired, and she served the dinner.

₹ $ £ €

Damayanthi went out to get vegetables and fruits to market beside the apartment. Bobby checked the bank; the KYC was successful; he logged in and changed the password. He went

176

through the latest statement; the last transaction was on the day he interacted with her over WhatsApp. The total was one crore, ninety-one lakhs, and thirty-two thousand. He downloaded the statement and saved the PDF on his laptop. He opened his personal trading account, which is already active and with one lakhs ten thousand, and at once changed the password. Then he logged in to two companies' trading accounts, and they too were in active mode

Now, Bobby was skeptical about taking the trades in the company's account that's in his name. He checked the funds in two accounts; one has rupees one lakh thirty thousand and the other has rupees one lakh ninety-two thousand. He changed the passwords of the accounts and logged out. It was like a trap; the fund was not paid out from the accounts. Was it to catch him red-handed while he was in trade? Or to track and hand him to the Hyderabad police on a murder charge? It was noon, and he was feeling thirsty and hungry after a long time. He took a chilled beer can and gulped half the can; his thoughts were running more than the alcohol's ABV, and after two minutes he drained the remaining beer and went into the bedroom.

Damayanthi returned, saw him snoring in the bedroom, and went into the kitchen. After half an hour, she woke him and served the lunch. He took another beer, and finished his meal, and locked himself in the bedroom. She realized that he was more heartbroken after she told him about Nikitha's death. She did not disturb him and was busy in the kitchen for another hour. Later, she relaxed on the sofa in the living room, thinking about how to help and support Bobby get out of the legal charges.

In the morning, he was waiting for the pre-market to open. At nine past thirty minutes am, he took four trades in his account and two in Damayanthi's trading account. Her account's trades were successful in Fin Nifty and Nifty bank options and squared off the trades. But his trades were moving sideways; he squared off two positions, deployed the straddle, and was waiting for premium decay, and favorably, the decay was faster in the present weekly expiry. After a while, he called Damayanthi; she replied that she would come after the bath and pooja. He closed his trades and went into the balcony and sat in the warm sunlight. She returns and gives him the banana that was offered to God, and they walk into the living room. He taught her how to deploy the Straddle and Iron Condor, and how to check the premium and the theta decay and placed orders in her account.

First, she was not prepared to trade the options in the market. He explained to her to go with just one lot. She did, and at once, the call premium shoots up, and she squares off her trade. Yet, she expressed her dislike, and he did not force her, as she was well experienced with day trading with the shares. She excuses herself, saying she has to prepare lunch, and goes into the kitchen. Bobby checked his emails and found that all contracts were scrapped except the Employee's Personal Trading Compliance—EPTC, and that was in force for another week. That was an advantage for him to break the ego and financially competent Sointhara.

He placed orders in two trading accounts of the company and was scalping for another two hours. The profits were lower compared to his earlier trades. He felt he was not brisk and quick while booking the profits; it was obvious that his ability decreased after all his bad experiences. Yet, he made a good profit of fifty-two thousand through intraday, and two positional trades were in profits of twelve thousand each by lunch time. After lunch, he closed the positions and initiated a payout request for rupees fifty-five thousand into the company's account. At three thirty pm, he took trades in currencies, and by five pm, he made a good profit and logged off. He took a nap until six, and later, he started watching the Natural Gas and Crude charts. The trades he took in them were not as per his observation; the demand and the supply gave a different view while the actual trades were moving in reverse. Similarly, he witnessed the same scenario in the Nifty and Nifty Bank charts. The shares of Nifty were rising but the Index was losing, and it was the same in Nifty Bank too. As he was off the market for a long time, it took him some time to adjust his trade strategies today. Damayanthi sat beside Bobby, observed his trades, and asked him.

"Bobby, why did you trade in the company's accounts today? I am scared... And again, they might start hunting and make you run away from me."

"Relax Damayanthi I have a plan; *first*, I want to prove that the money is not of the damn company. *Second*, they must realize that the murder took place while I was in Mumbai and trading with the company's fund. *Third*, I will lay down a few terms and conditions that Sointhara and Fulkeery must oblige, and if not, I'll be the whistleblower for their speculative deals in the stock market of the previous years. Now, it's my time to make them run... For me."

"Whittle blower?"

"I'll explain to you later, and now I shall not be staying with you here, they might track me by the IP address."

"What? Then, I won't be staying here... I'll go with you Bobby please."

"My love, wait for some time, and you said that you posted the delivery in your name and to this address, right."

She nods and holds his hand; he sees the tears rolling down from her eyes. He hugs her, and they stay for a short while. And later, he speaks,

"Damayanthi, give me just a few days, and also I want you to collect the delivery right from the post office, open it, and inform me besides, don't let anyone know that you're staying here, okay?"

28. Medussa & The Elephant

Sointhara and Fulkeery promptly reviewed their emails, their minds focused. Three emails were not just warnings but rather indications of potential threats, prompting Fulkeery to meticulously assess his deals from the past year. He was reviewing the financial reports from the previous year. It had been quite some time since both friends had met with such perturbed minds, apprehensive about their social standing. Their challenges, bets, and egos were all in jeopardy with a single word from Bobby posing a threat to them.

"Soin, it's not a good time for us, say yes and I'll see that he's vanished forever, or ask your investigator to get him."

"No, Fulk, we can't act that way now, did you go through the issue of repaying the SEBI turnover fees, stamp duty, and STT five times for deploying the five scalpers? although it's negligible, it makes sense because the Pump and Dump strategy was deliberately applied."

"We didn't post or persuade the brokers or traders to follow our trades. There was no manipulation at all."

"Yesterday he took a few trades on two accounts of the company and promptly remitted the profits. I wonder at his courage and confidence. At least for the sake of his loyalty and faithfulness, we must excuse and help him out with a cool negotiation. What do you say?"

Sointhara carefully considered the situation. Repaying the amount could be interpreted as an admission of guilt and might result in legal action, potentially damaging their companies' reputation as stock market fraudsters. Despite the relatively small amount owed in fees, paying SEBI may declare them as an acknowledgment and an act of fraudulent activities and manipulation. Sointhara realized Bobby's intentions as a whistleblower. At present, it seems there is no viable alternative to simply pleading for a stop to his actions.

Finally, they decided to oblige him to give the statements that he was with the company and doing his job. The money in his account was not the company's, but his friend's, and he wasn't involved in the murder case of his girlfriend, Nikitha. They decided to meet and convince him to drop his request, lure him with some amount, and ask him to leave the matter forever.

Sointhara sent an email to Bobby to meet them personally and assured him they have no issues now and would like to discuss the matter in confidence. Later, both friends reviewed their business, and Fulkeery left after receiving a call.

₹ $ £ €

Bobby had his breakfast, packed a few clothes, and said goodbye to Damayanthi. She was depressed; he consoled her to have patience for a week and asked her not to bother about the issues. He crossed two streets, took a bus to Bandra, Kurla, and checked into an economical hotel. From the third floor, he could see the NSE building; he refreshed and opened his laptop. He read the email and opened his trading accounts and was busy for an hour. At noon, he ordered a meal and resumed his trade. The ITM, ATM, and OTM premiums were decaying faster than usual weekdays. Later, he traded in the currencies and sent the Trademel to his ex-company's MD. He left the hotel and checked into another hotel.

Bobby had checked in and out six times from different hotels and different locations in a week. Finally, he paid out a total profit of four lakhs and twenty-five thousand and emailed saying he would meet them at Elephanta Island, ten kilometers away from the shore, Gateway of India in the Arabian Sea, Mumbai. Fulkeery and Sointhara were shocked to learn of the meeting place Bobby had mentioned, the rendezvous. The next morning, they reached the Gateway of India; they had to wait for five minutes, and Bobby searched for their followers among the tourists near the ferry station.

After confirmation, he messages that they take a boat and reach Elephanta Island. Bobby and Damayanthi boarded the next boat and reached after them. The cloudy weather was pleasant, with showers now and then.

The two friends were discussing the place and waiting for Bobby to meet.

"Good morning; it's been a long time since we met. Thank you for accepting my choice of place, and let's go to the café and have some refreshment."

Bobby said from behind and they followed him into the café. They were observing him, and he ordered soft drinks. After a few sips, he starts the conversation.

"Sir, with due respect, please help me out. You are aware of what I am talking about."

He stopped and looked at them. Sointhara and Fulkeery exchanged their looks and smiled. They did not expect him to be so cool after the issues. Fulkeery was the first to speak.

"Great rendezvous and wonderful attempt to blackmail us. You deserve the courageous award act."

Bobby smiles at Fulkeery and speaks,

"Well sir, it's just to be safe in your presence. As I mentioned to Sointhara about the conditions, please be kind enough to give a testimony in the court of law, in Hyderabad."

Sointhara looks around at the others and turns to him.

"Was this planning necessary? Bobby, you could've come to my office and discussed."

"If you wouldn't, I would've traced and dragged him to the office. Kid, you are not requesting us but intimidating."

Fulkeery said, fuming at Bobby.

"You better take it as threatening. It's not appropriate, Mr. Fulkeery, especially for you. Do remember Gaikwad and his copy trades, and now, I think you have no right to rake up the murky deals of the past. You might be aware of unfair trade practices of the markets... I hope you understood."

Sointhara placed his hand on his friend's shoulder and tapped, asking him to control his anger.

"Ok Bobby, I will give the testimony, but you have to rethink of the repayments to exchanges. Just think about our fame, business, and social and business status."

Bobby nods, and Fulkeery bangs on the table with his heavy right hand, expressing his frustration. Sointhara requests his friend, saying,

"Fulkeery, relax; it's a long time since I saw you reacting this way, even in our business loss, you didn't lose your temper. Take a walk and enjoy the pleasant cloudy weather."

"Ok, Soin, I'd take a walk, but if he behaves arrogant, I promise, I won't spare him."

"That's the reason, I didn't want to meet you in your office because you're the Medusa there, and here, I am the Elephant of the Island with circumstantial evidence being recorded. I assume... You can't say no... And affirm that you're aware of the law... You can be charged for violation of Articles 14, 19, and 21 and also would be penalized for misusing Section 499 and 500... Defamation, please try to understand."

Fulkeery stared at Bobby for a short while and walked out of the café in anguish. Sointhara folds his hands and watches the tourists; Bobby smiles, observing his body language, and thanked Damayanthi in his heart for updating the legal information.

"Bobby... Why didn't you take away the money from the two accounts? And what's the other condition to discuss the deal?"

Bobby takes the last sip of his soft drink and skillfully aims the empty plastic bottle into the dustbin a few feet away. Later, he presents the prints of his trades with the date underlined and includes a comment emphasizing the last date of Employee Private Trading Compliance—EPTC. After taking the printout, Sointhara was astounded by his loyalty, honesty, and intelligence. Ultimately, he has no choice but to agree to all his terms and conditions. Bobby proved a successful businessman like Sointhara to be a naïve human before an ordinary person.

"Bobby, you always surprise me with your performance, say, let it be in trading or the legal knowledge. I've terminated all charges, litigations, and obligations, and surprisingly, till now I didn't remember this agreement. Thankfully, my selection of a scalper is a rare gem and perfect, and my heart fully appreciates it. Bobby, I feel sorry for making your life miserable for the past year... I am ashamed."

"It's my fate. Forget it, sir, and take a look... I may not be excusing Gaikwad, and also you might not for his fraudulent, inhuman, and criminal act... Here's the proof."

Bobby says and throws the papers on the table. Sointhara's shocked seeing his signatures on the blank letterheads with the official seal. Bobby tells him the rest of the story. Meanwhile, Fulkeery returns, Sointhara gets up and takes out his wallet, and Bobby takes the bill and smiles.

After both friends left, he returned to Damayanthi. She's still sitting at the table a few feet away; where Sointhara and Fulkeery were sitting facing her while she was recording their discussion. Bobby decided they should leave immediately and did not want to witness some unforeseen incidents.

29. The Evidence

Damayanthi and Bobby took different local trains; she goes to Colaba, and he takes the MSRTC bus to LTT Railway Station. He checks into a hotel and books a second Ac ticket to Hyderabad bound train. He calls Damayanthi; she says she's at the Head Post Office and disconnects the call.

She meets the Head Post Master and requests him to give the delivery and shows him the lease agreement as residential proof. He takes a copy, files, and asks the clerk to give the post. She takes it and returns to the flat. She opens the crippled envelope and finds a broken screen mobile and a multi-folded legal document inside. Tries to switch on the smartphone, but it is dead, and she plugs in for charging by her battery charger. She goes through the Will, astonished to see the name of Bobby; it mentions him to be the Sole Beneficiary for her bank accounts, shares, her new house, and her coffee shop. A small sticky note showed the screen lock code to unlock the screen. Damayanthi was excited and read the document twice and wanted to call Bobby, but he asked her not to call until he reached Hyderabad. She took the snaps of the document and lay on the sofa.

After a short while, she checked the mobile, and it was charged fifty percent; she unplugged and switched it on. After two minutes of Android updates, it was active, and SMS messages and WhatsApp messages started downloading and the backup of the mobile was in process. The screen of the mobile was cracked from one side, but Apps were visible. After the backup, she unlocked the mobile, checked all the messages, and later opened the Gallery and tapped the recent video. The video made her aghast; she could not believe her eyes what she was viewing and placed her hand over her mouth and continued till the end. Sointhara and Edward were having a meeting and a call disturbed them and Sointhara asked to send in the visitor. The black coffee and biscuits are served to them. After a few sips, Sointhara leans back on his chair and stares at Edward.

"Sir, is there any problem?"

Sointhara sighed and replied,

"Edward, what we were and are imagining of Bobby is a blindfold game that someone else is playing, and we are all in it right now."

"Mr. Sointhara, I didn't get you?"

"Look at these."

He tosses the blank letterhead papers on the table. Edward takes them, and later, he removes the self-inking stamps from his belt pouch and places them on the table. Sointhara takes them in his hand, stares at his signature, and throws them on the side table. Both understood who the culprit was, and there was silence until someone knocked on the door.

One of the staff excused himself and told that there's a visitor, who wants to meet him personally. He waves his hand to let her in; Damayanthi enters in and wishes them namaste. She's in a white cotton chiffon sari with a bag hanging over her left shoulder; Edward stands up and shows her a seat beside him. She wraps her upper sari around her shoulders and nervously occupies the chair. Sointhara asks her,

"Please feel comfortable madam. Who are you?"

"Sir, I am Damayanthi, Bobby is my... fiancé, and I have come to you with the expectation that you might help me out."

Sointhara folds his hands and watches her; she lowers her eyes and is silent.

"Damayanthi, are you aware of who Bobby is? And what he did in the past few months?"

"Sir, I am aware of and that's the reason I want to meet you and beg to forgive his misdeeds."

He takes the blank letterhead, stares for a while, and looks at her. She was upset, realizing that if he knew about the video recording of the meeting in Elephant Island, her endeavor would be in vain. She composed herself and was looking at the papers on the table.

"Indeed, Bobby is an intelligent man, but his over-smartness made me hate him. However, he didn't incur any financial loss to my company, and he impelled me to oblige a meeting in private. And do you know? He threatened me and my friend and not just that, I missed an international negotiation of my business for the sake of his threat."

Now, she's confirmed that he did not see her and spoke in a pleading way.

"Sir, whatsoever happened I request you to ignore it and have mercy on him because he's in no way involved in Nikitha's murder. I have the evidence with me but I can't approach the police now. Only you can arrange an advocate to get him out of the charges."

She said and took out the mobile, unlocked it, played the video, and placed it on the table, Sointhara leaned forward and took it in his hand. The footage was five minutes and later, there was no action, and the recording ended. He was shocked, looked at her, and passed the mobile to Edward. He played the video twice and felt there was no morph, yet he was not confident of the brutal murder being shot so perfectly. He placed the mobile on the table and was observing his boss.

"Sir, may I ask her a few questions?"

Sointhara waves his right hand and Edward turns to her.

"Ms. Damatri, sorry if I pronounced your name wrong please don't mind."

She gives a pale smile, and he continues,

"Ma'am, how did you get this video, is this your mobile? And why didn't you go to the police?"

She folds her hands, observes his face and peering eyes, and turns to Sointhara.

"Damayanthi, he works for me. He's a private detective and an ex-cop from the USA."

"Ms. Damyathi, please feel free and tell me the complete story."

Sointhara speaks over the intercom. An office boy enters with the soft drink and water, she has some water; clears her throat, and speaks.

"Sir, I received a delivery when I was staying in Bobby's house in Hyderabad. And till today, I didn't open it as I was unable to contact him, and finally, I dared and opened the crippled envelope. Found this cracked screen dead mobile and a will on Bobby's name."

She deliberately did not tell them that they were together in the morning and did not want to until she heard their answers. Meanwhile, Edwards opened his notepad, turned a few pages, and asked her.

"The delivery boy Mutu gave you the envelope, on Friday, am I correct? Ma'am, were you in Bobby's house, then?"

"Yes! And how do you know him, sir?"

"Don't bother... That's my job, and who sent It.?

"Sir, there's no sender's name or address, and by the time I noticed it, he left. Here's the envelope."

Edward takes it and checks the front; the name and address are handwritten with a shaky hand, and the back has the dry marks of birds dropping and stains. After referring to his notes again, Edwards clarifies.

"Sir, I saw Mutu in Nikitha's coffee shop and followed him. Fortunately, I found him near the hotel where I was staying at the Secunderabad railway station. He told me, showed the message in Tamil that she messaged and requested him to deliver an urgent letter to Bobby."

"So, this envelope contained the mobile and the will. Damayanthi, show me the will."

She took the documents and gave them to Sointhara, and he was going through them. His face expressed an intensified look and knew the mystery behind the murder of Nikitha. He gives the will back to her and questions.

"I didn't understand. Who's the person who strangled, raped her, and who's the woman who hit her with a beer bottle? Only her back and hand are visible and. How did Nikitha record all this after the incident and who posted this package? An interesting, mysterious murder case. Edward, I think we have to get that poor soul out of it and fulfill her request. What do you say?"

"Sure sir, Ms. Damyathi, can you share the video with Mr. Sointhara and to my phone?"

She took their mobile numbers, saved them on her mobile, and shared the video through the WhatsApp application.

"Don't worry, Damayanthi, I'll see what can I do, maybe not for him, but at least for your happiness. Now, you can leave and we shall be in touch if you are required. Take care."

She got up, said namaste to them, and left the office.

₹ $ £ €

Bobby gets down at Begumpet railway station, takes the Metro rail, and checks into the hotel in HITEC City. He has his breakfast and hires an auto to Sidhu's office. Leaves a message to him with the security officer and waits in the waiting lounge. He calls Damayanthi, and she speaks happily and tells him about Nikitha's mobile and the will in his name. He was distressed physically and emotionally after hearing her words.

"Bobby... Bobby, can you hear me?"

"Yes... Yes, Damayanthi, and what you said is unbelievable. Are you sure that my name's in the will, and if so, I am dead? And there's no chance of getting out of the murder case."

"My darling, I sorted out everything here..."

"But, how..."

"The delivery contained her mobile, and it has a video? And two people killed Nikitha, I have the evidence. And I met with Sointhara and told him the complete story"

"Damayanthi, are you crazy? What was my plan, and what did you do?"

He was annoyed with her, and meanwhile, he saw Sidhu walking towards him and disconnected the call. They hugged each other, and Sidhu was happy see to his friend after a long time. They walked into the cafeteria and ordered coffee and Samosa.

"Bobby, what's all this, buddy, what happened to you, and do you know about Nikitha's death?"

"Yeah, Sid, I was told recently, and by the time I wanted to meet her, the police and my former employer were after me."

They had coffee; Sidhu placed his hand on Bobby's hand and squeezed; Bobby gained confidence and smiled at his friend. He told him about the fraud, and who was behind it, and how he was compelled to run away. Sidhu received a call; he disconnected and asked for Bobby's number. He gave the number, and Sidhu said he would meet at eight pm. Bobby bought a few cans of beer, took an auto, and reached his hotel.

There was a video call from Damayanthi. She appeared happy, her eyes expressing her excitement.

"Bobby, please don't get annoyed with me. I did what I felt was right, and that might get you out of all this mess. By the way, where are you now?"

"At HYTEC City, Hyderabad, in the morning I met with my friend and we shall meet in the evening. Now, tell me what's going on there?"

Bobby has a gulp from his can and stares at her. She passes a flying kiss and continues,

"After you left Colaba, I collected the envelope from the post office. I opened it and found a mobile and will documents. The mobile has the recording of the rape and murder, one's male, and the other is the hand of a woman hitting on the head of Nikitha with a beer bottle."

She stopped and went into the kitchen, switched off the gas, returned to the living room, and continued,

"At once, I remembered Sointhara and went to his office and met him. There was also a foreigner, a detective, whose name's Edward, ex-cop from the USA."

Bobby starts laughing and has another sip. She speaks,

"Why are you laughing? It's a long time since I saw my love laughing so cheerfully."

"So, they made me an international fraudster... The great Charles Ponzi?"

She smiles and continues,

"Later, I explained them and requested, and finally, after watching the video and the will documents, Sointhara agreed to help you."

"What did you tell them about you and our relationship? Did you tell them about the recording of my meeting?"

"I told him that you are my fiancé and shortly getting married. The meeting at Elephant Island and your threat irritated him."

"So, you are my fiancée now. I need you Damayanthi. I am in a state of confusion and not able to think or plan my next move. I'd check the flight for the evening or tonight; pack your things, and be ready, ok."

"Why flight? Book a train ticket."

"My fiancée deserves flights from now onwards, not trains. Ok bye. Also, send me the video of Nikitha's murder."

"Ok. Bye, my love."

The call ended, and Bobby checked evening flights; one was available at half past nine, booked, and sent the link to her mobile. He asked her to web login on her laptop and inform him in the evening. Bobby and Sidhu met in a pub, and they spoke of the past issues, police, and Edward's private investigation. Later, Bobby showed him the video of Nikitha's murder and Sidhu was speechless.

30. Nikitha's Murder Decoded

Bobby and Damayanthi visit the Birla temple at Lakdikapool and offer prayers. Later, they return to the hotel and complete their lunch. Meanwhile, Edward calls Damayanthi and tells her that she should convince him to meet him and Sointhara to discuss his case. She assures him that she will tell him when he calls her and disconnects the call. Bobby was asleep; she checked over her laptop and knew the difference between a suspect and an accused. Later, she learns about the arrest, bail, and court proceedings.

After Bobby's awake, she spoke with Bobby and said that they had to go and meet Sointhara and get his help. He thought and said he didn't want to get trapped again. That too was right, she thought and messaged Edward that he was trying to get an advocate for his case. After an hour, Edward called her and asked where she was and told her that the Sointhara's advocate would deal with the case on Bobby's behalf. The mobile was in speaker mode and Bobby heard their conversation and waved his hand to say yes. She did and he said he and advocate would visit in a day or two. She stared at Bobby; he looked like he was in a dilemma whether to accept the deal or not. She speaks to him,

"Bobby, I know what you're thinking, I believe it's better to go with an advocate's advice and I think Sointhara, being a famous businessman, would come and give the testimony in court and"

She checked her laptop and continued,

"We have *two options*, one is... if the police officers agree, convince with the letter stating that you were employed in Medussa and the rental agreement of your flat should suffice. Then, I think we don't have to go to court."

Bobby was surprised at her knowledge of the law; he took her hand, kissed her and said,

"Damayanthi, you do whatever you think it's right. Now, I am exhausted and not feeling well."

"I can understand. Earlier, I used to feel the same way until, I met you, Bobby. And the *second option* is... you surrender, get arrested, and stay in police remand... and show the evidence, get the bail in the court."

"What? No, no... I prefer the first offer, it's better, I don't want to stay in jail else, I will run away from here."

Bobby said and placed his head in her lap; she placed the laptop aside and tapped over his shoulder. After a few minutes, he was in deep sleep.

₹ $ £ €

As Damayanthi guessed, Sointhara didn't come, and Edward and advocate Advi arrived in Hyderabad. Edward sent a message to her saying that they were to visit the local police station and asked her to be ready with the IDs and proofs of Bobby. It was nine am; she checked the copies of IDs, rental agreements, and passport. At ten in the morning, Edward picked her up, and she asked Bobby not to leave the hotel. In the cab, he introduced the advocate; she said namaste, and later, he briefed her on how they wanted to deal with the police. Damayanthi was thrilled listening to them, and their idea was similar to her first option of a termination letter and his rental agreement.

They got down at Nikitha coffee shop and occupied the last table beside the entrance. She was speechless looking at the setup of the interiors, the arrangement of the tables, and the LED lighting, and especially loved the ambiance of the coffee shop. The streets and the main road were broadly visible from three sides through the plane glass panels. To her calculation, the total floor area would be more than three thousand square feet. In one corner, the beautiful smiling Nikitha's photo frame was hung with garlands, and the oil lamp and incense sticks were lit. She remembered her first job as a waitress in a similar cafeteria in Cuttack. Meanwhile, the manager recognized and wished Edward and took the order.

Unknowingly, the tears appeared in Damayanthi's eyes; she wiped them with her Dupatta. Edward realized her feelings and said,

"Even, I pity for Nikitha's untimely death. I was told that she was hard-working and loved her staff and the customers."

The waiter served hot coffee to her and Edward and a sandwich and milkshake to Advocate Advi.

Later, they sorted the requisition letter and Xerox copies of the IDs and removed the unwanted copy of Bobby's passport. Edward turned to Damayanthi and spoke,

"Ma'am, you are just like an assistant to us. Do not speak, I repeat do not reveal about Bobby and his relationship with you. I think you got me."

Advocate Advi explains her,

"Damayanthi, maybe it's the first time for you at the police station, bear in mind, no emotional or requesting type of conversation. The officers might act arrogant and provoking when they see an advocate in their office. If you speak anything to persuade them, they will make you slip on your ground of justice."

She nods and remembers a few incidents of her past life. Edward paid the bill and booked a cab to the police station. Advi and Edward displayed their cards to the staff and were waiting for Circle Inspector. After a few minutes, the CI came and took his seat. They wished him, and Advi gave the requisition letter and the set of copies to him. he read the few lines, placed the papers aside, and spoke,

"Did you get the FIR copy? If not please obtain it and then meet me, anything else Mr..."

"Advocate Advi..."

Advi replies formally and gives him his card. He takes it, reads it and drops it on the pen stand.

"Well, Advi you practice in Mumbai courts and what brings you come to Hyderabad and take up the murder case of Nikitha and"

He stops and asks with the constable standing aside; he mentions the name.

"Bobby, the famous film a long time ago, the hero's charged with multiple charges... fraud, intimidation, threatening, money laundering, rape and murder."

He sighs and asks,

"Now, what can we do? Also, you are not allowed to practice in other states... you may be aware of it."

"Sir, as per section..."

"Ok, there was an amendment, right? Sir, as of now, we can't do anything, until the suspect surrenders and gets into our custody."

"Sir, you can check the company's letters and the rental agreement copies, else..."

The CI interrupts and repeats Advi's words,

"Else, else what would you do? Tell me, advocate Advi, what would you do... threaten me?"

"Sir, relax... I mean to say else, the company's prestige and business prospects might get damaged. That's all."

By the Advi's humble words, his expression showed more arrogance and he was waving his hand to get out of my office. Damayanthi got irritated, she was to get up and answer. Meanwhile, Edward held her hand, and she realized and sat in silence.

The CI noticed her movements and questioned them,

"Another Nikitha?"

Advi counters his casual talk and speaks in a cool way.

"Sir, you're crossing your official limits..."

"So, what... will you file a case on-duty officer? I am not scared of your legal threat, you are wasting my time, and now, get lost."

Advi and Edward exchanged looks, and Advi reacted.

"Well CI... Mr... Never mind with the name. I know your job and why the officers are frequently transferred..."

"Hey?"

Advi cuts his words and speaks harshly.

"You Mr... Advocates don't threaten anyone unless provoked by an illegal practice or unofficial behavior. If so, they drag responsible officers legally and challenge the trial in the court of law. You better understand that ok?"

The CI was staring at them in anguish until they left his office.

₹ $ £ €

Edward suggests meeting the Commissioner and Crime Branch, and Damayanthi books a cab. She explains to them her experience a few days ago with the police and leaves for the hotel, and they too understand and ask her to stay in contact. Advocate Advi gives his card, introduces himself to the Commissioner, and explains the issue they faced at the local police station. He plays the recording of the conversation between him and the CI at the police station and the Commissioner gets annoyed. He calls PA and asks him to speak to the SHO. After a few minutes, the secretary walks in and gives the mobile to the Commissioner.

"Yes, what was the issue and what are you talking about?"

"Sir... sir, they were rude, and the advocate, Advi, was threatening me."

The Commissioner interrupts and speaks in anger,

"Did you send the DSR? Immediately mark the changes and the leads you're following, make a separate list, and send it."

He gives the mobile to his secretary, turns to Advi, and speaks in a soft tone.

"I think you can understand the work pressure, Mr. Advi. Just give us some time and leave the documents and the undertaking by the company stating it is reinstating the missing employee. But where's our suspect, employee? How would you contact him?"

"Sir, if your office allows, say relax the rules for a short period the company would first give an advertisement asking him to resume the office and later, you can go through with your investigation."

Advi takes out the undertaking document and gives it to the Commissioner; he goes through it and other papers, pins them along with the visiting card, and hands it over to his PA. Advocate Advi thanks him, and they leave the office. On the second day, Edward visits the police station and collects the conditional authorization papers to employ Bobby. Advi and Edward decided to call Muthu, as he was the witness who could give the statement stating that Bobby wasn't present in Hyderabad.

Edward calls Muthu to come down to Hyderabad and asks him to provide a statement saying that Bobby was not in the house when the letter was delivered. The next day, Muthu arrives; Advocate Advi, Edward, and Muthu visit the Commissioner, and the case investigators interrogate Muthu. Later, Commissioner and the officers agree to uphold the murder case for a short while. But before leaving, Advi presents a copy of Nikitha's Will, takes out her mobile, plays the video, and gives it to one of the officers, and he passes it to the Commissioner. He viewed the video twice and passed it to the other officers. They were shocked looking at the crime.

One of the officers inquired as to how they got it and Edwards explained that it was in the delivery sent to Bobby. Later, Commissioner inquired as to who filmed it, and Edward stated that she may have felt the murder attempt on her and intentionally placed her phone on an elevated surface to capture the scene while it was filming. After half an hour, the Commissioner summoned the police and homicide detectives to an urgent meeting.

The Commissioner warned them not to leak the video on any media; hence, they might take action for the breach of the code of conduct of the legal system. Advi smiles and nods; after receiving the acknowledgment letter of evidence, they leave the office. They returned to the hotel, and Muthu left for Chennai. On the way, Advocate Advi was disappointed and said,

"Edward, we won the war without the trial battle. I am not satisfied with this case, as it didn't have any arguments, sections, or the advocacy I had planned earlier. I love the lower courts, and that's the reason I felt disappointed."

"Well, Mr. Advi, come on, it's settled coolly, and Sointhara would be glad hearing Bobby is now off the records of suspect and accused."

"Just for the sake of his request, I had to close the case early, and however, feel happy for Damayanthi for getting her fiancé back."

Later, Edward called Damayanthi and narrated the meeting they had with the Commissioner and she was happy and thanked them twice. He told her she might get an email, a copy of a letter from the Commissioner's office saying the charges on Bobby are dropped. Besides, he asked her to keep him informed, and he suggested that if she met him in Hyderabad; he wanted them to go and meet Sointhara. She assured him and said goodbye.

31. Execution of Will

A few days passed away easily for Bobby and Damayanthi. They visited the Lord Venkateshwara Swamy, offered prayers, and have been staying at a guest house in Tirupathi for the past few days. Both were in routine and participated in the stock market regularly. One day, she received an email from Edward. He asked her to get Bobby to Mumbai, and she said that she wasn't in Hyderabad. She lied to him and said that she was returning to Mumbai after visiting the pilgrim places in the city.

There was another email and he was asking her to convey the message to Bobby to register himself as a beneficiary for Nikitha's Will. She understood his idea, as he wanted to know the whereabouts of Bobby, and sent a reply thanking him for the advice. She told Bobby about Nikitha's Will and he still did not believe himself despite looking at the original Will in his hands. She made a calculation of the cash in his bank, Nikitha's new house in Jubilee Hills, and the Coffee shop's net worth. The amount of money and assets astounded them.

Bobby remembers Armaan's offer and calls him and agrees to part finance the large tender he was bidding for electrification of the expanded area in Visakhapatnam and Karwar port. Later, he told her about the deal, and she too was happy with his decision. Bobby asked Sidhu to find out about the Will registration. Bobby and Damayanthi had returned to Secunderabad and were staying in a hotel. After a few days, Nikitha's Will had been executed in the name of Bobby Shacal, and all relevant assets were legally transferred in his name. Bobby recalled the train accident and told Damayanthi how the elderly couple in Rathipur, Bhubaneswar, saved him. Now, he wanted her to accompany him when he pays his gratitude for his survival. She agreed, and they left for Bhubaneswar. They left the airport and went shopping; Damayanthi selected a few saris and gents' clothes for the elder couple. Later, she bought the famous sweets, Malpua, Chhena Gaja, and Rasabali, and some snacks from Bhubaneswar, and hired a cab to Rathipur. Meanwhile, Bobby drew three lakhs and was looking for a cab.

Damayanthi has a weird feeling that someone is watching her and following right from the shopping mall. She thought it was due to stress or anxiety and tried to hide her face with the sari and wore the sunglasses too. Yet she was feeling insecure, remembering her earlier acquaintances.

₹ $ £ €

The cab arrived at Swamy Das's house after being guided by a farmer at a crossroads. An elder woman, with a part of her sari tucked inside at the navel, appeared from the house. She walked closer to enquire; she recognized Bobby and asked where he went without telling them and said they were worried about his health in the Odia language. Damayanthi wished her namaste and replied in Odia and said that he had to meet her in Cuttack. They spoke of his job, health, and the false fraud case implication on Bobby. In the course of their intimate discussion, Damayanthi started calling Laxmi as Amma and helped her prepare the rotis and the curry.

Damayanthi boiled the water over the firewood and showed the bathroom to Bobby. He took a bath and had a happy feeling like he was with his parents. At one pm, Swamy Das returned and was surprised to see Bobby and Damayanthi. He washed his face, hands, and legs and all sat in the room. Damayanthi called him Papa—Father and again told him what had happened at the office. Swamy said he too thought similar and pitied him for being dumb. Bobby and Damayanthi started laughing, and his wife too started laughing along with them. Swamy was surprised, and later, Damayanthi told him the reason for not revealing himself; he asked her to make him talk, and Bobby spoke in Telugu and

Hindi. Swamy took Bobby's hand and said that he thought he might have lost his voice forever after the accident. They had lunch, the roti's made out of Jowar—the sorghum, potato curry, rice, and the curd. Swamy took an onion, placed it on the floor, smashed it into pieces with his right hand, and placed it aside. He told them to have it with the meal and explained the benefits of having raw onions with the meals.

After the lunch, Damayanthi asked Bobby to offer the readymade dress to Swamy, and she presented the sari and sweets to Laxmi. Damayanthi waved her hand at Bobby; they bent to touch the feet of the elder couple. Swamy refused; Bobby spoke in Hindi and asked them to bless. They touched the feet of the elder couple, and they blessed them to get married and have a happy family life. Swamy and Laxmi remembered their son, wiped their tears, and asked Bobby and Damayanthi to have some rest.

In the evening, Bobby accompanied Swamy to the field and helped him by watering the field. They wrapped the dry grass in rolls and fed the cow and the calf in the cattle shed. They sat for a while and discussed the yield, fertilizer's use, and the bank loans provided to the farmers. Swamy showed the railway track expansion works going on the other side of the field.

They returned by six pm, and Bobby and Damayanthi were getting ready to leave for Bhubaneshwar. Swamy asked them to stay for the night, but Bobby politely lied to him, saying he had to meet his friend regarding his job. Damayanthi was not willing to leave; she was feeling like she had come to her maternal house. She too requested Bobby to stay, and finally, he agreed. After the dinner, Swamy and Bobby went for a walk around the lanes and returned. Meanwhile, Damayanthi arranged the beds for gents in the front room, and she and Laxmi slept in the small storeroom.

Swamy went to the field early the following day after Damayanthi had made him breakfast. Bobby finished his tea and went to the Co-operative bank that provides the loans to farmers. He enquired with the head clerk, repaid Swamy's loan amount, deposited some in a savings account, and took a bus to the city.

Swamy, Laxmi, and Damayanthi spoke of the village and the city life, the dressing, and the food habits. Laxmi asked how she spoke fluent Odia and wanted to know where she was. Damayanthi anticipated that she knew a woman's *inquisitiveness* and told them she was born in Mumbai and later brought up in Cuttack. Laxmi told about her parents, her marriage, and her son living away in the city and suggested that a woman is the only person after the marriage to take care of her family. They both spent some time remembering the memories of the past. Finally, she questioned about their relationship. Damayanthi said that they were to get married and said the company filed a false fraud case, and he ran away to hide from the police. Laxmi expressed her sympathy and thanked God for help. She told her that they were getting married shortly, invited them, and Lakshmi could see the blush on Damayanthi's face and smiled.

A small transport van stopped in front of the house, and Swamy thought the driver might have taken a wrong turn. Then, Bobby appeared from the other side and asked the helper to offload the items. Laxmi and Damayanthi came out of the house, and Bobby asked Damayanthi to guide the helper to place the refrigerator, air cooler, and refillable gas stove. He took kitchen items and placed them inside. The elderly couple were watching at the items in shock. In the evening, before leaving, he told Swamy that his loan was repaid, and he deposited some money in his account for their regular needs. Swamy was speechless, and tears dropped from his eyes. Damayanthi consoled him, saying that they have no parents and that from now onwards they would treat them as their parents. Bobby took a new cash box with a lock and key, opened and placed some money, and handed it to Swamy. He took it, hugged him for his generous act, and blessed him to live forever. Later, Damayanthi saved her mobile number and the Hyderabad address in Swamy's old mobile and asked him to visit them. The cab arrived, and they said goodbye.

₹ $ £ €

Bobby and Damayanthi took a flight to Goa and reached Canacona, South Goa. In the evening, they spent some time on the Palolem beach. The next morning, Armaan Bhatia took them to a natural harbor in Karwar, Karnataka, and with the permission of the port authority, took them on a tour of the premises. In the afternoon, he took them to the Agonda beach, had lunch at the shack, and they signed a few papers. Later, he dropped them at the hotel and said that he had to take a flight to Mumbai and said sorry for not spending time with them. Bobby ordered a few beers and dinner while Damayanthi was busy packing as they were leaving for Hyderabad the next morning. He called her and offered the drink, but she refused and said she wanted to stop having the drinks. He raised his eyebrows and had a sip. She took a soft drink and gave him company.

They returned to Hyderabad the next morning, and Bobby went out to get the vegetables, and Damayanthi was cleaning the house. Meanwhile, a tall and lean man with a face mask over his long grey beard was searching for the address near Bobby's house in Madhura Nagar. He saw Bobby crossing the road, walked to him, and asked for the address, mentioning the door number. He saw the number on the paper and asked him to go a few feet away after the grocery shop. The stranger walked away a few feet and observed Bobby going into his house. He didn't see any person inside the house; he took a snap of the house and the street on his mobile and left the premises.

Damayanthi was fasting and had been visiting the Balkampet Yellamma temple and offering prayers from the last week. The next day, after one week's pooja, she turned to a normal routine lifestyle and started cooking non-vegetarian food at home. Bobby too was happy with her devotion and supported her by giving her fruits, juices, salads, and nutritious food. He remembered his mother and said she appeared more like his mother; she smiled and returned to the kitchen. She surprised him by preparing the famous Hyderabadi Biriyani.

One morning, an old housemaid over sixty years old visited Bobby's house and asked if they needed a maid and he recognized her and called inside. She was the maid when his parents were alive and after they passed away, he asked her not to come. He spoke with her, and she told him her story; he politely said he would call her if he required her help and gave thirty thousand rupees. She refused; he told her that he owed her for her hard work when his parents were alive.

Damayanthi heard their talk while cooking and called Bobby; he told her about the loyal housemaid who worked when his parents were alive. She didn't like him paying her without attending the household job and asked,

"Bobby, why did you give the money to her?"

"I told you she's an old lady. Her son kicked her out of the house and she's staying along with her widowed sister and without any income."

"You should have asked me whether I require a housemaid or not?"

Bobby didn't understand, stared at her, and she continued,

"Moreover, you have become quite generous after getting the bequeathed wealth."

He disliked her words and walked into the living room. After finishing her work, she leaves the kitchen and goes and sits beside him. He pretends as though he did not notice her and makes himself busy on his laptop. She couldn't tolerate his behavior; she felt guilty for her words and questioned him.

"Bobby, just tell me? Do I have a right to say something against you that you might not like? If so, please leave me to my fate."

He ignored her words, shut his laptop, leaned his head over the sofa, and closed his eyes. She spoke in a requesting tone,

"Bobby, dear, don't take my words the wrong way. I mean to say that if you pay anyone without a reason or job, they get habituated and try to ask for more tomorrow. That's it."

He agreed she was right, but her expression and body language made him anguished. Nowadays, all his decisions and judgments are from the point of view of Damayanthi, and the words bequeathed wealth were not appropriate to say as he paid from his own money.

"Damayanthi, just rewind your words. What did you say?"

She realized and folded her hands and said,

"I am sorry, I shouldn't have uttered that word . . . Please forgive me."

"Right from my teenage years, I never was dependent on someone's money and, you should know, I used to play TT and Badminton at college and social sports events on teams, *betting* with money for my friends... And earned my pocket money... My father gave me a good education with his small salary."

Both were silent for a while; a cooker's whistle disturbed their thoughts. Damayanthi ran into the kitchen, switched off the gas, and returned.

"Damayanthi, you are unaware of my job at Medussa Company; daily I used to play the market in Crores of turnover. Just imagine someone else was there... Within a week he would have emptied the company's bank account."

"I meant to say you should've taken the money from my account."

"Please. Please... I believe even my money is not mine; it's yours, and Nikitha's wealth might be of yours too. And also, of the staff who are still keeping her dream alive today, and also of Muthu Raja, who delivered the prime evidence. Risking his young life. I never aspired for a large sum of money in my life."

Bobby's eyes were wet; he wiped them with his hand, took his mobile, and left.

Bobby and Sidhu met at their favorite bar in the evening, and Bobby told him how he played blackmail game with his boss, Sointhara, and about Damayanthi. He spoke of the Swamy Das in Rathipur who saved his life and how Damayanthi was taking care of him now. later, he narrated the stunt of Muthu, who saved him by producing the evidence.

He expressed his wish to take over Nikitha's coffee shop and also to finance the young entrepreneurs. He also said that he wishes conduct the free practice for trading of elders and pensioners, of course first with his money.

Sidhu was glad to hear his new aspirations, ideas, and plans and appreciated him. They had a wonderful time, and both said goodbye after a while.

32 Bobby Hospitalized

Damayanthi decides it's the right time to ask Bobby about their wedding; she meets a priest at the Ameerpet temple. He asks her to meet at eight pm after the evening rituals in the temple. Bobby was creating three strategies for the next day's market.

Nowadays, he's not actively trading in the stock markets; the trend reversal, with huge premiums and the premiums adjustments of the option, has become difficult. Besides, the change in lot sizes proved not so beneficial for the traders and investors. The new rules for FPIs and discrepancies at the NSE and an international research firm's allegations on SEBI were the national and international debates. Day by day, one or the other issues were racking up the whole market scenario. The brokers and retailers were unwilling to take a trade, and volumes decreased, and the prices and premiums appeared unjustified.

He saved the strategies, closed the laptop, and turned to her. She looked beautiful in an orange sari with new earrings and a short-sleeved white blouse.

"Bobby, can we talk?"

She stopped and looked at her palms. He took her closer, hugged her and she said,

"I think it's the right time we should"

"We should get married, yes. It's the perfect time for us to start a family, a new family life. What do you say?"

"I met a priest, and he asked me to meet him, saying he would suggest an auspicious Muhurat for the wedding."

"Should I go along with you?"

"No... No, sometimes I feel scared of your words and also, I forget what to ask when you stare at me."

"The love and the shyness often make one overwhelmed by emotions, right?"

He winks; she kisses his cheek and walks to the temple. Bobby gets up, takes a bottle of strong beer, and settles in the living room. He played his father's favorite Hindi song, 'Tere mere sapney . . . Ab ek rang hai.' Suddenly, the compound gate opens, and a tall man with a mask appears with a six-inch-long butcher's knife. Bobby gets up in surprise; the intruder runs inside, checks the room, and walks into the living room. Before Bobby questions, he stabs him in the stomach three times and yells at him,

"Where's she? I'll kill her. Where did you hide my wife, my source of income?"

The intruder pushes Bobby over the chair, and his head bangs to the wall and starts bleeding. The stranger runs out, and an old woman shouts and calls the neighbors for help. Bobby carefully gets up, sits on the chair, and looks at his wounds. He cannot figure out who his wife is, and his words have left him perplexed. My wife... source of income. And what was his source of income? The burning pain was unbearable; he closed his eyes and decided to wait for Damayanthi to return.

There was a screeching sound of the tyres; a car hit the stranger, and by the impact, he was thrown under a truck coming in the opposite direction. He was lying on the road with a head injury and his lower body crushed under the tyres. A stream of blood was flowing on the road. Damayanthi witnessed the accident and heard the old woman's voice in front of her house. The old woman, Ramanamma, tells her that Bobby has been stabbed with a knife; at once, she runs inside and leans to the door. For a few seconds, her mind goes blank, and later, she goes closer and observes that his shirt's torn and his stomach has a large cut. He held his hand over the wound.

Ramanamma, the former housemaid was the eye witness, she brought a cotton towel, wrapped it around the stomach, and tied a knot. Meanwhile, an ambulance arrives, and the paramedics pull the gurney, lift Bobby, and lay him on it. Damayanthi took Bobby's mobile and got into the ambulance. A police officer arrives and inquires with Ramanamma and takes the details of the assault. She described the complete story to him; he takes her statement and speaks over his mobile. He turned to her and asked her to move away from the crime scene and closed the door. She told him that she used to work as a maid a few years ago, and he took her number and address.

₹ $ £ €

Bobby and the intruder were admitted to the same ICU. The condition of Bobby was critical, and he was unconscious for the last few hours. His stomach and head were bandaged, and a drip was hanging beside his bed. The oxygen mask, the hum and beep sound of the equipment, and the graph on the monitors scared Damayanthi. The head nurse came and asked her to wait in the visitor's lounge. She left the ward and saw two men standing a few feet away. She saw them and vaguely remembered the face of Sidhu.

"Damayanthi Bhabhi . . . I am Sidhu, Bobby's friend."

She could not control herself and started crying. Sidhu walked her to the row of chairs, made her sit, and sat beside her. He wiped his eyes, and she stopped weeping and saw him.

"Bhabhi, I spoke to the duty doctor, he said Bobby is ok, but they are waiting for him to respond to the treatment. Don't worry, we will shift him to the multispecialty hospital after the preliminary diagnosis."

He convinced her and could not say more than those words. She wiped her eyes and placed her hands together, saying namaste and pleading with him to help her. Sidhu's cousin Lakshman spoke and said he knew a doctor and he would request him to attend. Two policemen arrived and took the statement of Damayanthi. One of them left, and the other sat on the chair and was speaking on his mobile. Sidhu spoke to the head nurse, took Damayanthi to the cafeteria, and bought some snacks and soft drinks. He gave her the packet and soft drink and asked her to have it; unwillingly, she drank the soft drink and returned to the ward. Sidhu's cousin Lakshman received a call; he said he would come in the morning and left.

At eight am, a nurse said that Bobby was responding to the treatment. Lakshman bought the breakfast and coffee for them to eat. Damayanthi refused, said that she would eat after the pooja, and asked Sidhu to have it. She said she had to go home, take a bath, perform pooja, and return. Lakshman volunteered to stay, and Sidhu went along with her. A constable was guarding the house. Sidhu requested him to allow them to take the clothes; he warned them not to touch anything except the clothes and escorted them inside.

₹ $ £ €

In the afternoon, Ramanamma, Swamy Das, and Laxmi visited the hospital and searched for the ward. A nurse showed the ICU ward, and, meanwhile, Damayanthi came out of the ward; saw them, and started weeping. Laxmi hugged her, and both were in tears. Ramanamma told Damayanthi that they were searching for her at the house. Later, Sidhu came, and Damayanthi introduced the old couple, and he thanked them for saving his friend. He placed the lunch box and water bottle on the chair and said he would get the lunch for the others, but they refused.

Bobby was conscious and was shifted to another ward. The police officer took the statements of him and Damayanthi. Sidhu returned with the prescription and medicines, and Bobby held his hand. He smiled and tapped Bobby's shoulder, assuring him he would do well. He went out and returned with Swamy Das, Laxmi, and Ramanamma. They spoke with Bobby, asked him not to worry about it, and said Lord Jagannatha would save him. Ramanamma said she offered prayers at the Yellamma temple. Damayanthi requested Sidhu to book a room in a hotel for Swamy Das and Laxmi. She gave her card and asked him to use it for payments, and he refused.

"Laxmi, give her this, and let's go."

Swamy says and takes out a packet from his cloth bag, gives it to her, and turns around. She takes it and stares at her husband.

"Papa, what's this? And where are you going? You have lunch and take some rest. I shall see you after giving the food and medicines to Bobby. Amma please, please, you stay with me, and I am alone here."

Laxmi sees the tears in her eyes, returns the packet, and convinces her husband. Sidhu booked a hotel room and took them. Damayanthi went into Bobby's ward. He was sleeping; she held his hand and prayed for recovery. She was recollecting, how many people she had called last night in the frenzy moment after the incident. She checked her mobile and scrolled the calls and checked Bobby's mobile; there was a call to Sidhu, but she did not find the number of Swamy Das. She was trying to guess how they knew about the incident. A male nurse entered, told her there were some visitors, and asked her not to allow more than one person. She walked out and was surprised to see Edward and the others. He stepped forward, took Damayanthi's hand and spoke in anger.

"Damyathi, how did this happen? And who's that bastard? I would cut him into pieces. Did the police find him?"

Helen walks to him, asks him to stay calm, and reminds the Doctor's advice. He softly released Damayanthi's hand, and introduced the others.

"She's my daughter, Helen, and my adopted sister, Saritha wife of, I don't want to use that bullshit name now, who framed Bobby."

"Dad, control yourself and we have come here to visit Bobby."

Damayanthi observes Helen; she's in a white Salwar Kameez, with beautiful blue eyes and a red bindi on her forehead. Then, she looks at a woman in Maharashtrian attire with a green nauvari cotton sari who appears much older than her actual age. Her sunken eyes with black marks under her eyes were displaying her severe health condition. She said namaste to them and asked them to be seated. Meanwhile, Sidhu arrived and was happy to see Edward.

"Edward, when did you arrive? Did you meet your favorite suspect?"

Edward hugged him and said,

"Sidhu! How are you kid and where's my fugitive hero?"

They walked into the ward, and Bobby is sleeping. Edward is astonished to see Bobby for the first time, as he had worked on this case only with a few clues, photographs, and witnesses. He walked closer, observed him, took his mobile, and checked the photo. It was his first case that had been solved without any action or any physical confrontation with his suspect.

Damayanthi bought the coffee and biscuits and offered them. Helen spoke in English and Marathi and expressed empathy and asked not to hesitate for any help. Saritha got up and sat beside Damayanthi. She placed her shaking hand over her shoulder and stared at her. Emotions tensed up within both women as Saritha talked about her husband Gaikwad and cursed him for fraud. She praised Bobby for his benevolent attitude and help when she was critically ill and alone in her house. Meanwhile, Edward felt his blood pressure rising, started sweating, and was also shivering. Helen gave him the medicines, spoke to Damayanthi, and then left.

Later, the head nurse comes and takes Damayanthi to the next ward.

33. Naganath's Dead

Damayanthi stares at the patient with the bandage around his head, on one hand, and both legs. She asks the head nurse who the patient was, and a police officer walks towards her questions.

"Do you know this man?"

She moves her head sideways saying no and the officer speaks in a loud voice to identify him. She walks closer to him, observes, and suddenly, the patient opens his eyes and calls her name.

"Damayanthi . . . my beloved wife, don't you recognize me? Your husband . . . Naganath?"

She was shocked seeing him on the bed; she feels the giddiness; her legs were not supporting, and she is on the verge of collapsing. The nurse and the officer hold her and make her sit on a chair. The ward boy gives a bottle of water, and the nurse sprinkles a few drops on her face. After a short while, Damayanthi comes to her senses, wipes her face, and drinks the water. The officer pulls a chair, sits opposite her, and asks,

"How are feeling Ma'am? Are you okay now? If not, I shall wait for a few minutes; can you hear me?"

"I am ok, now."

"I have a few questions to ask and be honest and answer."

She nods, and he turns the page of his notepad and questions her.

"I believe he's your husband, right? Now, tell me why you ran away with his money and jewelry. If you didn't want to stay with him you could have filed a divorce case in court."

Her tears were flowing out of her eyes; she took her sari's end and wiped them. The police officer was waiting for her answers. Meanwhile, a doctor visits with a report and inquiries about the patient. Naganath interrupts and asks the doctor.

"Doctor, are my legs ok? Can I walk again?"

The doctor looks at him and the others, calls the head nurse aside, explains his condition, and shows her the report. Naganath raises his head and tries to look at them and yells out with pain in his neck. The Doctor walks to him, checks the pulse and the heartbeat and records it on the case sheet, and leaves. With frustration, Naganath bangs his hand on the side table, and the drip stand falls along with the medicine tray. The nurse and the ward boy held his hand, and the officer walked to the bed. He stares at him and asks the nurse to tell him of his condition. She remains silent and he says,

"Tell him, sister, I heard what the Doctor was telling you. Don't worry he has no more life left."

Yet she stays quiet; she's not supposed to disclose the matter to others and the officer tells him,

"Naganath, tell me the truth, I know you are aware of your condition; at least be true to yourself before you. I think you know."

One of the staff inserted the drip on his hand. Naganath starts crying and hits his head with his hands. The ward boy held his hands tight and asked him not to do so and he stopped crying and started telling.

"Sir, we were living happily for a few years."

He looked at Damayanthi, turned his head and continued,

"Sir, I was diagnosed with Erectile Dysfunction and impotency, and I was ashamed to tell Damayanthi about it. I could not get out of the trauma, addicted to alcohol, was avoiding her at night, and pretended as if I was tired of the heavy work in the loco shed. Later, I convinced and forced her to drink and she too was giving company and drank, for the sake of me regularly. A few months passed and I was suspended for drinking at work. My hand loans turned from hundreds to thousands and one day one of my officers made a deal to revoke my suspension. In return, he asked for my wife.”

He stopped and wiped his tears and continued,

“One night I drugged her, and my case was solved. Later, to repay the loans, I used the same drug and offered her to others. Finally, after a few days, she found out and injured my head with a hammer and left.”

“Were you not ashamed of yourself for doing so? bastard.”

“Nurse... Nurse, now please leave us for a few minutes.”

The head nurse pitied Damayanthi and left the ward with the ward boy. The officer asks him,

“It was easily curable; why didn’t you go for the treatment?”

“I was scared. I thought she might laugh and insult me, and if she leaves, I would be left with no money.”

Later, he told the officer that one of his friends, who’s a cab driver, saw her with a young man traveling to a village in Bhubaneswar, and by the time he went, they had already left. He said he got her the mobile number and address and took some money from the old man and returned. The blood was dripping from behind his ear and his pillow was soaked.

The officer watches Damayanthi; her tears were dripping, and she did not bother to wipe them. He speaks in a soft voice.

“Damayanthi, you don’t have to weep now. It’s his turn in jail with a limbless, amputated life... Forever.”

Suddenly, they heard a shrill cry and turned to Naganath; he was hitting with his hand over the surgical scissors that were used for cutting and dressing the wound. It pierced almost three-forth into his chest from in between his lower ribs. The blood was flowing out from the puncture. The nurse and the other staff rushed into the ward, were trying to remove his hand, and he pushed the rest of the scissors inside his sunken chest. Later, the beeps stopped, and his hands loosened their grip on the scissors.

Edward and his family were leaving; his health was further deteriorated, and the new medicines did not control his high blood pressure. Helen gave the personal folder containing Bobby's educational certificates and told Sidhu about her father's health issues. Sidhu was to see them off at the airport, but she refused, asked him to take care of his friend, and left. Meanwhile, the head nurse recognizes Sidhu, tells him about Naganath, and takes him to the next ward. The police prepared the report and asked Damayanthi to claim the body. The police officer briefed about the death of Naganath while Sidhu was in shock. He started nodding at the police officer's words silently.

Sidhu walked Damayanthi into Bobby's room and asked her not to talk about her husband. She sat watching Bobby for a long time and Sidhu said he would take care of Naganath's dead body after completing the official formalities. He said they are transferring Bobby to the multi-specialty hospital at Banjara Hills. She was expressionless and a bleak future gave her no choice to think further. Sidhu called his cousin and prepared to shift Bobby, and she just followed them, leaving her *dead husband* behind.

After the checkup, the doctors prescribed a few new medicines. Bobby spoke with Sidhu and requested him to take Damayanthi to Nikitha's new house. He agreed and took Damayanthi to Jubilee Hills in his car. On the way, he asked her not to talk about her husband's death and promised he would tell him after he recuperated from the accident. They went to Madhura Nagar, collected Ramanamma, and asked her to clean the semi-furnished Nikitha's house.

Bobby was sedated for most of the time with the new medicines. Once, while he was conscious, he enquired about Swamy Das and his wife. Sidhu told him that he accommodated them in the hotel and Bobby wanted them to be shifted to Jubilee Hills along with the Damayanthi. He also questioned why she had been gloomy for the past few days and said he did not like seeing her in a white sari and without bindhi. Sidhu reminded him of his accident and said she was worried about his health. Bobby gave a smile and dosed off.

₹ $ £ €

During the house chores and the frequent questions of the maid, Damayanthi's occupied mind was slowly retracting to the present circumstance. Ramanamma was talking about the parents of Bobby and his habits and said she worked for fifteen years until she left with her husband for another district in the state. Bobby's childhood was similar to Damayanthi's and were from the same conservative family's livelihood. She realized why she liked him; now, it's a different story with the new issue of her husband's intrusion into their life.

Sometimes, hearing the third person's view and appreciation makes people feel compelled to inhabit and adopt a similar lifestyle for happiness. But now, her case was a mismatch to continue the relationship.

The old couple was shifted from the hotel to Nikith's house. The next day, Laxmi said they had to leave as the neighbors were going to attend a marriage in Bhubaneshwar and there was no one to take care of the cattle. Swamy Das hesitated to speak; she realized and spoke.

"Papa, I know why you are angry. I know what Naganath would have told you and took the money from you."

Swamy Das and Laxmi were surprised, and Damayanthi told the rest of the past.

"Damayanthi dear, please excuse me. After hearing from him, I was made to believe that you gave us his money. And in anger. I bought cash along with us."

She took his hands, kissed them, and said the money belonged to Bobby. Laxmi wiped her tears, and Ramanamma didn't understand what was going on. She was in confusion as they were speaking Odia and said,

217

"Damayanthi Amma, we should not send our relatives in tears, just pray to God for a safe journey."

Damayanthi translated her words into Odia, and they said she was right. She packed their food for the journey and requested them to use the money for their needs.

The train left the station; Damayanthi sat watching the trains and at one moment wanted to jump before a moving train and end her misery. She blamed herself for not informing Bobby about her husband and his dirty job as a pimp. Many times, she tried, but he wasn't interested in listening to her, and being a few years older than him made her feel guilty for not persuading him to understand her real life. Now, hearing about Naganath, he might not tolerate her staying with him; not only he, but no person would compromise to such a circumstance. However, she's decided to serve him, pay the gratitude, and after he gets well, she's decided to end her life. Meanwhile, there was a call, and she ran out of the railway station and took an auto to the hospital.

₹ $ £ €

Bobby leaned on his pillow and was looking out of the window. Sidhu was busy on his laptop for a while and later shut it. Bobby saw him and said,

"All these days, I was just thinking that I was helping a distressed woman, and she tried to tell me about her husband... And it was my arrogance that made me not listen to her. At least, if I did, I would have helped him out and tried to compromise them to live together. I would have paid for his treatment."

"Don't blame yourself, man. Anyone would've done the same if they were in your situation."

"Sid, be practical man. If you were in my place, would you do the same?"

Sidhu looked into his friend's eyes and questioned.

"Yes, I am practical buddy. First, I would have thought and then would have taken a decision. Now, you tell me. Did you ask her opinion about getting married to you? You didn't even bother, and she being a helpless woman and has been with you for your sake. Comforting you, she built up a close relationship, and I'd rather call it a sexual relationship. And with the hope to convince you to marry her someday."

He stops and continues,

"It's a personal and private matter. Bobby, would you dare to tell others, if you were in her place?"

"Yes, Sid. Yes, it's my fault. I should've been a good listener rather than a useless speaker."

Bobby replied, and later, he went blank and dropped on the floor. Sidhu called the nurse, and after the examination, the doctor told him he had a small hip fracture. Later, the doctors performed a hip surgery and brought him to his ward.

34. The Scalper's Future

*'The times heal, and the calm minds must adjust to the present day
for a better life.'*

Bobby is moved to Nikitha's home after a month, and the
hospital provided a female nurse. She comes in the morning
and evening, gives him the medicines, assists him with a few
exercises, and takes him for a walk with a walking stick. After
a week, Damayanthi convinced Bobby that she would take
care of him, thanked the nurse and said that she could handle
him, and settled her payment. Nowadays, Bobby was feeling
his restricted leg movements and felt ashamed taking her
help. And she was living with a vengeance on her own life
and was waiting for him to take care of himself.

One day, Sidhu visited with a few beers and chicken and
asked Ramanamma to prepare the spicy chicken. Damayanthi
heard him and went into her room. Now the time was
approaching for her to say goodbye, she thought, and her
mind was playing tricks while making the decisions. After a
few sips, both friends started their discussion over the issue
of marriage. Sidhu said his father was in the idea of getting
him married to his far relative's daughter. He said she too was
in IT and working for an MNC. With the second round, the
topic changed to the Hindu laws of re-marriage, and the
doubts were whether one could remarry a widow. If so, how
and what were the norms to follow? It was a serious
discussion was taking place in Telugu, and Damayanthi and
Ramanamma were listening to them while cooking the
chicken. After serving a few pieces of chicken to them,
Ramanamma took liberty and spoke.
"Son, I am not well educated. Nevertheless, my
grandmother taught me, and listened to the priests preaching
the Dharma and the practice of a married life."

"Wow, Amma, you are amazing as your spicy chicken. I am eager to listen to what you were taught."

Sidhu said, and she was feeling nervous. Bobby took a beer bottle, poured a glass full, and offered her. She refused, and he insisted on her and made her remember how her father used to give her the leftover alcohol while she was leaving after work. Sidhu pulled a chair and told her he'd drop her off after the party and while leaving. He asked her to sit, and she sat beside Bobby on the floor. She was convinced, and she sat beside Bobby on the floor. She saw them and nervously had a gulp and wiped her lips.

"Sidhu, you were telling about the Garuda Puram?"

Ah, yes, but I don't agree."

"What don't you agree?"

"It says that a woman should be given only one chance to get married in her life."

Ramanamma has another sip and answers,

"Even, I don't agree with it, then why did Loka Sanchaari Narada say that a woman has to be given a chance to get re-married when her husband dies without producing a child?"

"She's correct, Sidhu; even I heard that when my mother was talking to a neighbor."

The subject of remarriage was a hot topic and what Ramanamma said is related to the Narada Smriti. Bobby was recollecting one of the Bodhayana Dharma Sustras that allow a woman to remarry only, if her husband is impotent. Similarly, Sidhu was thinking of King Chandragupta Vikramaditya, who married his brother's wife and produced a child. They had a few sips and finally, she broke the silence and questioned,

"Biddaa—Son, if it's not allowed, then how did Mandodhori married her brother-in-law... After the Lankadipathi, Ravanasura's death?"

"Bobby... Does Damayanthi Bhabhi understand Telugu? It's not good discussing all these matters here."

Bobby smiles and replies,

"She knows Marathi, Odia, Telugu, and English and also Tamil, I think."

In the other room, Damayanthi placed a pillow over her ear and was not interested in hearing the discussion. Now, that her life had become a topic for them with drinks, she never thought she would ruin herself to such an extent and the lives of others who are associated with her. Her agony was unbearable and was taunting with various dreadful memories. She's now decided her death is an inevitable solution to live with guilt amongst the good people.

Bobby asked Ramanamma to feed them; she went into the kitchen and returned with the rotis, rice, chicken gravy, tomato dal, and curd dishes and placed them on the table. Sidhu took the plates, served the food, and was looking for Damayanthi. Ramanamma went into the room and called her for the dinner. She said she would have after they finished, Sidhu went and stood at the door, and she got up from her bed and said,

"Please, Sidhu I'll have it later. I have a severe headache. . . Please. you all complete your dinner."

They had dinner, and Sidhu took Ramanamma and said goodbye. Bobby was searching for tablets; Damayanthi went to the table, opened the box and gave him three tablets. He took them with the water and walked into the hall with his walking stick. She placed the dishes in the kitchen, cleared the dining table, wiped, and returned to her room. Both had a guilty feeling and only time had the answer to allow them to reconsider their wishes.

₹ $ £ €

The next day, Ramanamma's grandson brought a priest on his bike to the house. She spoke with him and Bobby came into the hall. She introduced the priest; he asked for the bride and bridegroom's names, and Ramanamma gave him the names, and he checked his Hindu Panchang. He fixed an auspicious date, took the fee, gave his card, and left. This unanticipated act of goodwill was making Bobby nervous.

She observed him and told him that's the reason an elder has to be with the children for such good occasions. He remembered his mother and went into the room. Damayanthi was busy in the kitchen; she heard and ignored them. Ramanamma completed her work and before going, she spoke to Damayanthi.

"Damayanthi beta, I saw the feelings of your parents, and before something happened, I want you both to get married as early as possible. If Bobby's parents were alive, they too would have done what I am intended to do now. My child, I'll come an hour late, please have your meal and make him have his diet food, if not the medicines won't heal faster."

Damayanthi completed her cooking and went into Bobby's room; he was busy on his laptop, and she did not disturb him. At noon, they had lunch in silence; she gave him the tablets, and she was busy with the other work. In the evening, after the tea, Bobby calls her, and she comes out of the kitchen and looks at him.

"Damayanthi, come here, sit. The burial service took care of the rituals, and now, everything's sorted out I think., What do you say?"

She sat on the single chair and spoke, watching the sunset.

"Bobby, you still have a choice; look for a young beautiful wife and get married. Why do you want a used and thrown woman from the street?"

Bobby was annoyed, stood up, walked with the help of his walking stick, and stood beside her. She turned her face away, and he placed his hand on her shoulder and spoke.

"Yes, I have a choice, and what about you? You have no choice of getting a selfish person other than me, what do you say?"

She looks into his eyes, places her arms around his waist, and hugs him. After the sunset, she walked him into his room. Bobby took her hand and said that they were getting married in two days. Bobby and Damayanthi got married in a Registrar of Marriages Office, and they visited the Balkampet

Yellamma temple and liberally donated some money for the temple's development. Later, Sidhu picked up Ramanamma, and the newlywed couple went to the hotel for lunch and said the treat was from him for their wedding. Damayanthi was happy; her life's desire was fulfilled, and she called herself proudly Mrs. Damayanthi Bobby when there was a call from the bank.

₹ $ £ €

Damayanthi altered a few routines of her husband, and she adjusted to the new life as a wife in Nikitha's house. Bobby obtained permission and transferred the Nikitha Coffee Shop to Damayanthi's name, but the coffee shop's name remained the same. Now, she's the new proprietress, and Bobby took her along with him daily. After a few days, she was managing the inventory, the staff, the daily requirements, and the customers after being assisted by the staff. The manager and the staff are satisfied with her style of running the business.

Bobby occupies his favorite table and trades till afternoon, and later, Damayanthi drives the new sedan with her husband and reaches their home for lunch. She took up the expansion work and constructed two large rooms on one side of the entrance of the coffee shop. These rooms were specially designed for small corporate meetings and other functions.

Bobby financed the new entrepreneur's startup of the new software design for the latest GPU—Graphical Processing Unit for ChatGPT applications and the Artificial Intelligent Interface. At home, he constructed an AC hall in the portico and was giving free classes for the elders, pensioners, and senior aspirants who were interested in trading in the stock markets and mutual fund investments. And the institution was named Nikitha's Boot Camp. And generously donated a part of his daily scalping profit to the members for free practical trading with his money. He also allocated some percent of the earnings to the coffee shop's staff for their children's education, their marriages, and for unforeseen incidents. Meanwhile, Armaan Bhatia, Sidhu, and Bobby met in the Coffee Shop and worked out new partnership businesses. The total estimation of the fund was around eighty crores for the software development, roads and tunnel electrification, and maintenance project, and were in the idea of the establishment of the chain of hotels and Tiffin centers in three states.

After a few months, Damayanthi called Edward and invited them to her new home, Nikitha's house with his family. She took Muthu Raja's mobile number from Edward and called him. He jokingly said that he wouldn't be delivering any letters. He arrived in Hyderabad, met Bobby for the first time and was surprised and told her that he imagined him like his favorite Tamil movie hero.

Damayanthi spoke in Tamil and said they were offering him a job as he had the earlier experience of working in a small cafeteria. He was excited at the job offer as the manager of three Tiffin centers in the prime locality in Chennai.

Ultimately, Bobby Shacal's targets achieved, and all positions were squared off for the better future.

THE AUTHOR's BIO

The author retired as a Superintendent, after 37 years of service from one of the top telecom service providers in India. His long pending project at last, transformed in the final draft, Bobby — The Scalper after a few years.

He wrote five books, also creates and designs his own titles and book cover for his books.

His stories, script, screenplay, and dialogue are registered with Screenwriters Association—SNA, Mumbai.

Two stories, scripts and screenplays are readily available for TV, Web-Series, OTT and movie production houses.